TEXAS WIND

"You've no reason to help me," Katherine said.

"You're wrong."

She turned back at the quiet pronouncement, and her heart thudded at the look in Slade's eyes. Then she knew she was mistaken in thinking she saw tenderness there as he added, "If you want to hire my services, that's reason enough."

"Are you for hire, Mr. Slade?"

He shrugged. "For the U.S. Army, the Texas Rangers—and maybe for you. If the price is right."

"I haven't gold."

"I don't want gold. Not from you." He stepped closer, and his forest-dark eyes held fire but no light.

Her own trembling angered her, and she said sharply, "I am not for sale, Mr. Slade, or for trade!"

"Then you'd better think of a damned good substitute, or you and your brother are out of luck."

WINDS ACROSS TEXAS

SUSAN TANNER

LEISURE BOOKS **NEW YORK CITY**

A LEISURE BOOK®

February 1994

Published by

Dorchester Publishing Co., Inc.
276 Fifth Avenue
New York, NY 10001

Printed in the United States of America.

For Carolyn

Chapter One

Texas, September 1857

Katherine walked swiftly along the wooden sidewalk, ignoring the looks, sidelong and sometimes hostile, cast her way. She was used to the stares; they could no longer make her cringe. But the child she held in her arms was clutched tightly, as if in an effort to shield it. In the street, mud churned beneath horses' hooves and wagon wheels and was carried on boots to the already caked walkway.

"Katherine! Katherine, wait!"

Reluctantly, she paused and turned, her graceful figure poised on the edge of movement. To stand still in this town was to invite an opportunity for others to wound. At least that was true for Katherine.

The girl who had hailed her was running to catch up, the exertion giving her ivory skin a glow of rose. Elizabeth Kern was perhaps the prettiest girl in New Braunfels, Texas, and it was no detraction from her that she was well aware of the fact.

"Weren't you even going to stop in?" Elizabeth asked in accusing tones. "You never come to town anymore." She knew the reason for that as well as any, and better than most. It was not shame that held Katherine Bellamy close to home. Not shame, but a burning bitterness, almost a hatred.

"Aunt Dee needed some lengths of material from Leggett's—for Shea." Instinctively, Katherine hugged the little girl close to her breast, her expression hard.

Elizabeth winced in sympathy. "You mustn't mind Mr. Leggett, Katherine."

"He thinks the same as everyone else in this town."

"Not everyone." Elizabeth's reminder was gentle. "I know some are deliberately cruel, but most just don't understand. Or they're afraid."

"Of Shea?" Katherine smiled bitterly. "No, they aren't afraid of an eighteen-month-old baby girl. They've just made a judgment as to what her place in this world should be."

Elizabeth could not argue the point. There *were* townsfolk who felt that way. They were the same ones who judged Katherine Bellamy, judged and condemned her.

12

"Let me hold Shea," she pleaded. "It's been weeks since I've seen either of you. And Mama will be disappointed that you didn't come by to see her. You know how she loves Shea."

Elizabeth held out her arms enticingly, and Katherine relaxed her defensive hold on the child. Shea went to Elizabeth without hesitation, reaching for her with plump, short arms. At eighteen months, Shea was outgrowing her babyhood much more swiftly than Katherine could have imagined. She was almost too big to be carried for any length of time. Her skin was soft and golden, her hair dark and straight, her eyes unexpectedly gray.

Elizabeth held her lovingly. "Have you heard from Ford?" She asked the question in a studiedly casual tone. "I thought he expected to be home weeks ago."

"You'll learn that time doesn't mean a great deal to my brother," Katherine said dryly.

Shea struggled in Elizabeth's arms as she spied a horse moving within touching distance. Her tiny hands reached for the animal.

"Shea, no!" Katherine spoke sharply, her eyes challenging the rider. He shifted his disdainful gaze and rode on.

Katherine took the baby from Elizabeth, and Shea grew quiet and watchful, the coveted horse forgotten in her mother's rare displeasure.

"I have to go, Elizabeth. I'll send word as soon as we hear from Ford."

Elizabeth shook her head. "Please don't. Ford will come to see me if he wants." The unaccustomed dignity was becoming in her. "Be sure to tell your aunt I said hello."

Suddenly anxious to be gone, Katherine nodded. She didn't want to be home so much as she wanted to be away from town. In truth, she had not felt truly at home anywhere for a long, long time. But anywhere was better than here. Elizabeth's sympathy was sometimes hard to accept. Katherine despised anything resembling pity for herself or for the child everyone believed to be her daughter.

She reached the buckboard and lifted Shea up before climbing agilely to the seat. Lifting the reins, she straightened and encountered an intense stare.

Her chin jerked up defiantly. "Good morning, Mrs. Addis." She watched as the woman's eyes slid from her to Shea.

A fleeting, quickly suppressed grimace crossed the woman's face as she stared at the baby. "Good morning to you, Katherine," she responded stiffly, turning her gaze back to Katherine. The starched brim of her bonnet scarcely moved with her nod of greeting. "How are you and your aunt faring with your brother away for such a long time?"

"We're just fine, Mrs. Addis." Katherine's eyes were cold. "All three of us."

The woman's pale blue eyes moved back unwillingly to Shea at this forced recognition of her existence. "She is a healthy-looking baby," she admitted. "It's a shame she doesn't look more like you."

"And less like her father, you mean."

Mrs. Addis reddened slightly but stood her ground. "Exactly. It would be better for her, after all."

Katherine stared her down. "Don't you really mean you would be less uncomfortable if my daughter didn't look like a murdering Comanche?"

"I'm not the only one." Her tone was defensive.

"No," Katherine agreed quietly, "there are a lot of stupid people in New Braunfels." Before the other woman could reply, she clucked briskly to the team, leaving Mrs. Addis to stare after her.

Though her mood had turned savage, the hand that steadied Shea on the seat beside her remained gentle. In a normal situation, Mrs. Addis would have admired a child with the bright intelligence and engaging smile of Katherine Bellamy's daughter, but hers was not a normal situation, and to people like the Addises and the Leggetts, Shea was not a normal child. She was a half-breed; unforgivably damned by blood as red as that of any person in the state of Texas. Nor would Shea ever be forgiven her mother's great sin. For Katherine had been taken from the Comanche by force, cursing the very men who considered themselves her rescuers.

And Katherine, herself, had learned to be as unforgiving and unyielding as those who condemned her.

Across the street from Katherine's encounter with Mrs. Addis, a stranger propped his shoulder against a corner post. No one glancing his way would have realized the intensity of his gaze as he studied the lone girl and the child. His look was neither condemning nor pitying. Nor was it disinterested.

As the buckboard reached the far end of town, he swung up into his saddle. The horse, a buckskin gelding as hungry-looking as his rider, responded to his signal, and they followed the buckboard with just enough space between to remain unnoticed.

Katherine never glanced back. She was fighting the haunted feeling that swept her too frequently and with devastating force. There seemed no normalcy to her life, no steadiness. From the moment the Comanche of Broken Arrow abducted her and another girl on that long-ago day of death and violence, she had lost all semblance of peace and a normal life. During her months with the Comanche she had come close. And then the soldiers had come. She did not believe she could ever feel secure again. She could pretend for Shea's sake, but it was only pretense, and that easily shaken.

For months after her return from the

Comanche, Katherine had refused to take Shea into town with her. She rarely went herself. Lately, though, she'd had second thoughts. If the people of New Braunfels did not come to accept Shea as a child, they never would. The stamp of her father's looks grew steadily more obvious. The promise of it was there in her face, in the sculpture of her bones. His bones. Wolf Killer.

His image went through Katherine's mind in a blaze of painful memory. What had he felt when he returned to find his flame-haired wife dead and his tiny daughter gone? His proud image was followed by others, even more painfully. Even now, months later, Katherine was haunted by the night of the massacre on Stone Creek. The screams of women and children, the leap of flames licking at the lodge as she pulled Sleeping Grasshopper from the trembling arms of the baby's dying mother. Too weak to escape, she had entrusted the life of her child to Katherine.

Katherine's breath caught in her throat. "No," she whispered. "No." And her mind obeyed, for she had trained herself well. The memories receded, to be replaced by familiar surroundings. She had not realized they were so close to home. The grove of pecan trees to her left marked the boundary of their land. She sighed, thankful for the dependable team that needed so little guidance to bring them home.

Guilt washed over her as she became aware

of Shea's bewilderment. Her arms clung to Katherine's knee, and her little body was tense with fear.

"It's all right, Shea," she soothed as she reined the team to a full stop before the barn. "We're home, love. We're home." The words brought far less reassurance to her than they did to Shea. They were home, but it was not all right. Not for her.

The creak and rattle of the wheels brought Yates from his fence-mending to the barnyard. Old Ben Yates had the strength of a man half his age and the experience of one twice his fifty-two years. Knowing Katherine, he did not offer to help her down. He waited while she leaped to the ground and then caught Shea, who jumped fearlessly into her mother's ready arms.

"I'll unhitch and unload," he said stoutly. "Go on in to your aunt. She's fretted the whole morning for the two of you."

"There's nothing to unload, Ben," Katherine admitted. "I didn't get anything I went in to town to buy." She turned away from his searching look and headed for the house.

A safe distance away, under the shade of a small stand of trees, the stranger waited. Before he dismounted, he would watch. If there were others here besides the old man, he wanted to know.

His horse shifted, needing water, smelling it,

but he would not make a sound or a move that would draw attention until the man allowed. They were dust-covered, the two of them, and weary from long miles. The man knew there would be no rest here, but the animal hoped.

Katherine's aunt was in her kitchen, where she could be found during most of her waking hours. It was her firm belief that work was sped by pleasant surroundings, and the kitchen offered that. It was a homey room, cozy in winter, with windows placed to catch the best of a day's light. She put aside her mending, one of Shea's worn gowns, as Katherine and Shea came through the door.

"So then, you've brought my darling back safe and sound."

Katherine stood Shea on her feet and watched as the little girl ran to her great-aunt with widespread arms.

Dee lifted the child lovingly and eyed her niece's set mouth. "It was not a pleasant morning for you, then?"

Katherine knew her face would be answer enough.

"You should never have taken the child into town with you!"

Though Dee spoke sharply, Katherine knew her soft heart was aching for the two of them. "Shea's got to know what this world is like, Aunt Dee. She might just as well learn it now."

Dee shook her head sadly. "Take the child

upstairs for a wash, Kate. She's dusty from her ride. We can talk later, after dinner. There's no need for us to be upsetting Shea with a quarrel."

"Hungry." The little voice was adamant. "Shea's hungry."

Dee's face relaxed its worried lines as she took a biscuit from a plate at the back of the black iron stove and gave it to Shea. "Now off with you, sweet."

Katherine took the baby and headed for the stairs, but her aunt's voice stopped her at their base.

"I don't suppose there was any word in town—about Ford, I mean?"

"No, Aunt Dee," Katherine answered, trying to keep concern from her voice. "Not yet." She did not have to see her aunt's face to know the worried look was back.

Chapter Two

Dee stared at Katherine's retreating back, held characteristically stiff with pride. That pride caused a great deal of Katherine's heartaches—but not all. Dee worried about her, and now she had Ford to worry about too.

He was more than a month overdue. He'd left in the first part of the summer with two men from neighboring Seguin to drive a small herd of beeves to Fort Clark. Accounting for every possible delay, the men should have been back weeks ago. October was beginning, and there had not been so much as a word from them.

Dee couldn't even contact the families of the other men, for she knew only that one of them was named Tupper and the other Adam. Though Ford was, admittedly, a reckless soul, he was not cruel. He would never frighten her without good cause.

He was so like his father that at times her heart ached with the resemblance. There were nights she dreamed of Tilford Bellamy still. Ford, as he was called and his son after him, had sent for her when her sister, Alaina, had contracted a fever after a miscarriage. Dee had been twenty-two then, with three rejected suitors behind her. She had left her aging parents in Aransas Pass, on the coast of Texas, and arrived in the new settlement of New Braunfels in time to help Ford bury her sister.

No one had ever known of her feelings for her sister's husband, and no one took it amiss that she stayed to care for the children Alaina had borne him. Katherine had been eight at the time, with serious, wood-smoke eyes and a face as pale as her dead mother's. She had been a sharp contrast to her brother, not quite a year younger, who had not lost his quick smile, though he grieved for his mother more openly than did Katherine.

After only a month or so Ford Bellamy had set out for Oregon, leaving Deirdre McKenna with his children and the understanding that when he returned she would go to Oregon with them—as his wife. She had known that it would be a convenient, affectionate arrangement for him, but it would have been so much more than that for her.

They never saw him again, though Dee had

received word of how and where he had died. He had been on his way back to them, ready to let his wanderlust take them on to new land. The hunting blade that slipped in his grasp had not made such a great gash. He had traveled a day or two more before the poison from the dirty steel overtook him. He had died among strangers, leaving three to grieve anew.

No one had called her Deirdre since Ford. She had loved the rolling sound of her name on his lips. She missed it still. She was Dee McKenna to the people of New Braunfels, a good-looking woman of thirty-four with a youthful body and the sturdy bones of the McKennas. She had the McKenna coloring in her curling, brown, red-tipped hair and dark, almond eyes.

No one in New Braunfels had known her Irish family, and the truth was, she had little family left by the time Ford died. Her parents had died not long after she had left them, within months of each other. The constant losses took their toll, though she found solace in caring for her niece and nephew.

For years she had believed her heart was forever buried in a lonely grave somewhere along the Oregon Trail. Of late, however, there had been a man whose company she had not refused. A man by the name of Doyle Shanley.

"Mrs. Bellamy?"

At the low sound of the voice, unexpected and totally unfamiliar, she whirled to find a man in the room with her. His face was as unfamiliar as his voice.

"What are you doing in here?" Her tone was sharp with fright and anger.

"I knocked," he said with no trace of apology, "and I called from the door. You didn't hear."

She knew it was possible, but there was no softening in her manner. "I am not Mrs. Bellamy. I am Miss McKenna; Dee McKenna."

She heard Katherine descending the stairs behind her and felt a sudden, intuitive apprehension, a warning. The stranger's eyes lifted, waiting for the footsteps to reach the bottom; waiting, it seemed to Dee, to see if it was danger that approached. She watched him closely. He was neither a good-looking man nor an ill-favored one, but he did look as if he knew the meaning of ruthlessness. Dee did not need to be told that it was not chance that brought him to this house.

Katherine stopped on the last step, and Dee saw her through the stranger's eyes. A handsome girl, as sturdily boned and slenderly fleshed as Dee herself, her face framed by sun-streaked brown hair. When Dee glanced back at the stranger it was not admiration she read in his face.

"Aunt Dee?" Katherine's voice held a questioning concern, while her gray eyes appraised the stranger with hostility. Dispassionately, she acknowledged his masculinity, the sensual appeal in muscle and sinew held in lithe control. But Katherine had schooled herself long ago. The men of her world wanted no part of a white squaw. And she wanted no part of them.

Dee gave her niece a nod of reassurance and addressed the intruder more calmly. "Have you business here, Mr. . . . ?"

"Slade. I'm with the Rangers, in a manner of speaking, and yes, ma'am, I do have business here. I am looking for the parents of a young man by the name of Ford Bellamy. In town, the young lady," he jerked his head at Katherine, "was pointed out to me as his sister."

Dee paled as Katherine asked tensely, "My brother! Has something happened to him?"

"It would be better if I spoke with your folks about him." His manner dismissed her right to any knowledge.

"He has none," Dee cut in before Katherine could erupt in the fury Dee knew would come. "Or, at least, I am as near that as any living. I raised my niece and nephew from childhood. Their parents are dead. Now then, will you be so good as to tell us what you know about our Ford?"

He kept them waiting, his eyes reading the girl's controlled anger and the woman's inner strength. "Your nephew is in trouble; bad enough, maybe worse."

"Go on."

"He sat in at a poker game at Fort Clark. Lost some money and called the game crooked, which it likely was. There was a brawl, and a man was killed. Next morning it was set straight and judged an accident, but your nephew didn't wait around to find out. He ran out during the night."

"If it was judged an accident, why should that matter?" Katherine asked heatedly.

"It doesn't." Slade eyed Katherine speculatively. "But he didn't have sense enough to ride for home. He headed north and took up with a man named Elzy Rusk, a renegade white man. They're holed up with Broken Arrow's Comanche." He was watching for Katherine's reaction as he spoke. There was none; at least none that was discernible. "He's with Rusk and two or three others known for dealing in whiskey and rifles where it ain't legal."

"Ford wouldn't." Dee's voice was adamant.

Katherine could not speak past the tightening of her throat at mention of Broken Arrow's people. Shea's people.

"You might not think so, Miss McKenna," Slade returned, still watching the girl, "but the United States Army is persuaded differently. We had a time quieting that band of Comanche after Stone Creek. We can't afford to have it started up all over again."

He got his reaction in the flare of nostrils and the quiver of firmly pressed lips. He recalled everything he'd read or been told about Wolf Killer's woman.

Stone Creek: The words conjured up horrors Katherine had never learned to forget. She set her jaw against the pain of remembering. The man facing her had deliberately evoked that pain. She knew it without understanding the knowledge, without understanding why he would do so.

"What exactly are you doing here, Mr. Slade?" Dee spoke with force. She was more fearful of Katherine's response than ever. She wanted this man gone. "Why come to us?"

"I thought the boy's pa might be of a mind to ride with me. Might be he could have brought the boy out sitting a horse, 'stead of slung over his saddle like Rusk is sure to be."

Dee was shaken, no longer thinking of Katherine. "That is decent of you, Mr. Slade, but . . ."

"Hardly decent, Aunt Dee! I would say that Mr. Slade came looking for someone to make his job easier, maybe even do it for him."

"Stop, Kate!" Dee's alarm made her sharper with Katherine than she had intended.

"It makes me no mind how the boy comes out of this. I'm going after Rusk's bunch. If Ford Bellamy is with them, I'll get him too. However is necessary."

"Alone, Mr. Slade?" Katherine's words were tart. "Broken Arrow's people are no tame band.

27

I suggest you take a cavalry troop with you, and maybe some of the same brave men who attacked a village of helpless women and children a year ago."

"And get myself scalped and peeled so you can have your revenge?" His eyes were cold on Katherine's callous face. "You know damned well that's what would happen if I blundered in there with a mounted troop. You would prefer it that way, though, wouldn't you, being a white squaw?" The intended insult was drawled and deadly.

Dee's eyes snapped with anger. "That is much more than enough, Mr. Slade! My niece and I care nothing for the talk that is given to every stranger who passes through this town, but we will *not* have it flung in our faces in our own home. You have given us your information concerning Ford, and you have received all of the hospitality you'll have from us. Now go!"

Dee McKenna was rarely angered, but once roused that anger was a rare thing to witness. She was reaching for the rifle that hung above the mantel when Slade's hand gripped her wrist with ungentle strength.

"Easy, lady. I'm headed out now." His flat gaze slung around to Katherine. For a moment their gazes held—challenging. Then he was gone.

Dee saw Katherine tremble as the door closed behind him.

"Yon's a dangerous man, Kate. Ford had best look to himself, whatever it is he might be doing."

Katherine had no answer for her but an anxious frown.

Upstairs, Shea wailed in fury at being left alone so long. Dee started up to her while Katherine went out to help Yates with the evening chores.

With the sun dropping swiftly, the temperature out of doors had cooled. Katherine's gaze searched the yard and beyond, but there was no sign of the stranger.

Yates was in the barn, tossing hay from the loft to the stalled animals below. Katherine settled in to do the milking, and the familiarity of the task was a comfort. She rested her cheek against the cow's soft, warm flank. The energetic rustling of Yates in the hay above her and the gentle sound of milk against the pail was soothing. Here where the body warmth of the animals broke the chill encircling the aging barn, for a brief time, she could forget.

"Stranger didn't stay long." The booted feet were sure on the rungs of the ladder as Yates left the loft.

"No need." Katherine still smarted from the stranger's deliberate insults. "He wasn't welcome and neither was his errand."

"I heard."

Katherine glanced up in quick surprise.

The old hand shrugged. "Mean look about

29

him. I stood outside and was just before giving him a bellyful of lead."

"It wouldn't help Ford any. The army would just send someone else."

Yates snorted. "Ford's nineteen, and man enough. It's just womenfolk that would worry about him. He'll come out of this well enough, but that Slade hadn't ought to have insulted you like he did."

She glanced at him wearily. "He didn't say anything that hasn't already been said. I lived willingly with the Comanche, and Shea is a breed. I'm just beginning to realize that's all we'll ever be, at least around here." Her jaw squared determinedly. "I won't have that for Shea."

She stood and hefted her full bucket, topped with white foam. "Don't worry about me, Ben. I can take care of myself and Shea just fine."

"You're a fine-looking girl, Kate. You ought to be the wife of a good man, with children no one would shun."

"How likely do you think that is to happen now, Ben? Folks around here, in all of Texas, have reason enough to hate Indians. And one look is all it takes to know Shea is half-Comanche."

Yates followed her as far as the barn door, and his gaze followed her out into the yard, his expression brooding. Katherine had been a sunny little thing as a child, always smiling and

happy. These days, her smiles were few and far
between.

Katherine gathered the hens' lay and swilled
the pushing, grunting spring litter of hogs,
lingering at her work until the last soft light
had faded. By the time she was ready to return
to the house, Dee, with Shea's full interference,
had supper ready for the table. Yates took
the meal with them, as he had for the last
half-dozen years.

Through the hours since Slade's unwanted
visit, Katherine's thoughts had been revolving
around one seemingly inevitable decision.

Dee, equally concerned for Ford, resolved to
a course of action of her own. "Katherine," she
said as she helped Shea maneuver her spoon,
"I think it best we ask Doyle to help us in this
matter."

"No."

So quiet was her answer and so unemphatic,
Dee was not at all certain she had heard right.
She looked up from Shea's efforts to eat alone.

Katherine met her gaze calmly. "No, Aunt
Dee, that won't do. I respect Mr. Shanley, but
this is a family matter."

"Well," Dee returned with some asperity, "no
doubt you've realized Doyle would like to make
this family his own."

Katherine sighed, not wanting to wound her
aunt in even the slightest way. Dee had given
her youth to two children not her own; her
youth and the greatest part of her love. "He

31

wants to make *you* his family, Aunt Dee. Ford and I have lives of our own. This does not concern Doyle Shanley."

"Now, Kate." Yates's look held admonition.

"It's all right, Ben. Katherine meant no disrespect, I'm sure." She studied Katherine. "I suppose you've already decided what is to be done?"

"I have."

Pointedly, Katherine resumed eating. Not until Yates had retired to his room in the barn and Katherine was preparing to take Shea up to bed did Dee broach the subject again. "I don't consider this discussion at an end, Katherine."

Fortunately, Dee did not expect an answer. There was a faint furrow between her brows, however, as she cleared the table by the warm light of the kerosene lamp.

Once upstairs, Shea was not quickly settled. "Mama sing," she demanded after she had splashed and played her way through her bath.

The fire in the hearth accompanied Katherine's husky voice with a quiet, comfortable crackling. No child of New Braunfels had ever heard the lullabies Katherine sang to the little girl. They were the songs a Comanche mother sings, songs Katherine had heard Little Feather sing to her daughter many long months ago. That was a time when Katherine had believed she would live the rest of her life among the

Comanche—and had hoped Wolf Killer would take her as his second wife. Little Feather had never recovered from the birth of her daughter. As Little Feather had slowly weakened, Katherine had taken over Shea's care, loving her as fiercely as if she were Katherine's own.

A chubby little hand reached up and patted Katherine's face softly. "Shea's mama," the baby asserted.

"Yes," Katherine whispered. "And Mama loves Shea." There was a lump in her throat to equal the hurting pressure in her chest. She had never regretted for one moment the pain her lie had caused in her own life. If the soldiers had not believed Shea to be her child, Shea would have died at Stone Creek. If they had realized the truth later, Shea would have been wrested from her arms, probably to die of neglect as she was shipped to the government lands reserved for the Indians.

And Katherine had lied to her family and friends, fearful they would never accept the little girl otherwise. Who was left for Shea but the woman she now firmly believed was her mother?

The decision Katherine had made with such confidence earlier in the day was suddenly frightening. But she couldn't turn her back on Ford. He needed her. And when she found Ford she would find Wolf Killer. The thought would not leave her. There seemed to be no future for her and Shea in New Braunfels. Perhaps there could be one with the Comanche.

"Mama's going away," she whispered. "Just for a little while." She began to sing again as Shea's face puckered at her words. The child had heard them before, and she didn't like to be left behind even though it had never been for more than a few hours. Katherine was thankful Shea did not realize that this time it would be for much longer than that.

She fell silent as Shea drifted into sleep, and she clung to her daughter for a long while after that. At last, however, she made herself lay Shea in her own trundle bed. Carefully tucking warm coverlets about the sleeping child, she left the fire for Dee to bank or feed as she wished. For tonight, Dee would have to sleep here with Shea.

Quietly and slowly, Katherine shed her somber homespun gown and put it neatly away. When Katherine was younger Dee had loved to clothe her in brightly dyed materials, but since her return from the Comanche Katherine had preferred quieter hues. The dark shirt and breeches she drew from the clothes chest she had appropriated when Ford had outgrown them. The hat was her own, as was the rifle she removed from pegs over the door.

She took a leather pouch full of shot from a smaller chest which held, also, mementos of her mother and her father. Her hand strayed toward a small portrait before she removed it abruptly.

Her powder horn was full; she had no further excuse for lingering.

Fighting tears and an insidious weakness, she kissed Shea's silky, cool cheek. It was hard not to take the baby up in her arms once more as she studied the small features. Black lashes lay gently against her soft cheeks, and her lips were parted with quiet, even breathing.

Katherine found it hard, very hard, to force herself to leave her daughter there.

The upper floor, with its three small, cozy rooms, was given access by only one flight of stairs, which led to the kitchen. Dee turned to speak as Katherine descended those stairs, but her words died, forgotten. She stood motionless, staring in sudden, knowing apprehension.

"No, Katherine," she said when she finally found her voice. "I'll not have it!"

"And I'll not leave Ford to the mercies of a man such as Slade. And there is no one else to do it."

"Doyle," Dee began determinedly, but Katherine cut her short.

"It won't do, Aunt Dee. You must see that. Please . . . please, just listen. Ford would never be with the Comanche to stir them with whiskey to murdering his own kind—nor would he be providing them with the means to do so. And I don't believe he would ally himself with men who would, unless he had another reason for it. He surely agreed to ride with this Rusk as a way to get to the Comanche. I think Ford must have known that Wolf Killer is a member of Broken Arrow's band. Ford had to be looking for Wolf Killer."

Dee's face was a picture of dismay. "But why? Why, Kate?" Her niece met her gaze inflexibly, and she sighed. "Ah, Katherine, well I know how unhappy you've been, but why would Ford believe you would countenance such a thing?" Dread came with realization. "Sweet Lord, no! Kate, you could not mean to take the child back there?"

"Shea is Wolf Killer's child, Aunt Dee, and I didn't leave him willingly. You know that."

"So, you asked Ford . . ."

"No! No, Aunt Dee, I didn't. But Ford knows well enough how I feel. That I would never have left Wolf Killer unless forced to it. That I feel outcast by this town—and Shea along with me!"

Dee sank back into a chair, and Katherine was washed with pity, until Dee spoke again.

"And have you forgotten, then, that the Comanche took you by force? That you would never willingly have left us? At least you poor children were allowed to live, not murdered like poor Dave and Anne. How many times I have regretted the day I allowed you to visit the Pearsons and placed you in such horrible danger. The things you suffered because of that . . . Have you forgotten that day?"

"No!" Katherine cried. "I've forgotten none

of it. And I've not forgotten that it was soldiers who killed little Davey Pearson! Good, decent, white-skinned men of Christianity! Damn them!"

"They didn't know Davey was a white boy!"

"And that makes it right?" Tears glittered in Katherine's eyes. "It was right that they slaughtered a sleeping village of women and children and men too old to defend themselves? Comanche or white, Davey was still only eleven years old. Would it really have been right if his skin had been brown? And the babies . . . Oh God, the beautiful babies. Like Shea. If Shea hadn't been in my arms . . ." Her throat ached from holding back sobs.

Dee flinched, grieved at hearing put into words things she had only suspected when Katherine had been returned to her, wounded and suffering in heart and soul. But she didn't interrupt. In God's truth, she didn't know what to say. How hard it must have been for Katherine to keep all of this buried within herself all these months.

"The commanding officer at the fort told me that they were supposed to drive the tribe back; the settlers needed more room. It didn't matter to him that the land belonged to the Indian. It didn't matter to him when I told him his men had murdered the helpless and the innocent. They were following orders, he said. I told him about Davey, clubbed from behind. It was regrettable, he said. Regrettable!" She was near hysteria and she knew it. But it had all been held back for too long, released only in terrifying nightmares.

Katherine stopped abruptly, then continued more quietly. "Do you know the soldier who chased me down was going to sling Shea into the creek? I lied to save her. I said she was all white, and he let her live. He let my baby live." She caught her breath on a sob. "Is it any wonder I ran away from the fort and the soldiers, tried to run back to the band—what was left of it?"

Dee rose stiffly. Katherine's words might have been physical blows by their effect on her. Methodically, she began to take staples from the open shelves and place them on the table.

Without comment, Katherine stowed them in the saddlebags that hung near the door.

Dee included a skillet and a coffeepot. "Do you have money?"

Katherine nodded. "Enough."

At the door, they embraced. Reluctantly, Katherine broached one last painful subject.

"Aunt Dee, you know Wolf Killer has never known where to find me. And I never found him after the soldiers took me away. If he comes, with me or alone, it will be because I have sent him—for Shea." Her look hardened at her aunt's expression of horror. "She is his child, Aunt Dee, and mine. As much Comanche as white, and at least she will belong to the tribe. She will be accepted."

"You are going to stay among them, then? Raise your child among savages?"

"I don't know. I never asked to be taken from the band, but I don't know if Wolf Killer will want me after so long a time. Or if I will want him. But if it is to be so, you must give Shea up, Aunt Dee. You must."

"Very well, Katherine." The words were cold. Reaching up, she slipped a thin chain of gold from her neck. A tiny cross swung gently upon the golden strand. "She is your daughter, but I will not give her up to anyone who cannot show me this."

Katherine's face was a mask of pain. "Love her for me, until I come back or . . ."

"I always have, Kate, and I always will. Just as I have loved you and Ford."

When Katherine had closed the door quietly, irrevocably, behind her, Dee sat alone in the silent kitchen, the baby sleeping peacefully abovestairs, and watched the lamp slowly burning on its wick. She remembered the long days after they had been told of the Pearson massacre. Her despair now was almost as great as it had been then.

Chapter Three

New Braunfels was quiet but not deserted when Katherine passed in front of the hotel with its downstairs bar. The Saturday-night customers were almost always local men. There was low-keyed music and talk and laughter, none of it any more disturbing to the night than the soft kerosene light streaming from dull windows.

The mud slowly dried in the street, for there had been no rain in the last forty-eight hours. There was not a man in the area who didn't hope October would prove drier than September had been.

Katherine stopped her horse in front of the livery stable, and Evan Burch, the owner's son, met her at the entrance. Too many years ago to remember, she had been Evan's first love.

"Take your horse, sir?" He held his lantern

higher, and suspicion edged his voice as he asked, "You just come by this mare, mister?"

Dismounting, Katherine laughed softly. Evan had not recognized her dressed as she was in Ford's clothing with her hair tucked under a hat, but he had recognized her horse. "Eight years it's been, Evan Burch, since your father promised me his chestnut mare's first foal."

"Katherine? Whatever are you doing in that rig? And it's long past dark. Is there trouble at your place?"

"No, Evan, no trouble. I'm looking for a stranger who was through here today. Might be he's still here. He rides a big, raw-boned buckskin."

"The buckskin, sure. I remember him." Evan recalled horses quicker than he did people. "But I thought the stranger would have been out to your place earlier." Evan looked puzzled. "He left his packhorse here around noon and was asking where he might find the family of Ford Bellamy. You were just across the way talking to Elizabeth, and I pointed you out to him. He followed you from town."

"He made it out to the house," Katherine said grimly.

"I worried he might be bringing bad news about Ford, but he wouldn't say. Not to me, leastways."

Katherine sighed. "It was bad news, Ben. That man is with the Rangers, and he claims Ford is in some kind of trouble. I intend to get him out of it, if I can. That's why I need to find him—Slade, that is. He must know where to start looking for Ford. I don't."

Evan looked dubious. "He came back for his packhorse, late, and rode on out of town. It was close on dark."

"I was afraid he'd have set out already. I'll just have to try to pick up his trail."

"In the dark?"

"He won't have gone far before stopping for the night, and he has to be headed north." She was talking now more to herself than to Evan. "Broken Arrow keeps to his own territory."

"Ford's mixed up with that black-hearted bastard?"

"Don't judge Ford just yet, Evan Burch, or you'll ruin this town for him like it's been ruined for me." Without waiting for him to answer, she swung up into the saddle and touched the heels of her boots lightly to the mare. All the bitterness she had felt earlier and forgotten in her worry for Ford and the pain of leaving Shea came flooding back. People who had befriended her as a child had turned their backs on her when she returned home carrying a half-Comanche baby in her arms. Evan Burch, a boy who had long been a friend of Ford's, was ready to condemn him now with no facts to back that condemnation.

How could she raise Shea amid such hatred? No one could change the color of her skin, the arrangement of her features. What kind of life was there for her in this place? Katherine lifted her chin. There had long been a thought that stayed at the edges of her mind, a stark and bitter thought, but one that now seemed right. She would find Wolf Killer and see if he wanted his family.

Katherine rode at a steady pace, determined to come upon Slade's trail at dawn. He would surely have bedded down soon after dark, but he would have been able to ride more swiftly than she while it was still daylight. Katherine was puzzled that he hadn't stayed the night in town, starting out at daybreak. It was possible he had no money, she reasoned, but more likely he simply shunned people. He'd not seemed a person to seek the company of others.

Fortunately, because of Katherine's distraction with her own thoughts, her mare gave her no trouble as she rode. Sadie could be a fractious-minded animal when the notion took her, but she was Katherine's, heart and soul, and totally responsive to her moods.

Reluctant to stop, Katherine finally had to acknowledge the futility of pushing ahead any farther in the dark. She rarely had reason to venture in this direction, even by daylight, and the moonlit landmarks had become totally foreign to her. If she bypassed Slade in the dark, she might never find his trail. She chose to stop at a stand of cottonwood trees, softly silver in the starlight, and unsaddled Sadie, hobbling her loosely for grazing.

Unrolling her blanket, she spread it upon the ground beneath a tree. She propped her back against the trunk and drew her shirt collar up closer to her chin. The openness of her surroundings, with the wind brushing her face and the sound of Sadie's grazing nearby, forcibly reminded her of her time among the Comanche. It reminded her, also, that the quiet sound of her daughter's breathing was miles away. Not since the moment Little Feather had handed Shea to her waiting arms had they slept apart. It was a lonesome realization.

Despite the lateness of the hour and her need for rest, she dozed only briefly through the night. The first rays of the morning sun brought her to her feet. She stretched numbly and felt the ache in her muscles from the position in which she had slept and the cold night air. When she stopped again for the night she would most certainly sleep wrapped warmly in her blanket and not sitting on it.

She whistled to Sadie, who stood sleeping a few feet away. The mare roused as she approached. "Good morning, girl." Sadie lowered her ears to be scratched, and Katherine obliged.

As she resaddled her, her fingers worked deftly, independent of her mind. She shelved thoughts of Wolf Killer and the future, and even of Shea. She had to concentrate on tracking Slade and probably matching wits and wills with him when she found him. And she had to concentrate on Ford—finding him and helping him.

She checked the position of her rifle in the saddle holster, looped her reins, and mounted.

Luck was with her. Within the hour she found a creek for watering Sadie and a quick, soul-chilling wash for herself. And almost immediately after crossing she picked up Slade's trail. Just beyond that she found his campsite. The shallow firepit was still warm, and Katherine's stomach protested her cold breakfast eaten in the saddle.

She marveled at his choice of a resting place, completely open to friend and foe alike. And she could not imagine his having many friends. She wondered, also, that he had started a fire. Most travelers felt a little more secure if there were no evidence of their passing. It was autumn, the time of raiding. But she acknowledged that Slade was not like most travelers. There was a hardness to him, a fearlessness, and she knew Aunt Dee was right: Slade was a dangerous man.

The trail had to be Slade's. The hoofprints of the first horse were large and far-spaced. A big animal—like the buckskin. The second set of prints were placed at just about the position of an animal being led, his packhorse. Katherine held Sadie to a walk. She didn't want to come on Slade, had no desire for an encounter at all. She just wanted to follow him, at least for now.

Throughout the day the weather held good, the wind cool through the sunshine. They splashed through several water courses, whether separate rivers or forks of one she had no way of knowing. Crossing wide fields, Sadie crushed dried stalks of bluebonnets and mountain pinks beneath her sharp hooves. Soon their colors, along with the white pools of tiny daisies that lingered, would be lost to winter.

Slade held to a northerly direction, and she relaxed her close watch of his tracks, content to study them several times during the day. He never varied his pace; the horses' hoofprints remained steady and measured, and she knew he was pacing them carefully for a long journey.

In the last hour before dark she was startled by the crack of a single rifle shot. Startled; and then unreasonably infuriated. Her own cold meal seemed even skimpier, knowing he was enjoying hot, fresh meat. It occurred to her that sooner or later she would be forced to lag behind so that he could not hear the shots she used to supplement her supplies. She had not carried much with her.

That night, again, she dared not build a fire that Slade might be close enough to see or to smell. She did not see the glow of his campfire, but the cracked bones scattered by the cold ashes of his fire taunted her the next morning.

Sadie pricked her ears at Katherine's low curse.

Though the second day was a repeat of the first, the third day brought a change. It began sunnily, but by noontime a solid band of clouds massed in the northern sky. A bitter wind swept across the rolling hills, and the temperature began to drop. Katherine was forced to don her coat early in the afternoon, and she found herself grateful for the heavy lining Aunt Dee had insisted upon when Katherine would have been better satisfied with far less at the time. Bulky and cumbersome as Katherine had complained it would be, it was also blessedly warm.

For a while Slade followed along a riverbank, then crossed it. For Katherine, at least, the crossing was miserable. Cold water crept slowly upward until, suddenly, Sadie plunged into a swim. Katherine cursed and held on against torrents that had been fed by weeks of continual autumn rains. That the muddy river was not wide seemed to be its only good point. Katherine hoped vindictively that Slade had fared no better and no drier than she.

His trail began again almost at the point where Sadie touched the bank. Pulling upward, the mare slipped sickeningly before she regained her footing.

Katherine's teeth were chattering as it began to grow dark. She almost winced when she heard the sound of Slade's rifle, though she had been listening for it. She had the option of bedding down there in the open or riding until she reached Slade's camp, where there was sure to be a windbreak, a fire, and hot food. She kept riding.

She smelled Slade's fire before she reached it. When the glow was faintly visible she hailed him clearly and then waited. Sadie stamped her feet impatiently.

"Come ahead."

She did. The windbreak was an outcropping of rocks to the north, while a stand of trees stood as shield to the west. A thin stream hurried between the tree trunks.

Slade's fire was dug low and burned steadily out of the wind. Slade sat next to it, his blanket around his shoulders, his rifle lying loosely across his knee. He watched in silence while she unsaddled and hobbled Sadie. Katherine left her saddle near his but pulled her rifle and blanket from the pack. When she came closer he jerked his head toward the fire and the remains of his meal.

Without scruple or fastidiousness, she took up his plate and refilled it with tough wild turkey and hot beans. She used his spoon to eat. Across the fire, he laid his rifle aside and was still. She thought he might be sleeping. She cleaned the plate and filled it once again.

Finishing more slowly now that the pangs of hunger were stilled, Katherine stared at Slade in sudden suspicion. He would not have prepared this much food just for himself.

"You planning to find that brother of yours before I do?"

She was glad she had not jumped even though his voice had startled her. Looking up to find him watching her, she lowered the spoon she had been lifting to her mouth. "I aim to try."

"You think it likely?"

Because his voice held no inflection, she couldn't tell if he was angry or mocking or simply curious.

She shrugged. "You know where Broken Arrow's Comanche have made their winter camp. I don't. But I do know that maybe you won't be able to get in there. I can."

"So . . . you think Wolf Killer will welcome you?"

She stiffened, not answering. It was easy enough to imagine the thoughts behind the words, but she didn't care what he thought of her.

"Wolf Killer and his bucks have burned out a dozen homesteads in the last year." Slade watched her with hard eyes as he spoke. "Some more than once. Some as far down as Tehuacana. We made a peace of sorts with most of the band, thanks to Broken Arrow's wisdom. Only Wolf Killer has held out because of Stone Creek. If he gets the guns Rusk is promising, there'll be no stopping him. He's out to kill every white he can."

"He has reason."

"Because the pony soldiers took his woman?"

Katherine hid her satisfaction. So, the great white man's army had never discovered her lie. They still thought she had been Wolf Killer's wife. "Because they took me—and his daughter. And because they murdered his father, an old man, and his brother's son, who was only a child." Each word was drenched in venom. "Oh, yes, Mr. Slade, Wolf Killer has reason for every drop of blood he spills."

"He murdered before that. Long before. The Pearsons," he paused deliberately, "and others."

Katherine set her plate aside, no longer hungry. "You seem to know a great deal about Wolf Killer. And about me."

"Reports," he said tersely, "army reports on your disappearance, and on your return." He had read them all, every word.

She noticed that he did not use the word rescue, and thought the reports must have been very complete.

"And there is a file on Wolf Killer alone." His emphasis was clear. Those reports he had read more than once, trying to fit everything together so that he had a clear understanding of what drove Wolf Killer.

"I can imagine," she said bleakly. "But what have those reports to say about the actions of the United States Army?"

"Probably just what you are thinking." At her expression, he shook his head. Though he shared her outrage at the lies, that admission

51

was a luxury he could not afford. "Nobody has the right of it, but the killing has got to stop somewhere. And somebody has got to do the unpleasant parts to see that it does."

"And what is your part?" It was a taunt.

"To stop Rusk from making matters worse than they are." Which was one of the reasons he had baited her earlier, tested her. To see if she could be used to prevent any more bloodshed. Regret for his taunts was another luxury he couldn't afford. If her wounded feelings saved a life, he'd have to count it worth the cost.

"If Wolf Killer wants rifles, he'll get them." Katherine was convinced of that. She had never known Wolf Killer to fail in anything.

Across the fire, Slade's eyes were speculative. "When I came to New Braunfels I was looking for someone who might have some influence on Ford Bellamy. Maybe convince him to help me take Rusk. Looks like I almost missed the mark. The one I really need to influence is Wolf Killer. Rusk can't sell rifles if he has no one to buy them."

"You can't think I would help you?" She laughed derisively; the army had brought her nothing but pain. For her, Slade and his kind symbolized needless death and destruction. She would never help them in their slaughter of the Indian.

"Won't matter. Wolf Killer will be grateful if I bring his woman back to him."

"Nobody is *bringing* me anywhere! I'll follow

you as long as you're useful to me. But if I have to, I'll find Wolf Killer and my brother in my own way. And be damned to you!"

"Maybe. But even if you manage that, are you going to want the father of that little girl of yours murdering her own kind?"

"My daughter has no kind. She is neither white nor Indian, but the Comanche will take her and make her their own. The whites will not. And I don't care if Wolf Killer drives every white person out of the state of Texas," she ended with savage honesty.

There was dead silence, and then Slade resettled himself in his blanket. "You'd better get some sleep, Katherine Bellamy." His voice was almost gentle.

Never a fool, Katherine wrapped her blanket around her and lay down close to the fire. She kept her rifle reassuringly at hand.

Just before she slept, Slade's voice came again. "You running back to the Comanche— or away from the whites?"

She did not bother to answer.

Chapter Four

A soft whimper brought him to consciousness, a sound so faint it was almost nonexistent. Slade lay very still, trying to discern the animal that was its source. Reaching far back in his memory, he likened it to a baby's cries before it was fully awake. And then he knew it was the girl, Katherine. Still, he did not move, listening, knowing she slept. And dreamed.

He stifled the first faint twinges of sympathy that he had felt for her; and then marveled that he recognized the feelings at all. It had been a very long time since he'd had to remind himself to remain hardened to his prey, and to those he used to stalk his prey. He knew the cost of weakness. Plans went awry and innocent people died when men in his position gave in to things like sympathy.

What he did allow himself to feel was admiration. Katherine Bellamy was as proud and fierce as any Indian. The Comanche had named her aptly: Fierce Tongue. Her eyes looked a man clear through to his heart, while her tongue slashed at his soul. The army report filed by the young captain who led her "rescue" had described in detail her furious struggles to escape but only hinted at her beauty. And though she was beautiful to Slade, with her narrow waist and full breasts, he suspected her features held too much strength for most men.

Slade turned his mind abruptly from that line of thinking. There, too, lay danger. He would have to ignore his body's instinctive attraction to this girl. She was Wolf Killer's woman. With a skill born of long years of practice, he pulled his blanket closer to his face, closed out the sounds of the soft whimpers from across the camp, and slept.

The first time Katherine woke it was to the slow, faint graying of dawn. She sensed rather than saw Slade opposite her, fed the fire, and slept again. The second time she woke daylight had cracked the horizon, and Slade was rolling up his blanket. She crawled from her own, feeling stiff and grubby. Her eyes ached and she did not feel rested.

Slade disappeared into the trees, and she rekindled the fire, feeding it slowly until the flames were steady. The salt-cured slab bacon she lay onto the skillet was from her pack.

When Slade came back he carried a pot full of clear water into which he measured ground coffee beans. For the life of her, Katherine could not think of anything to say to him. She left him to tend their breakfast and escaped to the relative privacy of the sparse trees. The stream water was stingingly cold against her face and neck. She longed desperately for a bath.

The bacon was off the fire and Slade had rummaged in her saddlebag until he found her tin plate and mug. They were filled and waiting for her.

They were nearly finished eating when he spoke. "I have to meet someone in Camp San Saba before I go any farther. You coming?"

"Will you tell me where to find Broken Arrow's camp?"

"No."

She shrugged. "I'm coming."

Slade stood and tossed the last of his coffee on the fire. Katherine wolfed down the remainder of her breakfast and scrambled to wash and repack their eating utensils and pots. The cold hurt her hands as she tightened the saddle girth on her mare, but she thought the day likely to be warmer than the one before it. She gathered her reins and saw Slade waiting impassively. If he thought her slow, it did not show on his face. She was beginning to think nothing ever did. Not anger, not irritation, not anything. His eyes were equally unreadable, narrowing when he was considering but otherwise unrevealing. Only his voice ever reflected what he was feeling, and that rarely.

Just before he nudged his horse forward, his glance met hers. "You have nightmares."

It was half statement, half question. Katherine knew then why her head and her eyes ached. She did not look away. "Yes."

"We'll make San Saba tonight." It was as if his first observation had never been made.

Silently, Katherine matched Sadie's pace to the buckskin's, wishing she could dismiss her nightmares as easily as Slade. She did not need to recall them now to feel their chill. Nightmares had followed her from the moment she had been taken by the Comanche. They had changed content and intensity after her violent rescue by the military.

The weeks that had followed the attack at Stone Creek had been a waking nightmare. Terrified someone at the fort where she was held would learn Shea was not her child, she had awakened every night to images of the baby girl being torn from the safety of her arms. Horrible memories of small bodies impaled upon bayonets became even more horrible when those slaughtered innocents stared at her through Shea's eyes. No prisoners had been taken at Stone Creek, and Katherine suspected only those swift of foot had survived. Her heart ached for all those she had loved, and who had loved her.

Shaking herself free of the painful thoughts, she focused her eyes on Slade's back. He would be an easy man to hate, she thought. There was no compassion in him; none visible, anyway. He reminded her of the commander who had called Davey Pearson's death a regrettable incident. All business, and the business was war.

She wondered how much ground they would be covering to reach Slade's destination, but she would be cursed before she would ask him. She dared not say or do anything that could be taken as a sign of weakness.

Slade led the way, again north, with only a slight westward veering. By midmorning the sun was warming the air to a temperature almost mild. Ahead of her, Slade shed his coat, and within moments, Katherine followed suit.

The sun was directly overhead when Slade reined his buckskin to a halt. Wordlessly, Katherine checked Sadie, watching as Slade rummaged through his saddlebag.

Her eyes met his as he handed her a chunk of dried beef. She would be damned if she would ask to dismount and rest.

"Do you have water?"

She lifted her canteen to test it and nodded.

"Good."

Her lips twisted wryly as he nudged his horse forward. She was a woman of few words; he was a man of even fewer. By the time she had forced the last of the beef down her throat, her canteen was nearly empty. And she was still hungry.

Though Slade paced the horses expertly, the animals were beginning to tire. The terrain had gradually changed from easy slopes to irregular hills cut by streambeds. She felt Sadie's muscles strain as she pulled upward from a gully filled with mud that dragged at her hooves.

The sun sank to the middle of the western horizon, and not too long afterward Slade made a sharp gesture toward Katherine and slid his rifle from his holster. Sadie stood obediently, willing to rest after the arduous climbs followed by the downhill sliding of the past few hours. Her ears twitched at the rifle blast.

Automatically, Katherine slipped from the saddle. Her knees felt stiff as she climbed the stony incline and grasped the jackrabbit's long, soft ears. Slade watched wordlessly as she returned and mounted. She held the rabbit against her knee and nudged forward.

"Wolf Killer trains his squaws well." His eyes swept over her lithe body, and he thought of other things the warrior would have trained her to do.

She flushed a dark crimson, and the glare she turned on him would have withered the hardiest Texas sunflower. She had acted out of instinct and felt furious now with herself and with him. "It wasn't Wolf Killer who taught me."

Slade felt her fury and choked back a grin. "One of the squaws?"

"His mother." Katherine winced in memory. The lessons had not been easily learned. She had been defiant until she had learned the inevitable, degrading price of that defiance. "I carried the marks of Old Mother's switch on my arms and shoulders for months."

Slade did not look sympathetic. "You try to run away?"

She shook her head.

"Then why did she beat you?"

"Because I was ignorant. There was so much I was supposed to learn. To understand Comanche. To speak it. To prepare the food to eat and preserve it so that it would last all winter."

Watching her face, Slade realized she had almost forgotten that she spoke to him. He had a fleeting image of what it must have been like for her, a young girl helpless among one of the fiercest of the Indian tribes. The Pearson massacre and Stone Creek had changed the course of her life, and not just for those few years.

"Old Mother had other ways to teach than beating," Katherine continued softly. "For a long time I could only eat when the others had finished. Usually there wasn't enough left to stop my stomach from hurting."

"Just for ignorance?"

She shot him a quick look, almost but not

quite a smile. "Because I wanted to stay ignorant. I was stubborn."

He could believe it. And he couldn't help but appreciate it. That stubbornness was probably what had ensured her survival this long.

"And for Wolf Killer everything had to be just so. His clothes had to be sewn one way only from skins tanned and softened just right. Then I had to take care of his war shield and his weapons. It was a long time before I realized how great an honor it was for him to even let me touch them." And it was then, too, that she had begun to picture herself as Wolf Killer's woman. But he chose red-haired Jeane, whose nature had never let her defy her captors.

This time it was Slade who shot a look her way, but she did not notice. He wondered at the faraway look in her eyes. She was an unsettling kind of woman, like no one he had ever met before. He could not decide if he admired or despised her.

Before dark, they halted near a stream. The horses were left saddled, but though Katherine hobbled Sadie, the buckskin was not restrained by anything but his training. While Slade skinned his kill, Katherine built a fire. It was neat and smokeless, the spit expertly constructed. Returning, Slade eyed her handiwork while she silently dared him to comment.

They ate while the flesh was hot enough to singe hair. When Slade was done he wiped his hands on his leather pants and stood.

"Let's go."

Katherine wondered if he was deliberately rude, and then decided he had too little manners to know the difference. Unhurriedly, she finished the last two bites of her half of the rabbit and rose.

They were in Camp San Saba before she realized it. Somewhat to her surprise, Slade did not ride toward the cluster of buildings ahead but circled until they reached a long double log cabin.

Katherine dismounted tiredly, looking around her. They were at the rear of the cabin, nearer the barn adjoined by a paddock in which a big bay circled nervously at their presence.

"Turn your mare loose in there." It was an order.

She did as he said, amazed to see him lift her saddle effortlessly with his and carry them both to the interior of the barn. It was the most consideration he had shown her yet, likely because he did not want to be bothered with showing her where to put her things.

Beyond the cabin, Katherine saw the glint of starlight on the river's surface. She turned slowly, establishing their position. Following Slade blindly, she knew it would be easy for her to lose her bearings. He reminded her of Ford's hunting hound: quick on the scent, steady on the trail, relentless and calculating, baying only when the prey was undoubtedly his for the taking.

Slade returned to her side and led the way. The door of the cabin was not locked, and Slade did not bother to knock. Katherine was too tired to be hesitant about following him inside, whether it proved to be an invasion of someone's privacy or not.

She did hold back just inside the door, giving herself a moment to study the room and its occupants. It was perhaps three times as long as it was wide, and as clean as it was bare. There were two heavy planked tables with benches. Shelves, well stocked with foodstuffs, filled one corner. There were no other furnishings.

Three men sat at one of the tables. A woman stooped over the fireplace, stirring the contents of a great kettle. She straightened her thin frame as they entered, and a broad smile covered her pleasant face.

"Slade! I'll be danged but it's good to see you." Her ladle waved in accompaniment.

"Things going good for you, Birdie?"

Katherine felt a slight shock at the warmth of his tone. It was hard for her to remember that he was more human than animal. She wasn't actually sure he *was*.

The woman noticed Katherine, still cautiously near the door. "And who is this you've brought with you?"

Slade turned to glance at Katherine, and suddenly she knew she made an outlandish sight.

Her hair, tied back with a leather thong, was stringy and far from clean. Her clothes were outright filth-laden. She did not consider that the most outlandish sight to Birdie might be the rifle she carried in the crook of her arm. She was fairly tall and strong-boned, but she was slender, and the firearm looked weighty and out of place against her.

"I wouldn't exactly say I brought her," Slade replied. "Her name's Katherine, and she just came."

Katherine's face burned at the way the truth sounded, but Birdie seemed to take nothing amiss at his words.

If Slade noticed her embarrassment, he ignored it.

"You'll be wanting a room and a bed for a while," Birdie said helpfully.

"Two rooms," Katherine asserted before Slade had a chance to answer. She felt amusement in the look he gave her, but there was none on his face.

Birdie did not take her request amiss either. Maybe Slade did not make a habit of bringing women here to share his bed. She wondered what type of woman would share his bed, wondered if any woman would not find him as cold and as dangerous as she did.

"Jeb been in yet?"

Katherine started at the sound of his voice. Now she was attentive, listening for anything that might affect her quest or its outcome.

"Jeb Welles? No. You expectin' him?"

Slade nodded. "Yesterday, today, maybe tomorrow."

"Then he'll be along, unless he's got hisself killed." Birdie did not appear overly concerned by the possibility. Apparently, she did not hold him in high regard, as she seemed to do Slade. "You two hungry? I was just fixin' to dish up for these here gentlemen."

The gentlemen seemed to have forgotten their card game and were staring with almost indifferent curiosity.

"No," Slade answered, "just tell us which rooms we can have."

"Any one, I mean, two you want." She saw the direction of his questioning glance and waved a hand dismissingly. "These boys would rather sleep on the hard ground than pay for decent beds."

One of them scowled at her tart comment, but nothing was said. Katherine wondered if it was because they did not dare. For all her slight size, Birdie looked well able to take care of any troublemaker. Katherine suspected she could not have survived in this business otherwise.

Birdie saved Katherine from having to make the request hovering on the tip of her tongue. "You'll be wanting a bath, I expect, if you've been traveling far. We'll get the water on, and I'll get these fellows fed and out of here. Slade, if you'll just fetch me a couple extry pails of water and that tub from around the side . . ."

"I can do for myself," Katherine cut in quickly.

Birdie's ladle stopped, suspended in air. "Tub's heavy," she warned.

"I can manage."

"I reckon the river will do for me." Slade was already moving toward the door. He'd had a quick mental image of Katherine stripped for her bath, and his body was responding accordingly.

"Buck's out there already," Birdie warned him. "You'd better sing out afore you hit the water, else you'll scare a month of my pleasure out of him."

Slade grinned, and Katherine blushed. She had thought herself long beyond blushing— and Slade beyond grinning. It made him seem almost human.

By the time the men were finished eating, she had dragged the tub inside and Birdie had her bath water ready. Birdie did not allow the men to linger over empty plates. "You ain't paying for any roof over your heads. You can get out as well now as later. This gal's looking for a bit of privacy." She noticed Katherine's anxious look as she bolted the door behind them. Moving to lock the door as well, she winked. "Don't you worry none. Buck could chase them out with an ax, and they'd still be back when they got hungry."

Soap plopped into the water, and a soft scrub brush followed.

"Well," Birdie demanded, "what are you waiting for? Men are locked out 'til we let 'em in."

Katherine had been waiting for her to leave, but she didn't say so. She stripped and stepped into the water, modesty be damned.

While she scrubbed, Birdie bustled about clearing the table. Katherine studied her back, hating to waste an opportunity but not wanting to arouse Birdie's own curiosity. Finally, she asked, "Have you known Slade long?"

Birdie never paused. "Years. Couldn't say how many."

That didn't leave Katherine much of an opening. She was considering how to make one for herself when Birdie asked a question of her own. "You travelin' far? Winter's coming on," she added by way of warning as well as explanation for asking. Katherine suspected Birdie wasn't one to nose about.

"Not too far," Katherine said noncommittally, giving up any hope of learning more about Slade from Birdie. To do so would open herself up to answering questions she didn't want asked.

When she finished bathing Birdie stood ready to pour the last pail of unheated water over her head. Katherine rose gasping, and Birdie handed her a rough homespun towel. Rubbing briskly, Katherine dried herself, turned, and shrieked.

Birdie jumped and looked up owl-eyed from dunking Katherine's filthy garments in the hot, soapy water. "Indians?" she gasped.

"Worse," Katherine said glumly. "You just soaked the only clothes I have with me."

"Landsakes, child, they'll be dry by morning!"

"What am I supposed to do 'til then?"

Birdie's eyes narrowed in laughter. "Sleep, hon, sleep."

Resigned, Katherine wrapped herself in the towel. "Where's my bed?"

Birdie pointed to the south end of the cabin, where four doors opened off the main room. "There ain't a spot of difference between any of 'em." She jerked her head toward the single door on the north wall. "That's me and Buck's room if you need anything."

Katherine's lips twitched. "I'm not likely to come looking for you until you bring my clothes."

Birdie's cackle followed her into the room she chose at random. It held a bed, a rug, and a hook for clothing. She closed the door and ran her hands along the inside frame. There was no lock. Feeling her way in the dark, she discarded the towel and crept beneath the coverlets. The linen was clean and smelled of sunlight. She watched the crack of light beneath the door, heard Slade and the man named Buck come in from their river bath, and fell asleep to the murmuring sounds of their conversation.

Dawn woke her through the oiled skin over the narrow slit of a window. Her first thought

69

was that she had no way to get to her clothes. She did not dare to call out. Someone other than Birdie might answer that call. Fortunately, she hadn't too long to wait before there came a rap at the door and Birdie's voice calling her name softly.

"I'm awake," Katherine answered with equal quiet.

Birdie stepped into the room and placed the neatly folded clothes on the foot of the bed. "Put 'em on while they're warm and come on out for your breakfast."

Leaving the warmth of the bed, Katherine scrambled into the clothes, which retained the heat of the fire near which they had been hung.

Birdie's table was piled high with steaming johnnycakes, fried pork, fresh eggs, and plenty of hot coffee. Slade and a man Katherine assumed was Buck were already eating. Slade only glanced up briefly as she took a place beside him, but Buck gave her a quick good morning. He was a perfect match for Birdie, no taller and no larger around. And like Birdie, his lined face was full of character, strong-jawed and honest-eyed.

The outer door opened, and with a waft of chill air, two men entered. "You got enough for a couple more, Birdie?"

"I got enough for a couple dozen more," she returned. "Help yourself."

Katherine felt someone watching her and lifted her eyes to the newcomer, who had not yet spoken. He stared at her without any self-consciousness. She stared back coolly. His face, not bad-looking, creased with a grin at having gotten her attention. He seemed not to care that her reaction was less than welcoming.

She felt Slade's sudden tensing at her side and glanced sidelong at him. His attention was also on the newcomer, his glare forbidding. Katherine was reminded of the times Wolf Killer had glared just so at other young bucks who had shown too much attention to Little Feather and herself, an animal staking its territory. With Wolf Killer, Katherine had felt the thrill of anticipation, believing the day would come when the warrior would claim her as his woman. He had been like a young god to her, then. With Slade, Katherine felt only a rippling chill of warning.

The young man moved to join his companion and the moment passed, but not Katherine's reaction. Though she was convinced Slade's claim on her was not sexual, that was only a little reassuring. He believed he could use her to accomplish his goal, but she had goals of her own. She did not intend for Slade or anyone else to get in the way of that, but she could not escape the feeling that Slade's plans might definitely prove at odds with hers.

Chapter Five

Slade was looking for information. He and
Buck rode into the outpost of San Saba before
the morning sun had dried the sparkles of dew
on the grass.

When Buck tired of listening to the creak of
saddle leather, he glanced sideways at Slade.
"That's a right pretty woman."

Slade grunted. He knew Buck meant Katherine, and he knew where Buck was headed.
He didn't want to go.

"Light on her feet, too. Kind of graceful-like."

Slade scowled. "She's my ticket into Broken
Arrow's good graces."

"You sure Wolf Killer wants her back?" Buck
didn't care to picture that light-haired girl shar-
ing a lodge with the likes of Wolf Killer.

"He's made a few forays looking for her. He

attacked the fort where she was held within days after she was moved from there."

"Could have been revenge," Buck offered.

"Wolf Killer wants his woman," Slade answered bluntly. For a while, before he'd seen Katherine Bellamy, Slade had considered that Wolf Killer's main objective was the little girl, even though it was unusual for a warrior to concern himself with girl children. Now that Slade had had a good look at Katherine, he didn't doubt for a moment that Wolf Killer wanted his wife back. Slade told himself he didn't care what choices the Bellamy girl made in her life. Not if those choices took him to Broken Arrow—and to Wolf Killer.

Buck finally fell silent in the face of Slade's ill humor. Of course, he consoled himself, sometimes it was difficult to tell Slade's good moods from his bad. He hid both equally well. Buck had always wondered what there had been in Slade's past that had taught him to bury his feelings so deeply, but Slade had never offered that information. And Buck, for as long and as well as they had been friends, had never asked.

Slade learned nothing in San Saba. There was no message waiting for him at the trading post, though the trader remembered him well enough. He'd held messages for weeks in the past, just waiting for the man known only as Slade to pick them up. He was always well paid for his caretaking of those bits of paper so important to Slade. Though he'd read one once, it had done him no good. He suspected it would have held meaning only to the sender, Slade, and maybe Slade's quarry. He'd decided long ago that Slade was a bounty hunter but never voiced that opinion. And never would.

Slade hadn't really expected to find a message in San Saba. Jeb would have left word with Buck and Birdie if he'd had word to leave. But Slade had to wait for Jeb, and he wasn't one to waste his time. There were always bits and pieces to be gleaned from trappers, traders, and regular army who passed through. He and Buck passed a pleasant enough day, drinking and trading stories with those who wandered through the trading post. But Slade heard nothing new.

Katherine reached for another tin plate and realized the cloth she was using to dry dishes held almost as much water as Birdie's rinse pan. It had been a long day. Birdie was a thorough housekeeper, but she didn't have any hired help and she wasn't above accepting any that was offered. And Katherine couldn't sit idle while another woman worked. Aunt Dee had taught her far better than that.

Much to Katherine's surprise, Birdie turned out to be a grand talker—once she decided Katherine was to be trusted. It had taken a full morning for that to happen. But after the noon day diners had cleared out, the dishwater appeared to loosen her tongue as easily as it did the food crusted on pots and plates.

"I got me a fine son," Birdie said proudly, scrubbing briskly at a pot. "He's army—Fort Gates—so I get to see him often. Never had a husband," she ran on, "and never missed one, having my boy. I reckoned at times it was hard on him—not having a pa. But then Buck came along some years back and helped to raise him right."

Katherine thought of Shea and Wolf Killer and wondered. Would Shea have a father? Once Wolf Killer had been proud of his girl child, perhaps only because of her red-haired mother. Would that bond still hold strong? Whatever happened, Katherine knew she had to protect Shea, think of her and her future above all else.

"You been traveling long with Slade?"

Lost in her thoughts, Katherine started at Birdie's question. "Not too long," she returned noncommittally. "He's headed north, and so am I."

"Army send him to escort you someplace?" Birdie asked curiously.

"I thought Slade was with the Texas Rangers," Katherine asked carefully, answering nothing.

She was rewarded by a keen look. "Well, he ain't Army and he ain't a Ranger. He works for the Army out of Fort Lancaster, scouting and parleying with the Indians. They loan him out regular to the Rangers, but he don't take on any job 'less he's of a mind to."

"Who is this Jeb Welles he's here to meet?" Katherine decided to take advantage of Birdie's willingness to talk. Besides, she would rather ask the questions than answer them.

Birdie snorted; but then she answered. "Jeb's a regular. Been with the Rangers for a few years now."

"You don't like him?"

"Don't dislike him. Don't know as I trust him. He's not a bad sort, but reckless. Oh, he thinks things through, sure enough, but most times he just goes ahead and takes the chance, whatever it is."

Katherine rinsed the last pot, studying the filmed water in the rinse pan as she absorbed the information. She wasn't sure she had learned anything of importance, but it was hard to know what questions to ask when she wasn't sure what answer she was trying to find. When she spoke again she deliberately turned the conversation to Birdie's own life. The woman seemed capable of drawing information from a person like water from a well, and Katherine had no more questions of her own with which to fend her away.

By the time supper was ready, Katherine was restless. Dusk was settling, and she had not left the cabin once that day. Slade and Buck had not returned from wherever they had ridden early in the morning, and she would have choked before asking even Birdie where they had gone.

77

She caught up a shawl Birdie kept hanging on a hook near the door. "I'm going out for a while to see about Sadie."

"Sadie?"

"My mare."

"Well, Buck takes fine care of the stock, hon."

Katherine smiled. "I don't doubt it. I mostly just want to walk out for a while."

Birdie frowned slightly. "Not too far or for too long, you hear. There's lots of strangers riding through San Saba."

With a smile for her fears, Katherine surreptitiously felt for the knife tucked in her boot. Satisfied, she straightened and wrapped the woolen shawl about her shoulders.

The night was more chill than she had anticipated in the deceptive warmth of the cabin. Even the setting sun held no look of heat as it rode in a motionless sky. As it lowered, the shadows of the trees deepened beyond the protective clearing that served as a yard for the cabin. Reflected light, glinting on the San Saba River, made the course of water look like frozen fire. There was no more than a breath of wind, leaving the night to a deep, still quiet.

Katherine strolled contentedly toward the barn, glad to be away from the stiflingly solid walls of the cabin and Birdie's neverending voice. The earth was firm beneath her feet though roughened by tough clumps of dead grass.

It felt good to run her hand along Sadie's

heavily coated neck, to tug the mare's forelock
and feel her warm breath against cold fingers.
Katherine laid a cheek against the broad neck
and fought homesickness. She missed Shea and
she missed Aunt Dee and she missed Ford, who
wasn't even there waiting for her. Dee would be
feeding Shea, now, or maybe bathing the little
girl while she played in the warm water.

Walking back to the cabin, Katherine carried her thoughts of home with her. Too little aware of her surroundings, she was startled by a hand planted solidly on her shoulder.
She stopped, certain it was Slade, and turned.
The man grinned, and she recognized him with
quick dismay. He was staring, just as he had
been that morning.

"Take your hand from me," she said firmly.

He leaned in close to her so that she was
surrounded by a woods odor, not unpleasant,
of brush and smoke and game. "Out here all
alone?"

She stiffened. "Look, mister . . ."

"Just call me Harris," he said, "with or without the mister."

His constant grin was beginning to annoy
her. "I have no desire to call you anything,"
she gritted, shaking his hand from her shoulder
and moving past him.

One arm, lean but strong, scooped around
her while his hand slid against her breast. She
had not expected so bold a move, but it did not
frighten her. She slapped him, a stinging blow.

79

That served nothing.

His hand worked its way down to the waist of her pants while his other hand warded off her blows. She thought of the knife in her boot and felt a moment's disgust at not having moved it to her waist. She had little chance of freeing herself long enough to reach it now.

Furious with herself as well as him, she balled her fist and connected strongly against his throat, feeling a sense of satisfaction at his grunt of pain. "I hope somebody gut-shoots you," she said between clenched teeth.

"I'm considering it." The quiet voice came from behind Harris.

Lifting her eyes, Katherine met the flat, hard look of Slade's.

"You going to shoot me in the back, mister?" Harris asked without turning, his hands withdrawing slowly from Katherine's body. "Or are you going to give me a chance to face you?"

"You'll be just as dead either way," Slade said evenly. "Gut or back. Try apologizing to the lady. It just might buy you some time."

Katherine thought for a moment that the man, Harris, would refuse, and that Slade would end up killing him. Finally, Harris lifted one leather-clad shoulder in a shrug.

"I'm apologizing then, ma'am."

She didn't say anything or even look at him. She was still watching Slade, recognizing the absolute lack of mercy in his stance and in his eyes.

Slade never lowered the Colt. "I hope you can find another place to bed and feed tonight. It's going to be cold before long."

"I'll manage," Harris said, turning for the first time to face Slade. He studied the revolver and met Slade's eyes. His face remained expressionless, but there was an ugly edge to his gaze.

When he finally turned and walked away Katherine's shoulders slumped in relief. Though she hadn't been afraid of Harris, she had been very much afraid Slade would kill him. She'd seen way too much death in her lifetime.

"Thank you. . . ." The words died in her throat as the expression in his eyes altered subtly. For the first time he seemed to regard her as a woman, seeing her as Harris had. She took an involuntary step backward, finding she infinitely preferred his hard, calculating manner of assessing her to this. It occurred to her that she might have been in less danger from a man like Harris.

The silence between them lengthened uncomfortably. Slade did not answer her stiff words, nor did he make any move either away from or toward her. His look was almost a physical touch to Katherine's wary senses.

Abruptly, she started toward the cabin. Her legs felt unexpectedly numb, not exactly weak but certainly not trustworthy. Even now, without seeing, she knew Slade watched her.

Just before she reached to open the door

of the cabin, she heard him behind her. She hurried in without looking back.

Slade wondered at his own reaction. The sight of Harris's hand fumbling at Katherine's breeches had hit him with an icy shock, followed by burning fury. Even now, his finger ached to squeeze against the trigger of his revolver. Her pride and fierce determination to defend herself had touched him. And he couldn't afford to be touched—he knew that. Deliberately, he reminded himself that Katherine Bellamy was a white squaw, choosing to follow him back to Broken Arrow's people. He pushed away the fact that he had instigated the journey. She'd made her choice.

Birdie looked anxious as they came through the door, and for a moment Katherine wondered if her face revealed the emotions of the encounter just past. She relaxed as Birdie began to scold her.

"I was thinking it would be all cold and tasteless before you two got in. Buck came in a bit ago and said Slade was out with you, so I didn't worry none."

Katherine heard Slade stop behind her. Automatically, her eyes searched out Buck. His wide, clear gaze was fixed on her. She felt heat rise to her skin as she considered what he might have seen or what he might think existed between Slade and herself.

After a meal she could scarcely taste she helped Birdie once more with the stack of dishes. During the meal there had been no glimpse of Harris or his friend. She felt no sympathy for the man wherever he was, sheltered or not, but she had no desire to see his blood shed on her behalf.

It was still early when she turned to Birdie. "If there isn't anything else I can do to help, I think I'll go on to bed."

"There's not a blessed thing, hon. Why, I haven't had so much help around here in years." As she was speaking, Birdie grabbed a basin from a shelf and dropped soap and a scrap of cloth into it. She handed the basin and a kettle of heated water to Katherine. "If there's anything else you want, just you let me know."

"Thanks, Birdie, this is fine. Good night."

A quick glance toward the table made her feel better. Slade wasn't paying her any heed. His attention was on Buck, a bottle of whiskey, and a deck of cards on the table between them.

When she reached her room, though, she hesitated before stripping to wash. It was as if Slade's eyes were still upon her, as if he could see through the wood planks of the door. *He's forgotten you even exist,* she chided herself. Oddly, the thought made her feel lonely. And that was an alarming realization. She was used to lonely, and she would have to remain used to it. Lonely was all she might ever know, except for Shea.

Slowly, she unbuttoned her shirt and bathed

her shoulders, arms, and breasts. A shiver took her, and she finished stripping and bathed more quickly. She did not like the thoughts that were disturbing her. She did not want to fear Slade, or to wish for his attention. They had too far to travel together.

Her hair resisted the comb she tried to pull through the silken snarls. Dispassionately, she considered cutting the tangles. Wolf Killer would doubtless look askance on a squaw with cropped hair, though it was not that thought that deterred her. Wolf Killer's authority would, perhaps, bind her soon enough. For the present, she was still free to do as she chose.

She tried to rekindle the feelings she had once had for Wolf Killer. Her young heart had been broken when he had taken Jeane to his tepee. Even then, she could not feel jealous of Jeane. They had been like sisters from the moment they had been taken from Jeane's home by the Comanche warriors. She had loved Jeane, but she had loved Wolf Killer, as well. Surely those feelings for him still existed, buried deep within her, more mature than the young girl's infatuation of that long-ago past. Or had they died with her youth the day she was taken from Broken Arrow's camp?

For this moment, at least, she could feel nothing at all. Wearily, she turned her thoughts to Shea and sank to the bed. What if Shea was frightened by her absence? The possibility tormented her. She didn't have to fear for her daughter's safety—Dee was far more cautious than she in that regard—but she had no such reassurance for her daughter's emotional state. Not even the most loving of aunts could substitute for a mother; Katherine knew that for a certainty. And she *was* Shea's mother, regardless of whose blood flowed in the child's vein. *She* was Shea's mother.

Combating an ache in her throat and the sting of tears in her eyes, she crawled beneath the bedclothes, naked and shivering. She lay wakeful for hours, and just as she was finally drifting into sleep, a sound brought her sharply awake.

Through the thin partition, she heard someone enter the room just next to hers. Slade's voice was recognizable, and she realized at once that he was not alone. For him to bring someone into the tiny space of the sleeping quarters, she knew he had a need for privacy. Was this the man he had been waiting to see? She sat up, listening, but the words were indistinct. Slipping from the bed, she pressed her ear to the wall, without shame or hesitation for eavesdropping.

"Have any trouble on your way in, Jeb?"

"No. I know I'm a little late, but not because of any trouble. Harding managed to squeeze in an extra job before I could head out."

"My orders still the same?"

"Word for word. Find Rusk and put a stop to

his trading. You've got a free hand in how you do it, but it ain't going to be easy even with me along."

"You?"

"Well, there is that one change."

There was laughter in his voice, and Katherine wondered if this Jeb was as good-humored as he sounded.

Jeb continued, "Harding put Jackson with Frank, so I've been sent up to give you a hand."

"You're damned welcome," Slade admitted. "I figured we'd just be crossing paths here. I won't be sorry to have you along."

Katherine heard the clink of a bottle neck against a glass.

"So fill me in. You find that Bellamy boy's kin like you planned?"

"Yeah, I found them." Slade grunted. "There ain't no menfolk, though."

He didn't mention Katherine, and she wondered how he would explain her presence when the time came. He'd find he couldn't lose her, if that was what he planned; not, at least, until she knew where to find her brother.

"Well, I don't expect we'll need any help with the boy, and I ain't too worried about Rusk," Jeb said, "but damned if I'm keen on dealing with the Comanche, particularly Wolf Killer. You know for sure where to find 'em?"

"They wintered in Palo Duro last year. Word is, that's where the traders expect them to be again this winter."

And in those two sentences came the information Katherine needed. There was more, but nothing so valuable to Katherine as this. She listened impatiently, hoping for something else she could use, but their conversation dwindled to the casual talk of drinking companions. At that point she straightened cautiously, for the cold had made her stiff.

Back in her bed, she pondered what she had learned and what it meant to her. For one thing, it meant there was a long, hard ride ahead of her, but not nearly so long or so hard as she had anticipated. For another, and more importantly, it meant she no longer had any need for Slade. Now, she had only to decide to continue as they were and make her move later or to try to get ahead of him now.

Finally, she decided to get what sleep she could and make her decision in the morning. But that did not prove easy. Sleep eluded her, for her restless mind would not be still. Thoughts of Slade and the way he had looked at her mixed with thoughts of finding Ford, and of seeing Wolf Killer. Wolf Killer. For so long she had thought she would never see him again.

It seemed hours later that she heard Jeb leave Slade's room. He did not go far. She heard a door open and close beyond Slade's. The quiet that settled then was intense, broken only by the faint noises of the cabin itself.

Slade's door reopened, and her breath froze in her throat as she heard him leave his room—

and stop just outside hers. She lay in the same taut position for long minutes, waiting for him to make up his mind, wondering what she would do when he did. She had faced the possibility of rape when she and Jeane were first taken by the Comanche, and it seemed to her there could not be much difference between a red man bent on having a woman and a white man with the same intent. Only this time, there was no Old Mother to wrap her in the mantle of her authority and protection. And she strongly suspected Slade was drunk, between the bottle of whiskey he'd shared with Buck and the one he'd shared with Jeb Welles.

Her breath finally came again on a long sigh when Slade's footsteps carried him away from her door. He'd made his decision, and he had made one for her as well. She had to escape him now.

Chapter Six

Slade was pulled to consciousness by the acrid smell of smoke. He lay still for only a moment, disoriented, before instinctively rolling from the bed to land palms down on the floor. Coughing and choking, he crawled to the door. The room beyond was edged in flames.

Cursing, he searched the dark for his revolver, tucking it into the waist of his pants. The cabin was built for security against intruders, not against fire. The single window was no more than a slit covered by an oiled skin. There was no way out except through the door and the blazing heat beyond. Slade had seen buildings burn before; he knew how little time he had.

Grabbing the pitcher of water from the stand, he doused his hair and clothes as thoroughly as he could. He caught a full breath of the cleaner air near the floor and left the room at a crouched run. Burning bits of ash sizzled against his dampened clothes and stung his neck and face. The hair on his arms, which were held over his head protectingly, burned; then the flesh. The heat of the blaze around him was so intense, the air itself was a painful contact.

He erupted from the door of the cabin gasping for breath. Behind him, a ceiling timber cracked and fell in a whoosh of showering sparks. Until that moment he had only reacted, responding as an animal faced with danger. Instinct was the only way he had survived over the years. The scene in the yard brought him back to reality.

In front of him, Birdie and Buck clasped each other, smoke-blackened and tearless. Jeb froze in the act of pouring a pail of water over his head.

"Damn, man." Relief was evident in Jeb's voice. "I was just coming in after you."

With a groan, Slade whirled back toward the cabin. Fire leaped from a gaping hole in the roof. "Katherine." Her name was a growl on his lips.

Jeb watched in stunned silence as Slade started for the door, the frame already wreathed by bright flickers.

"Stop! Slade, she's dead!"

Birdie's voice roused Jeb to action. He tackled Slade at a run, and they both landed near enough to the door to be in danger.

Slade spat dirt, oblivious to the logs crackling only inches away from his face. "You bastard! Let me go!"

He struggled to overturn Jeb, who was smart enough to scramble until his knee was on Slade's neck, pressing his face hard against the ground. Jeb knew he'd never hold Slade otherwise. He was a strong and dirty fighter when he wanted to be.

"It's no use, damn it! Whoever Katherine is, you can't get to her now. And if you could, she wouldn't be alive!"

Another timber gave way in a burst of searing heat, and Slade went limp. Jeb eased back cautiously, ready to pounce again if necessary.

After long moments in which no one moved Jeb touched Slade's arm. "Come on. We need to get you to the river. Most of your hide's burned off."

Slade shuddered at his words. He thought of Katherine's flesh, warm and healthy.

Lurching to his feet, he flung Jeb's helping hand away. After a moment's indecision Jeb let him go, watching him stagger toward the river. He'd never seen Slade out of control.

Buck was staring at the barn and the fire reflecting against aged wood. The horses within were growing more frantic with each moment, their shrill neighs ringing through the night.

"Help me, Jeb," he said heavily. "We've got to turn the animals into the paddock in case the barn catches fire."

Buck turned his back on the flames leaping into the air, but Birdie could not look away from her dying home. Tears now rolled down her cheeks unashamedly.

Jeb moved with Buck. "Who was Slade going after? Who's Katherine?"

Buck shrugged sadly. "She rode in with him. Her last name was Bellamy."

Jeb stared at him, struck dumb. He had no more questions because he had too many. And the next few moments were too busy for speech as they battled the terrified horses, who did not want to be forced from the safety of their stalls. Jeb was bruised and bloody by the time the last one was freed. Only Slade's buckskin had not fought, but moved quietly at Jeb's command.

Buck stood at the entrance of the barn and watched them circle the paddock. If they did not settle, he would have to turn them loose altogether before they injured one another. Abruptly, he stiffened. "The mare . . . she's not here."

"What mare?"

"The girl's." He wheeled, his eyes searching the dim interior of the barn. "And her saddle. Both are gone."

Slade waded into the river, clenching his jaw against the agony of water against raw flesh. A part of him welcomed the pain. Had Katherine felt such pain? He wished he could believe her smothered by the thick smoke that had lain a palpable shroud through the cabin. He wished he could know that she had never awakened to the blazing hell around her.

He lifted his eyes toward the star-glittered heavens. Why had he not remembered her existence in his race from the cabin? As for that, why had he taunted her into following him from her home? But for him, Katherine Bellamy would be safe in New Braunfels. It was the second time a woman had died simply because of the choices he had made. And that other time, too, Elzy Rusk had been involved.

Not that he could blame Rusk for the cabin fire. And not that it mattered. The girl was dead, and he, Slade, had been the one to let her die.

After the first shock of the water wore off he began to grow numb. Teeth chattering, he started toward the riverbank, shivering harder as the cold night air struck his bare chest and dripping pants.

Moving back along the path to what was left of the still-blazing cabin, his attention was caught by a flash of moonlight against metal on the far side of the clearing. He froze and watched until the faintest of movements convinced him someone watched the scene in front of the cabin; someone who did not wish to be noticed. Forgetting his injuries, he faded into the undergrowth alongside the path and began a slow, soundless passage through the woods.

* * *

Jeb's attention was pulled from the burning rubble of the cabin as Slade dragged a man, kicking and cursing, into the clearing. Slade flung him to the ground at Jeb's feet.

"What the hell?" Jeb frowned at the man. From his face, it looked as if Slade had fallen on him with every intention to kill. He was bruised and bleeding, his broken nose swelling.

Buck stepped forward, his arm slipping around Birdie's shoulder as she moved to stand beside him.

Birdie looked down into the face of the man who had sat at her breakfast table only the morning before, eating her johnnycakes and drinking her coffee.

Slade felt guilt press deeper. The man was Harris's companion. Harris, who had been backed down by Slade's loaded revolver.

"I told him not to do it!" the man babbled, "I told him!"

Slade nudged him with the toe of his boot. "Tell me where the bastard is."

A whimper answered him. "He'll kill me. Harris will kill me if I tell you."

"I'll kill you," Slade gritted. "He's already a dead man."

Jeb laid a hand on the only part of Slade's arm that did not look burned. "The girl isn't dead."

Slade's eyes flickered. He looked beyond

Jeb to the cabin burning in upon itself. "She's dead."

"She rode out. Her horse and saddle are gone."

Slade swayed away from them, absorbing the knowledge. He staggered as he headed for the buckskin. "I'm going to find Harris. And I'm going to kill him."

With a look back at the pathetic shape crouched on the ground, Jeb moved to follow.

Chapter Seven

Ford Bellamy stared into the solid dark above
him as another grunt came from the far side
of the tepee. He considered moving his bedroll
out into the open. Most of the time the randy
activities of his traveling companions did not
disturb him. In fact, there'd been a time or
two when he'd done a little grunting himself,
not caring that the others were within hearing
distance. But tonight his mind wasn't on the
warm, squirming body of a young Comanche
woman. His mind was on Elizabeth, and on
Aunt Dee and Katherine and home.

Things quieted down in the far corner of the
tepee, but not in his mind. Damn, he wanted
to go home! He felt like such a fool. If only he
hadn't decided to sit in on that poker game. If
only he'd gotten up when he started losing. If

only the other guy hadn't pulled a gun. If only.

A soft giggle broke the silence, and Ford flinched at the sound. Shit, Louis was going to keep that squaw giggling all night. "Damn it, Louis, can't you let a body get some sleep?"

"Sure, my friend," came the easy answer. "But is it sleep you want, or maybe you would like to join us?"

"Ah, hell." Ford rolled lightly to his feet. Snatching up his bedroll, he pushed open the flap of the tepee. "I reckon I'm bad as a woman at her time of the month, Louis; don't mind me."

A chuckle followed him out into the night air. He spread his blanket near the open fire. Elzy was propped against a boulder, staring into the flames, but neither man spoke. Ford wasn't sure how he felt about Elzy. He liked Louis well enough, and the others, but Elzy had a deep side to him that was darker than Lucifer.

Elzy had been good to him. He'd helped him escape Fort Clark, and he'd let him work several trading deals. At this rate it wouldn't be long before he had earned as much money as he'd lost in that crooked poker game. But then what? He couldn't take it home to Aunt Dee. If he did, he'd be arrested for murder.

Yet he suspected he wouldn't want to ride with Elzy for much longer. So far all the trades he had knowledge of could have been conducted in a Sunday-school class, but what were they doing here with the Comanche?

Oh, he'd been as eager as any of them to reach Broken Arrow, but for reasons that had nothing to do with any deal Elzy planned to cut. He had some vague idea of letting Wolf Killer know his wife and daughter were safe and sound. But he hadn't done that. The raw lifestyle of these people dismayed him. He didn't want Katherine and Shea living in this, no matter how gladly they would be accepted. Nor could he accept the image of the warrior Wolf Killer taking his sister's body in the corner of a tepee filled with other members of the family. He knew he was being hypocritical, all things considered, but he couldn't help it.

So he had avoided Wolf Killer, never mentioning to anyone that he was the brother of the white squaw who had been torn from the tribe at Stone Creek.

Chapter Eight

Katherine dreamed of food and woke to the pangs of hunger. Driven by a sense of urgency, she had ridden long and hard the previous day, not allowing any time for hunting. The few times she and Sadie had stopped to rest she had eaten parched corn.

She wondered what Slade had thought when he woke to find her gone. Wondered what he would think when he reached Broken Arrow's winter camp and found her there ahead of him. Most of all, she wondered why she kept thinking of him.

Rubbing her eyes, she stretched the stiffness born of a cold night and the hard ground from her aching limbs. As she glanced around her campsite, marked only by a single stunted mesquite, she knew it was not as well chosen as Slade's would have been. She smiled; and then frowned, irritated that thoughts of the man continued to surface now that she was free of his presence.

As she buried the ashes of her campfire, she regretted that she'd had no better use for it than the coffee that was all that was left of her supplies. And there was little enough of that. If she wasn't such a good shot, she might well have starved before reaching the Palo Duro canyon.

When the sun was high her keen eyes sighted a plump quail, and she eased her rifle from the saddle. Her mouth watered as she squeezed the trigger. She nudged the mare forward. "Time for breakfast."

She dined on jackrabbit the following day, and on a blue-winged mallard the next. Though she glanced often over her shoulder, there was never a glimpse of a single rider or even a pair following her. The rough hills gave way to sloping, short-grassed plains. On the fourth, or maybe it was the fifth afternoon, she detoured far around what looked to be a fort. She saw no sign of activity or inhabitation around or near it, but she had no desire to dare closer.

Llana Estacado, the Staked Plain, lay before her. The streams and river branches had thinned, and she was careful to conserve her water from one watering hole to the next. She was grateful for the continuingly clear though increasingly cool weather. Her coffee was gone now, but small game remained abundant, and

Sadie did not lack for grazing. Thus far, she had been fortunate enough to encounter no predators, either four-legged or two.

By midafternoon her stomach was tightening against cramps of hunger. She felled a wild turkey with one skillful shot. While she built a fire on a rocky slope, Sadie made the most of the stop, snatching avidly at the tough, dying grass. Katherine had the large, stringy bird ready for the fire when she heard hooves drumming over the rise ahead of her.

The turkey hit the flames lapping at charred buffalo chips as she spun for her rifle. She stood, lifted the barrel, braced her legs, and waited.

The rider was a lone man, heavy jowled, powerfully built, and even more powerfully odorous. He stopped his shaggily coated pony and stared down the bore of her rifle. With a surprising lightness, he left his saddle.

Her finger trembled on the trigger as he came within an arm's length of the killing end of her rifle.

He paused and sniffed the air as he stared down at her fire. "Dinner's aburnin'." This astute pronouncement was followed by a great shout of laughter.

Katherine stared.

"Got somethin' better'n that cooking. Sling that there rifle in your holster and come on to Ugly Jack's place."

She studied him warily, and her tone was

sharp as she asked, "I suppose you're Ugly Jack?"

"Nary a soul but me." He squinted his eyes in seriousness. "You ain't needin' to suspicion me. It's been so many years since old Jack Lawson's seen a white woman, he would be purely terrified of lying with one."

She burned at his candor but lowered her rifle slowly, not yet trusting and not at all sure what her next move should be.

Without waiting for her acceptance of his invitation, he began to kick dirt over her fire. "Grab your pony and let's get home."

Katherine cursed her luck. An inner sense warned her that if she refused to go with him, she would be forced. At least if she appeared willing, she would still be free. Still suspicious, she followed reluctantly as he rode out.

Home to Jack Lawson, she soon discovered, was a dugout in the swiftly dropping slope of an escarpment. The dugout was a trading place for the Comanche and the Kiowa. Ugly Jack had placed himself right at the edge of the Comanche homelands.

"There's been many a hostage I've helped to ransom. Yes'm, more than one young'un has made it back home to kin because of Ugly Jack. 'Course, most of 'ems folks was kilt when they was took, but there's always some kind of family left that's willing to pay to get 'em back."

Katherine was silent, knowing the ransom was paid in coin to this man. To the Indians, he would then give iron goods and blankets, probably whiskey, maybe guns.

Sprawled just outside his door was a vicious-looking animal, part dog, part wolf. With a hideous snarl, the wolf dog rose, hackles lifted, fangs bared, looking straight at Katherine.

Ugly Jack laughed at his reaction. "He hates strangers." He placed a broad palm on the creature's head, and the wolf dog subsided.

Katherine breathed a little prayer that he would not bother Sadie, who was penned with Ugly Jack's pony on one side of the dugout's entrance. She stepped quickly into the cabin ahead of Ugly Jack, glad that the wolf dog's obedience to his master overrode his hatred of strangers.

The trader's supplies were heaped on the hard earth floor against walls of damp earth. There were random piles of buffalo hides, harsh blankets of wool, bags of meal—doubtless bug-infested—and neat stacks of iron pans and kettles. No rifles were visible, and she wondered about that. Ugly Jack was as nearly outside the law's reach as a man could be and still be living. She wasn't ready to believe him too scrupulous to supply firearms to the Indians he served. She thought of Ford and his companions. No, she told herself, Ford would have no part of the dealings of which Slade had accused him, but she could believe it of this man.

Keeping his word, Ugly Jack dished up two full bowls of greasy buffalo stew.

"Odd I never heard of you," Katherine said around a blistering mouthful. She was too hungry to quibble over the false assurances Ugly Jack had made that his meal would be better than her ruined turkey.

"Any reason you should have?" Ugly Jack's look was shrewd despite the blandness of his tone. He had not yet asked what she was doing, a woman alone, at the edge of the Staked Plain.

She clamped her teeth over the truth and lifted her shoulders. "No reason, I reckon."

"Where you headed?"

Her spoon, made of buffalo horn, scraped the bottom of the bowl. "That's good enough for a second bowl." It wasn't, but her stomach still cried out for filling.

Amiably, he refilled the wooden bowl and handed it back to her. "Where you headed?" He eyed her patiently.

He did not intend to be evaded or ignored, she realized. "North." She waved her spoon in that general direction before dipping it back into the stew.

"Ain't nothin' out there but savages."

She gave him a level look. If she had been a man, her silence would have ended the discussion. A man's actions, however foolish and however wild they might appear, were accepted as his own concern and no one else's. Unfortunately, Katherine was not a man.

"Be a shame to have all that purty hair a hangin' on some lodgepole."

"The Kiowa could be a problem," she admitted.

"But not the Comanche."

She could have admired him for his perception if it was not so aggravating. Then it dawned on her that here was her protection from Ugly Jack himself. "The Comanche won't be," she agreed, "not if I can find Wolf Killer or some other of Broken Arrow's people. Even so, I can speak enough Comanche to keep their hands off me until my story can be checked."

"And it'll hold?"

"It will."

He sipped the vile brew he offered to her as coffee and studied her with squinted eyes. "Then I reckon you'd be Kate Bellamy."

She stared. "I am."

He chuckled at her reaction. "Oh, I've heard of you right enough. Any folks what's got anything to do with the Comanche around here has. Tell me, gal, what you going to do if it's Kiowa you come on first?"

She did not want to answer that one, but there was no way she could make him forget he'd asked. "Then I expect I'm in trouble," she admitted.

He was silent, and she sat watching him. She didn't trust the man, and she would have preferred that he knew nothing of her. Her connection with the Comanche would be no help to her against him. He did not look as if he would be frightened of even the most bloodthirsty of warriors. She wasn't sure why she instinctively mistrusted him, but she did. It wasn't because of the way he lived, nor even his rough looks. She'd seen worse. Her mistrust came from something Ford had always called a gut feeling, something you knew without knowing how you knew it. And that gut feeling told her Ugly Jack was going to be a problem.

He got up without saying anything further on the subject. "I'll feed that mare of yours along with my beast."

Alone, she cleared their dishes from the table, ignoring the scum that was caked on the table's scarred surface. Dark was closing in by the time Ugly Jack returned to the cabin. It seemed to her that he had been gone far longer than was necessary, but perhaps he had more to do than just feed two horses.

He scooped up a ladle of the stew and refilled his bowl, placing it outside the door for the wolf dog.

When he stepped back in she said, "I'll be leaving at first light."

"I'll go along 'til you get where you're goin'."

"No." She held her voice firm.

His eyes narrowed in his heavy, pitted face. "Ain't up to you, gal."

Her mouth grew dry and her palms clammy as she regarded him. This was what she had feared. She braced herself. It could be dangerous to stand up to him, but she couldn't back down either. "I won't take you to Wolf Killer."

He laughed hugely. "Ain't needin' you to. I know where to find him. And you're as good as buffalo hides or furs to me, gal. Ransoming hostages works both ways. Some the white folks pays for—some the Indians pays for."

"You bastard!" She was furious that she had let herself be trapped, her rifle neatly holstered on her saddle, which hung on a peg with Ugly Jack between it and her.

"That's just what I am," he grinned, "a bastard, but my mama didn't care, and I don't either."

He turned his back on her, obviously intent on placing his weapon and hers out of reach. Deftly, she slipped the knife from her boot in a smooth motion that did not catch his attention.

"Stand away from my rifle." She marveled that her voice came out as firmly as she intended.

Ugly Jack turned to stare incredulously at the slim blade. "You think that li'l thing can stop me?"

A huge paw came at her, and she slashed with the knife.

The trader roared and slung blood from the gash. "Damn me!" he exclaimed, more in surprise than anger. His fist caught her on the side of the head, and the knife went spinning from her fingers.

Tears blurred her eyes as she braced herself

to rise. She was nearly blinded with pain as she stood in front of him, proud and defeated.

"By God," he said, "I purely admire a woman with grit."

"You bastard," she said again. It wasn't original, but it suited her feelings of the moment.

Ugly Jack took both rifles from their holsters. "Might as well get some sleep, gal. You're caught for sure." He stretched out on the filthy pile of buffalo robes that was obviously his bed and was snoring within minutes.

Katherine reached for a chair and sat glumly. The rifles were under one monstrous arm and the beast stood guard outside the door. She leaned over to pick up her knife and regarded it ruefully before slipping it back into her boot. As a weapon it had proven something less than effective.

"Damn," she said aloud. For the first time she wished she had stayed with Slade. A knife kept handy would have prevented any unwelcome midnight visits. Slade was no mountain like Ugly Jack. He would at least have had respect for her weapon.

Breakfast was more buffalo stew. At least, Ugly Jack broke his night's fast, while Katherine looked on balefully. Her appetite had failed her when she watched his method of cooking; he simply added fresh meat and plant roots to the old stew. Her stomach quivered at the knowledge that she had eaten of it unsuspectingly.

When he was done he drowned the fire

beneath the kettle. She shuddered to think he would simply rekindle it on his return, eating the days', maybe weeks', old stew for his next meal. Leaving his dirty dishes on the table, he picked up his rifle and hung hers on pegs placed near the dirt ceiling braced with cured saplings. He gestured her out the door, where he petted the wolf dog and then shoved him toward the cabin. The beast leaped over the threshold, and Ugly Jack bolted the door from the outside. Any intruder would not live long enough to enjoy Ugly Jack's store of goods.

Ugly Jack had saddled the horses earlier, and Katherine quickly checked Sadie's girth to make sure it did not pinch. Her saddlebags hung in place, only her rifle was missing. She was furious at the loss but said nothing. It would do no good.

"Let's go." He spoke around a wad of the tobacco that had ruined his teeth years ago.

Traveling alone had been hard and sometimes a little frightening, but Katherine heartily wished she was alone again. Three days passed on the broad sweep of the Staked Plain, and there was never one opportunity to rid herself of Ugly Jack. She would have used any means to do so, but he was too watchful, too ready for her to make a move. She felt he was laughing at her inwardly, and the thought increased her rancor.

He never tried to make conversation with her, though he was fond of talking to his horse, a mean-tempered Indian pony.

Late one afternoon they reached the Red
River. The next morning, Katherine knew, they
would have to turn west, following the riverbed.
She was getting desperate to escape before he
brought her to Wolf Killer in the ignominious
position of hostage. It was a matter of pride.
It was, also, that she feared Wolf Killer would
never believe she had returned to him willingly
under such circumstances.

Wolf Killer was more than a fierce warrior.
He was a strong, proud man, as well. If he
believed her unwilling, she could not hope to
influence him. How could she convince him to
have Rusk sent away from the tribe then? Fear
made her want Rusk and his men gone. He
might—likely would—bring the soldiers down
on the band. Again. And the people of Broken
Arrow needed no more suffering.

Her gaze followed Ugly Jack's movements
across the campfire as he slowly sharpened his
hunting blade on a piece of sandstone. It was
a procedure he followed every night; one of
habit, she suspected, rather than need. She'd
had time enough to ascertain that he liked for
his actions to follow a definite pattern, one he
broke only when forced. In a few minutes he
would carefully feed the fire, roll up his blanket, and sleep, his rifle grasped in one thick-
fingered paw.

She lay down in her blanket before he could
put away his knife and sandstone. Not even

Aunt Dee could have sworn she was not far into sleep a few minutes later.

Ugly Jack completed his nightly ritual and settled into his blanket with a grunt. Katherine held her breathing steady and waited. The horses made small sounds of grazing while a nightbird's soft but unmelodious voice haunted the surrounding dark. And then, finally, the nightbird was rivaled by Ugly Jack's unlovely snores.

A few minutes more passed before Katherine allowed herself to sit. Her hand moved cautiously along the ground until it encountered one of the stones she had flung from the spot where she had spread her blanket. Her fingers closed around the rock, discovered it was too small, and moved on. The next seemed right. She grasped it firmly as she got to her feet.

Tiny, sharp stones dug into the worn soles of her boots as she crept around the fire. She stopped near Ugly Jack's head. His slumber was peaceful, but she did not dare hesitate. And she knew the danger she would be in if one blow did not suffice. His strength and the thickness of his skull were all that had held her from this course for even this long. He would kill her if she failed.

Blocking out her thoughts, and at the last possible moment squeezing her eyes shut, she stooped, bringing the stone against his brow with every ounce of her not inconsiderable strength. Her shoulder socket and elbow tingled

113

at the force of the blow. Her stomach quivered at the sickening thud. She flung the rock from her, nauseated by what she'd been forced to do. She had defended herself many times and in many ways, but she had never injured anyone not engaged in trying to injure her first.

For long moments she stood fighting the weakness that swept her, afraid to open her eyes and find she had killed him. There was a slight shifting near her feet; then, incredibly, Ugly Jack snored. Her eyes flew open and she backed hastily away.

Whirling, heart pounding, she gathered her belongings in haste. At the last minute she returned to Ugly Jack and held her breath as she eased the rifle stock from his slack fingers.

After saddling Sadie she turned the other horse free, though he did not seem inclined to pursue that freedom. She wanted nothing that belonged to the felled trader but the rifle. She deemed that an even trade for her own.

Chapter Nine

Dee turned away from the front-room window, angry to realize she'd been watching the horizon and worrying once more. She knew from past experience how very little could be accomplished that way. She'd watched and waited for Ford, Senior, and he had never returned. Watching and waiting for Katherine had not brought her home from the Comanche any sooner. Nor would it bring her niece and nephew home now.

The curtain swung gently into place, and Dee sighed.

You need a life of your own, Dee McKenna. Dee heard again the soft sound of Doyle's voice in her ear, and her lips curved in a smile. She suspected the man was right, after all. Doyle Shanley wanted to marry her, and judging by her reaction to his touch she suspected she would be wise to do so. Her body seemed not to recall that she was nearly old enough for Shea to be her granddaughter.

"Miss Dee?" Yates called to her from the back door, and she hurried to see how he and Shea had fared at egg collection. Shea wanted to do more and more as she tested the limits of her abilities—and Dee's patience.

To her relief, Yates was still smiling. Shea held out her little basket proudly. "See, Mama?"

"Yes, darlin', Aunt Dee sees."

Shea had begun calling her Mama several days after Katherine had ridden off in search of her brother. Dee corrected her each time, but without making an issue of it, which might upset the little girl. So far she'd had no luck in the correcting. Shea needed her mother, and Dee tried hard to ignore the soft, responsive chord that was struck deep within her each time Shea called her Mama.

"Ben, we'll be going into church this morning with Mr. Shanley. Will you kill a young fryer for me while we're gone?"

Yates nodded, and turned away with an unsettled feeling. Things were sure changing fast. Shanley was here every minute propriety allowed, which Yates didn't mind, because Shanley was a good sort. But taking the little 'un to church—well, he didn't know about that. Folks in town could be cruel.

Dee found herself humming as she readied herself and Shea for church services. She carefully tied a ribbon in Shea's silky hair and recalled with a pang the many years of dressing Ford and Katherine for Sunday worship. She and Ford had continued to go together through the long months of Katherine's captivity, when they had not known if she was even alive— and had feared it would be better if she was not.

Dee had not ceased to attend church until the first week of Katherine's return, when she had walked through the doors so proudly with her niece and nephew at her side. She had been so eager for her church family to share her happiness, her relief. What she had been met with, instead, had been the shocked dismay on so many faces, the outrage on so many others, as they realized Katherine Bellamy expected them to take her half-breed daughter into their midst.

Dee's bewilderment had turned to an outrage of her own, and when she and Katherine and Ford had left the church with Shea that day they had not returned. The pastor had made many trips to their farm, pleading and even exhorting for their return. But Dee had only to close her eyes to recall Katherine's wounded look, and her resolve was stengthened. The pastor was invited to join their own Sunday services at the kitchen table, but, no, they would not be back to church.

But Dee had suspected for some time that they had made the wrong choice. Doyle was certain of it. "You didn't give them enough of a chance," he'd insisted. "Everybody deserves at least one more chance after they've been stupid. Let them get to know Shea, and they'll love her."

Dee and Shea were ready by the time Doyle stopped his buckboard at the front door. Holding Shea's hand, Dee stepped out onto the porch and smiled at him.

Doyle's pride was evident when he climbed down to meet them. His smile was broad across his face. Dee felt treasured when he lifted her carefully up to the seat and then handed up Shea to her. He stood staring up at the two of them as if they were his reason for being— his own wife and daughter. The sun was shining on his pale hair, gleaming against his blue eyes, and Dee felt a pride of her own. She was thirty-four years old, encumbered by a child many men would consider an anathema, and the most eligible bachelor in New Braunfels sought her company at every opportunity.

Her body responded to his presence when he climbed up and settled beside her, elbow to elbow, his thigh barely brushing against her skirts.

With a flick of the reins, he started the team forward. Dee felt a surge of warmth as his muscled shoulder brushed against hers, and then she blushed at her own reaction. She might be able to convince a lot of the good folk of New Braunfels that she was being practical in finally allowing a man to come calling—after all, a woman had to look toward her future—but Dee knew she could never lie to herself. Doyle Shanley made her forget a lot of lonely things in her past and promised a future that tempted her more each day.

Only as they reached the little whitewashed church did Dee's spirits flag. Doyle seemed to sense her uncertainty as the building came into view. He cast a glance at the small knot of people gathered at the front door and took one hand from the reins to clasp hers briefly. He didn't so much as look at her, but by his action Dee felt protected and strengthened.

Shea, seated upon Dee's lap, began to bounce a little with her excitement as Doyle pulled the team to a stop and set the brake in the buckboard. He jumped to the ground, smiling at her chatter as he lifted his arms to catch her when she jumped exuberantly. Standing her at his knee, he instructed her to be very still. Then, with tender care, he lifted Deirdre McKenna from the wagon while a dozen pairs of eyes looked on.

When Dee stooped to take Shea in her arms Doyle stopped her. "I'll carry Shea," he said quietly.

Dee straightened slowly. His handsome jaw was set, and Dee knew he did two things by his action. He laid further claim to them as his chosen family—and challenged the church-goers watching to snub those he had chosen. Dee forced her stiff shoulders to relax.

Doyle, holding Shea lovingly against his chest, stood watching the woman he adored. When she smiled and placed her hand in the crook of his elbow he smiled broadly in return.

They turned together and walked toward the congregation.

Not a soul in that little church met Doyle Shanley's challenge.

Chapter Ten

Instinctively, Katherine avoided the Red River as long as possible. Along its path there were bound to be Indians, and not necessarily Comanche. The Kiowa came here, also, and though they were allies of the Comanche, she had no intention of testing their loyalty with her safety.

A chill winter wind swept the open mesa, causing Sadie to stagger now and again under its force. Katherine could only hope she was guiding the mare in the right direction, for the cold made her eyes tear, and the stars, her guideposts, danced in the blur. She longed to stop but did not dare. She told herself it was only exhaustion that made her doubt herself, that made her wonder if she had been foolish to strike out on her own and leave Slade behind.

Morning came but brought no warm sunlight. The sky was as coldly silver as it had been the day before. After midday she reined Sadie closer to the river course. By now, they were headed as much north as west. Her nerves tautened as she realized the river was deepening to a gorge. The Palo Duro Canyon was near, very near. So, too, was her hour of reckoning, the moment in which she would face Wolf Killer and make her decision.

Two hours later, Sadie stood on the rim of the deep, red-walled gorge. It was here Katherine had spent her first miserable months with the Comanche. Now she was returning by her own choice.

Below her was the village of Broken Arrow. She knew this with a certainty that had no source other than herself. The tepees, with their new lodgepoles and buffalo-hide covers, beckoned to her. She could see the movement of the people, hear their voices, faint in the immensity of the great canyon. She wondered how many of her old friends had survived that horrible night on Stone Creek.

She nudged Sadie down the slope, halted the mare at the sound of harsh laughter behind her, and turned. Her blood chilled to ice.

This time it was she who stared into the bore of a gun. Ugly Jack held the weapon, an unwieldy pistol of dubious reliability but wicked aspect. Reluctantly, Katherine lifted her gaze from the gun to Ugly Jack.

His eyes were slits of fury. "I should blast you right here, you little bitch!"

Katherine knew well enough that her only avenue of escape lay at her back. There was a worn, rough path downward, but on either side were down-dropping cliffs. Ugly Jack stood between her and flight across the plains. In one split second Katherine made her decision.

Sadie wheeled, startled by the savage handling of her reins from a mistress who had never been anything but gentle with her. Hard boot heels pounded her ribs, and she plunged recklessly downward, terror-driven.

Katherine's back burned in anticipation of the bullet that could not miss at so close a range. It did not come. Instead, she heard the stumbling of horse's hooves behind her. She prayed Sadie's feet would find only firm ground and that Ugly Jack's pony would stumble beneath his weight. She recalled the moment when she could have struck Ugly Jack a second and perhaps final blow and wished she had seized that opportunity.

They were near the base of the cliff, the first tepee not too far distant. Katherine's throat was raw, her chest aching from the tortured breaths she drew.

Sadie placed her foot on a stone, and it rolled beneath her weight. The little mare stumbled to her knees, pitching Katherine forward over her shoulder. Katherine hit the gravelly earth and slid downward, tearing her forearm, sleeve, and

123

skin, against a cactus. Her collarbone struck painfully against the rough trunk of a cedar. At the base of the descending path she scrambled to her feet and knew despair when her knees buckled with the effort.

Ugly Jack was on her before she could rise again. He grabbed a handful of her hair and jerked her head back so that she was looking into his face. His lips were curled, baring his teeth, and she was reminded of his dog. He waved his blade, so frequently sharpened, with threatening abandon near her face. Katherine closed her eyes, biting the soft inside of her lips so that she would not cry out when the blade bit into her flesh.

"What happens here?"

Her eyes flew open at the familiar Comanche words. The young brave stood watching, poised but not yet ready to intervene.

"A man treats his slave as he will," Ugly Jack answered capably.

Katherine saw the frown of the young warrior but knew it did not convey any concern for her. In a moment he would turn away. Ugly Jack was known to him and trusted, particularly as he was apparently alone save for the woman he called slave. Besides, a man could, indeed, treat a slave as he wished.

"Wait!" She called to him quickly, before Ugly Jack could silence her. The brave turned his eyes fully to her face, and she saw his faint look of perplexity, perhaps at the Comanche word on her tongue, perhaps in vague memory. He had known her a regal squaw in soft skins. He did not know this disheveled female in the clothing of the white man. "You must wait," she pleaded.

The hand in her hair tightened; the knife dropped lower.

The brave warned Ugly Jack with a growled "No."

Relief weakened her as she said to him, "Is the woman of Wolf Killer a slave?" It was not a lie. Though Wolf Killer had never taken her for wife, none of the tribe had doubted that he would. But Stone Creek had come before that day.

Recognition dawned as he drew nearer, but the brave held his reaction in tight check. "It is Fierce Tongue?"

Defeated, Ugly Jack drew away. Feeling his grip relax, Katherine got to her feet, ignoring every sharp ache and dull throb. "It is she." Her voice was quiet. Memories assailed her. Fierce Tongue, the name given her in anger and in jest when she had long ago defied her captors so fiercely.

"You will come." He ignored the white trader.

"My mare," Katherine said urgently, gesturing to Sadie, who stood quietly nearby.

Before Katherine could move toward her Ugly Jack slipped the rifle from the saddle holster. His smirk dared Katherine to protest. The brave seized the dangling reins, and Katherine felt reassured when Sadie followed him without a limp. The rifle seemed of little importance, now, and she did not speak of it.

Katherine was left to walk unaided. The physical discomfort, however, faded before her thoughts. What would Wolf Killer's reaction be to the sight of her? Only now, with him so near, did she feel afraid. She had named herself as his woman to this young warrior, but she did not know if she was prepared for the choice she had just made.

She straightened her shoulders and stepped forward proudly. She had done nothing wrong. She would not slink back into the camp of the People.

The scattering of tepees was sheltered by a grove of cedar trees near a clear stream that branched out from the river. The people outside fell silent at the approach of a white man and a white woman with one of the braves of the village. Some of them Katherine recognized at once; at some she took a longer look. She realized a year had made a difference in many things.

Broken Arrow's tepee centered the camp, and it was here they stopped. Broken Arrow was civil leader of this band of the People. In decisions of peacetime his word held sway. In disputes among the tribe members his arbitration was sought. His medicine was good.

One of the women who had been patiently scraping a green buffalo hide outside the lodge ducked inside at their approach. Within moments, Broken Arrow emerged. He had aged. One year could not have made such a difference. But the events of that year—the loss of many lives in a village helpless before the white soldiers' attack, the slaughter of a fine herd of horses, the burning of laboriously acquired necessities—these things could, and had, turned an honored though aging warrior into an old man. The tribe was not nearly as decimated as Katherine had feared, but it had not the look of prosperity that she remembered. It had been a hard year for all.

Broken Arrow needed no prompting as to Katherine's identity. "Fierce Tongue." She thought he smiled faintly. She bowed her head in mute confirmation.

His eyes looked beyond her to the white trader and the young brave. The Comanche Katherine remembered as Sun Stick stepped forward, drawing attention to his words.

"This man who has been one trusted by the People was with Fierce Tongue when I found her. His knife was at her throat."

"This is so?" Broken Arrow's plucked brows furrowed.

"She cracked my skull," Ugly Jack said sharply, "and she ran. Does not one of the People treat his possessions in his own manner?"

"What do you say in answer to this, Fierce Tongue?"

She sensed sympathy, though the hooked nose and thin, set lips revealed nothing. "I say this man," her look was contemptuous, "claims what is not his to claim. I am of the People. If I belong to any man, that man is Wolf Killer."

The old warrior nodded. "Then Wolf Killer must claim what is his when he returns."

Her heart plummeted. This was a contingency she had not foreseen. Her thoughts had been that if Wolf Killer did not desire her, she would return home. Would she, instead, be given over to the trader? She controlled a shudder, for all eyes were upon her.

There was a commotion behind them. Sun Stick yielded his place to an urgent gesture. Strong hands on Katherine's shoulders turned her around.

Her eyes burned with tears that blurred rich copper hair, dark eyes—McKenna coloring.

"Ford! Oh, Ford!" She felt him press her against his chest and hardly noticed the pangs of her bruised body.

"They were saying that it was the yellow-haired squaw who had returned," Ford said, squeezing her nearly breathless. "I could hardly believe it was you."

"Where is Wolf Killer, Ford?" she asked when she could speak again, conscious of Ugly Jack hovering nearby. She was not yet out of danger.

"He led a handful of warriors down into New Mexico," he replied. "One last raid before the

128

snows. I thought he'd be back by now."

Katherine was dismayed at how easily and lightly Ford talked of Wolf Killer's raiding. She became aware of the silence that was all around them and turned back to Broken Arrow.

"This is my brother," she said proudly.

The tribal leader nodded, unsurprised. "You will wish to speak in private. I will send word to you later."

Ford led her through the silent people who parted to let them pass. She did not look back to see if Ugly Jack was watching her. She knew that he would be. He would feel cheated of his ransom—and cheated of his revenge.

On the outer fringes of the crowd stood a young woman, a cradleboard strapped to her back. Her dark lips curved into a smile. "Fierce Tongue," she called softly.

"Beaver Talks!" Katherine stopped, choked by feelings too strong to allow speech.

This woman, no more than a girl, was her friend. For many months, Katherine could only believe her dead, and her then-unborn child with her. A livid scar across her temple was mute testimony of the savagery that had felled her. Katherine could still picture the soldier who had stood over her. He had been blond-mustached with eyes as pale and blue as a winter sky. And she could still see his expression, filled with hatred for a weaponless, heavily pregnant girl. He had been poised to scalp her when another officer had called to him for help. She blessed the unknown man who had been the unwitting savior of her friend.

The baby in the cradleboard was hidden from sight, but she was reminded achingly of Shea, who had once ridden in such secure comfort on the strength of her back through the long months of Little Feather's illness.

She felt Ford's impatience through the pressure of his hand on her elbow. "Later," she said, "later, Beaver Talks, we will visit. My heart is gladdened by the sight of you."

"And mine," the girl responded, but Katherine thought she saw a sadness lurking in her eyes.

Ford drew her on. They entered a lodge set apart from the others. Three men lounged within. Katherine had a jumbled impression of bearded faces and hard eyes and was reminded of Slade. He would not have been distinguishable from these outlaws.

"Found her, did you," one of them commented.

Later, Katherine would learn that he was Rusk. Now she knew only that she recoiled instinctively from his obsidian stare.

"Yeah," Ford returned. "Leave us alone awhile."

To her surprise, they complied with only slight grumbling, and that was good-natured. She realized then that the brother she had looked upon as yet a boy was regarded as a man and their equal by his companions.

As cold at it was outside, it was stifling within. Automatically, Katherine went out and adjusted the pole that was hooked to the smoke hole flap.

Ford smiled at her as she came back in, but the smile held sadness. "Right at home, ain't you, Kate?" He sat cross-legged in front of the fire, but Katherine remained standing, too tense to sit still.

"Yes," she said softly, "I suppose I am."

He nodded slowly. "I reckon I expected you would be, though I ain't sure it's for the best."

Katherine hesitated. "Does . . . does Wolf Killer want me?"

"He wants you. And he wants his daughter. But these are things I've heard, not anything he's told me. He doesn't know you're my sister. I've heard other things too."

Ford watched her, and the look in his eyes was knowing. Katherine sighed in answer to that knowledge. "No, Shea isn't my daughter, at least not by blood. But Little Feather—Jeane— was never strong after Shea was born. I took care of her almost from the first."

She couldn't read anything in Ford's expression now. "The soldiers would have killed her if I hadn't lied, if I hadn't told them she was completely white. By the time it was light enough to see the truth, the blood lust had died down. I told them she was my daughter by Wolf Killer.

All of Jeane's family was dead; Shea had no one but me."

Ford considered all his sister had sacrificed for the little girl he would always feel was a part of his family and nodded. "I understand, Kate. I'm proud of what you did." He frowned slightly. "But you were never Wolf Killer's squaw. . . . Are you sure this is the kind of life you want?" It was a rough one; they both knew that.

"What kind of life can Shea ever have in New Braunfels?"

"There are other towns," Ford offered.

"Would it be any different some other place?" Katherine asked sadly.

"I don't know," he admitted. "But I've always thought you judged too harshly and too soon. You blame the whites more for their crimes than you do the Comanche for the same acts. You've got your own prejudices, Kate, and you'll see that one day."

Ford found it hard to meet the hurt look in her eyes, but these were things he needed to say; things that needed to be said. "The people of New Braunfels aren't the soldiers of the Stone Creek massacre, but you came home determined to act as if they were. You expected them to be cruel to Shea, and you treated them as if they were even before they had a chance to make up their own minds about how they felt."

"How can you say these things to me?"

Katherine's voice was trembling. This wasn't what she had expected from her brother.

"Because they're true, and because I love you. I know there are some in New Braunfels who feel exactly as you think they do, but there are a lot more who don't. And you never gave them a chance. It can't be too late, Katherine."

"Yes," she said bleakly, "it is. Much too late."

"You could let Shea's father take her." The suggestion hung between them.

Tears burned in Katherine's eyes. "I don't think I could, Ford," she said in a low voice. "I've thought of it, and the thought is like ripping my own heart out. I love Shea. I don't think I could love her more if I *had* given birth to her."

She dropped to her knees in front of Ford. "The only way I could ever give Shea up is if I thought it would be best for her."

Ford stirred at the fire with a stick. There wasn't much left to say on the subject then. "How did you know where to find Wolf Killer?"

"It was you I was looking for," she said slowly.

Beginning with the day Slade came to the farm, she told him everything. Only one thing was omitted from her tale: Ford would never know of the moment Slade had stood outside her room, leaving her fearful of his intentions. She said only that she had overheard him tell his partner of Broken Arrow's winter encampment at Palo Duro, and that she had decided to set out on her own, only to cross paths with the trader Ugly Jack.

Her brother's expression changed moment by moment as she talked, first registering bewilderment, apprehension, some anger, and finally relief. One fact edged out the rest for him.

"I can go home?"

"Yes. The matter at Fort Clark is closed. That man's death was judged an accident."

"It was an accident," he said fiercely, "and I wasn't even holding the gun. But I was scared, Kate, and now I feel like a fool."

"Don't. It doesn't matter anymore," she answered softly, not wanting him to feel shamed before her, for he was no longer a boy. He was a man.

"I have to warn Elzy and the others." He saw her frown. "What else would you expect me to do? This man Slade doesn't mean anything to you, and Elzy Rusk has been a friend to me."

"He's wanted by the law," she said flatly.

"He minds his own business. He don't preach. And he don't give orders."

"A paragon," Katherine said dryly. "And how do he and his men make a living?"

"Trade. Cattle, horses, goods."

"Rifles," she added, when she saw he would not.

"I ain't seen any, and it doesn't matter now, does it? I can go home, which is just what I aim to do."

"You're right, of course. And you'll have to

leave soon, Ford, else you'll get mixed up in Slade's and Rusk's quarrel. I still can't believe that I got here in time to warn you. I'll miss you."

He looked uncertain. "I don't know as I should leave you with that bastard Lawson still around."

"You have to," she answered firmly. "Besides, I am under Broken Arrow's protection until Wolf Killer returns. And if, as you say, he still wants me, I need no other protection."

"He wants you." He almost wished it wasn't true. Then he could make her return to New Braunfels with him. To Aunt Dee and Shea, where she belonged.

Ford rose and gave his hand to her. She stood before him, her eyes roving his squared shoulders and his bearded face. She had never seen him unshaven. It suited him.

"When you see Aunt Dee tell her that I am well and that I've found my place. And tell her that when the spring comes, I'll be coming back—for Shea."

"She won't like that."

Katherine shrugged helplessly. "I can't have both worlds. She has to know that. Help her to understand, Ford, for me."

He took her slender, scratched hands in his hard, callused ones. "I'll try, Katherine Fierce Tongue. Now, wait for me here. I won't be long."

He was back within minutes, followed by his

three ousted companions. The one she had first noticed with a strong reaction of distaste spoke to her.

"We appreciate the warning, ma'am, even if it was just for Ford's sake."

She forced herself not to step back or show her repugnance.

He grinned. "Name's Elzy, 'case you ain't been told."

"I had guessed your identity, Mr. Rusk." She emphasized her use of his surname.

His smile thinned. "You tell your friend Slade, when he comes, that I've made my deal with these Comanche. And it'll stand. I reckon you'll be around that long. Ford, here, says you aim to stay with these people." His tone made the word *people* synonymous with *savages*.

She eyed him coolly. "You've been among them yourself, Mr. Rusk, apparently for quite some time."

"Yeah, but a woman . . ." He left it at that, the implication more damning than words.

Ford looked up sharply from stowing his belongings in his saddlebags. "Lay off, Elzy."

Katherine tensed uneasily, but Rusk laughed.

"Sure, Ford. No harm meant." He glanced over his shoulder. "You got my gear together, Louis?"

A swarthy man of small stature grunted affirmation.

Ford stood aside as the others left the tepee.

When he was alone with Katherine he pressed his lips to her forehead. "Good-bye, Katie-love. And good luck."

"Good-bye, Ford," she whispered. "Ride carefully." But he was already leaving, and she could not be certain that he heard.

Chapter Eleven

Almost before Katherine had time to wonder what was to be done with her until Wolf Killer returned, his mother entered the lodge. Katherine eyed her stooped frame warily, remembering the days of the cottonwood switch that had sharply punished every transgression, whether accidental or an act of defiance. It was Old Mother, not Wolf Killer, who had made her act, think, even feel Comanche.

Old Mother's dark eyes darted around the tepee, though she must have known that Katherine was alone. "Where is Sleeping Grasshopper?"

Katherine smiled faintly to hear Shea's Comanche name once more. "Safe, until her father can take me for her."

With such a simple exchange Katherine discovered that she no longer had even the faintest awe of the old woman. Only respect was left.

"It is good." The dry parchment cheeks crinkled into a smile of a hundred creases. "It is good, also, that Fierce Tongue has come home to her people."

Katherine knew a fierce, exultant hope. Her skin was white, but Old Mother saw a Comanche soul within her. There was a place for them here. Nothing would mar the life of peace she so wanted for Shea; for Sleeping Grasshopper. The correction came to mind effortlessly.

"Let us go home, Old Mother."

Old Mother laughed. "Home. Yes. Let us go home."

Because of his importance within the tribe, Wolf Killer's tepee was among those nearest Broken Arrow's. It was a good lodge, with stout poles carefully chosen by Wolf Killer and hides prepared by the women. Hides scraped and cured with great care and even greater pride. And, as in so many other tepees around it, the poles and hides were new, for the old lodge of Wolf Killer had been burned. Visions of those flames had been with Katherine a long time.

Her fingers brushed the buffalo cover before she lifted the flap, stooped, and entered. She straightened slowly.

The girl sitting close to the light of the fire was young and pretty. Her slim hands worked at beading a buckskin shirt. Her smile flashed shyly at their entrance.

Old Mother was watching Katherine with unmalicious interest. "This is my new daughter, Willow Dancing. When Wolf Killer comes home to his lodge you will share my little tepee, Fierce Tongue."

Katherine thought of Ford, and wondered why he had not told her of Wolf Killer's new wife.

"Welcome, Fierce Tongue." Willow's voice was soft and warm. "Sit. There is fresh meat."

As Katherine ate deer meat and listened to Willow's soft-voiced exchange with Old Mother, she hid her feelings until she could determine what they were. She wondered how long Wolf Killer had waited before choosing another woman to share his lodge and his buffalo robe. Katherine studied her own reaction but could find no jealousy in it, not even for Little Feather's sake. Life was hard but continued even in the face of tragedy. She did not feel any shock deeper than a mild surprise. The surprise was only because she had not thought of the possibility, not because of the fact itself.

Nor did Old Mother's suggestion that it would be Willow Dancing and not Katherine who slept with Wolf Killer disturb her. She acknowledged within her that somewhere along the way she had lost the youthful infatuation she had felt for Wolf Killer. She wanted only the protection of his home and lodge for her daughter. For herself, she craved only the serenity to be found in truly belonging to one way of life.

When Old Mother spoke of her granddaughter, Sleeping Grasshopper, Katherine watched Willow's face. It was peaceful.

Willow smiled at Katherine. "Soon Wolf Killer will have another mouth to feed." Her hand touched her stomach, only faintly rounded. "Sleeping Grasshopper will have a brother or a sister."

Katherine returned the smile. "It is good for a warrior to have many children."

She felt only relief that Willow did not perceive her as a threat. She wanted no quarrel with anyone, particularly not someone with whom she would be forced to share so close an existence.

During the next day she acquainted herself with every change that had come to Wolf Killer's lodge. The obvious one, Willow Dancing, created others. With his marriage to her, her family had become his responsibility. Her father was dead, killed when he had sought revenge on the white soldiers for a daughter and an infant son lost at Stone Creek. The remaining son was still young, though he was an able hunter. For now, Willow's mother and her brother had erected their tepee near Wolf Killer's lodge and listened to his counsel. Later, when the boy was grown and sought his medicine with a vision, he would marry, and his mother would remove herself to her daughter's shelter.

Not surprisingly, an easy camaraderie developed between the mother and the wives of Wolf Killer. Old Mother accepted Katherine as her equal now, and Willow was too docile, too well trained ever to need the sharp discipline of the old matriarch's tongue. She reminded Katherine a great deal of Jeane Pearson, for she was as clearly adoring of Wolf Killer as Jeane had ever been.

The three of them worked all day on a dress for Katherine. Willow held the soft skin against Katherine, and Katherine smiled as Old Mother tilted her head this way and that, finally marking the skin with the burned, smutted end of a stick.

"I will cut the skin," Old Mother pronounced, certain neither girl could do it as skillfully as she.

"And I will do the beadwork." Willow's soft voice asked more than told.

Katherine had seen some of Willow's work and knew she could not match it. Unfortunately, that left Katherine to do most of the sewing of the garment. She stifled a groan, still half afraid Old Mother would pull out a switch at any sign of what she would consider laziness.

Old Mother made the moccasins that covered the whole of Katherine's legs below the knee.

By late afternoon it was ready to be donned, and Katherine stood in front of Wolf Killer's wife and mother and ran her hands over the dress. Now, she began to feel Comanche. She realized she had begun to look more the part when Old Mother's face creased in a beam of approval.

Stifling the tiniest tingle of regret, she folded her buckskin shirt and breeches neatly and put them aside, but she was not surprised when Old Mother snatched them up. She choked back a protest when they landed in the fire with a whoosh of embers. Old Mother looked on in satisfaction as they began to smolder.

Willow touched Katherine's shoulder gently. "I will braid your hair."

Katherine nodded and sank to her knees in front of the young girl. Willow braided her hair, shyly admiring the pale gold strands as she wove them with leather thongs. "It is the color of the grass on the prairie when the sun first touches it in the morning."

That color marked her as different, Katherine knew, but she was not entirely sorry. Though she wanted to be of the Comanche, she did not want to lose her identity entirely.

Willow had barely finished the braids when Katherine heard Beaver Talks calling to her from outside. "Come see this! Please come, Fierce Tongue."

Katherine glanced at Old Mother, for she knew there was work to be done.

"Go on, then," Old Mother scolded with a show of irritation. "You will not work so well if you do not, but come back soon."

Katherine went with Beaver Talks, and they walked nearly to the other side of the camp, where an old man sat before his tepee. He was very old, with skin like a dried plum and hair that looked as if it had died long ago. In front of him was a small hide, perhaps that of a young deer, stretched on a frame of sticks. He was painting a story in pictures. His colors were all the shades that the earth could give.

Katherine studied the symbols, and when the story became clear to her she was left with mixed feelings. It was a story about her, and about Wolf Killer. The first was a picture of the raid on the Pearson place; the second showed her cradling Wolf Killer's daughter with Little Feather lying in the background. Next was the massacre at Stone Creek. A series of bloody scenes followed—Wolf Killer extracting his revenge from the settlers. Finally, she returned to a happy camp. The figures were crude; simple but effective. Each of these scenes showed her in dresses of white skin with light-colored hair hanging loose.

It was the last picture that disturbed her. She stood with arms outstretched toward the camp of the People. Her dress was brown, her skin was brown; even her hair he had braided and painted brown.

She looked into Beaver's eyes, saw her excited

pleasure, and smiled, hiding her own inner turmoil. "I am honored," she told Beaver Talks and the old man.

But, returning to Old Mother, she knew she was also filled with misgivings. She remembered Ford's words, and she thought of Slade, who had told her she was running away.

The sun was lowering in a silver sky, and the clouds darkened with each hour. The cold swept through even the warmest clothing. Old Mother sent both girls scurrying for extra firewood to last through the bad weather that threatened. Enough had to be gathered for Wolf Killer's lodge, as well as Old Mother's little tepee and that of Willow's mother.

The girls had not wandered far along the stream when Ugly Jack stepped in front of them. His bulky, shaggy appearance more than ever reminded Katherine of a great brown bear.

Willow gasped at his sudden appearance, but Katherine stared him down. "Let us pass."

Ugly Jack scowled. "Setting yourself up, ain't you, missy?"

Katherine lifted her chin, determined not to be intimidated. "As a member of Wolf Killer's family, I have a place in this tribe."

"If he wants you," he growled.

She smiled slowly, undisturbed by the suggestion. "I am not troubled by what Wolf Killer will do when he returns—are you?"

Her smile deepened as he turned away

abruptly without answering. So, the great white trader was frightened. Good.

Willow stared anxiously after him, and Katherine touched her arm. "It is all right now, Willow. Let us go on."

They were headed back to the lodge, arms loaded with branches and twigs, when Willow gave a glad cry. "It is Wolf Killer!"

Katherine followed her gaze upward.

Eight horses descended the cliff path, their heads and tails red with the same paint that streaked the bodies of the warriors and the parts of their hair. Impervious to the cold, their grease-stroked torsos were bare and glistening in the last of the pale sunlight. Three of the horses carried their captives: two young girls and a very small boy. Mexicans.

Katherine could see little of the children's expressions, but the lines of their bodies were slumped with grief, despair, and weariness. She pitied them now for their unhappiness, remembering her own, but she knew their life here would not be hard. They would be taken into families eager for children, especially those who had lost family at Stone Creek. There would be no difference in the way they and the Comanche-born children were treated. They would adjust and, in time, learn to be happy. Eventually, they would even forget they had once not belonged.

Wolf Killer was at the fore of the group,

his war lance held proudly, but even from this distance Katherine knew something was wrong. Willow seemed to notice nothing amiss, running ahead of Katherine, stopping only to deposit her burden of firewood at the lodge. Despite her foreboding, Katherine could not help but smile at the care Willow took even in her excitement. Willow would never forget her duties. Katherine's own steps hastened, but she did not go forward to meet the returning men. She went to Wolf Killer's lodge and waited.

If all was well, the returning warriors would go first to the council, where they would tell of their exploits in great detail, each man bragging of his successes and those of his companions until every event, large and small, was revealed and understood. It was a good thing for a warrior to tell of the brave deeds he had done, Katherine knew, for it gave confidence to all of the band and provided schooling for the young.

Restless, she hunted carefully through Wolf Killer's belongings until she found his comb. It fit comfortably into the curves of her hand. Always, at the end of a day, Wolf Killer had been soothed by her combing his hair. He had told her often that his thoughts came easier then, clearer. Then he had taken Little Feather to wife, and it had been she who had wielded the comb that eased Wolf Killer's mind.

Katherine turned abruptly and put the comb

away. That was now Willow's place, not hers. She could not have given a name to her feelings at that point.

Old Mother returned to the lodge, her steps slow and her face drawn with worry. "Come, Fierce Tongue. Wolf Killer would see you now."

Katherine followed, asking no questions. Wolf Killer lay in the lodge of the medicine man. It had taken the last of his strength to ride back into camp, victorious. He would not let himself be carried into camp. A litter was for an old man; Katherine could almost hear him say the words.

Most of the warriors of the tribe were gathered around the tepee, looking solemn, ignoring the moans of the women who had gathered there also. Katherine glanced around at the ominous expressions and ducked into the opening. It was stifling within. Wolf Killer lay on a soft pile of skins, Willow at his side. Willow's gaze lifted to Katherine, and her eyes held a hollow look of defeat. Katherine moved closer, her eyes searching Wolf Killer's nearly naked body. The wound was low, in the groin area, and it was very bad.

Katherine dropped to her knees beside Wolf Killer. His eyes were closed, and a sheen of sweat dampened his entire body. After all this time of trying to get to him Katherine realized that she did not know what to say to him. Especially now.

Wolf Killer opened his eyes and stared at her. The silence lengthened.

"Is your tongue finally silenced, Fierce Tongue?"

She found a smile in his eyes and knew then that she had missed him. "Once," she began quietly, "I thought never to see you again."

"You thought this when the soldiers took you from the banks of the Stone Creek?" Each word was an effort for him to speak.

She nodded. "When I ran away from the soldiers and was two, maybe three days coming back to our camp there, I found only charred, ruined buffalo robes and the bodies of the dead lodged in the trees, and no trail. Then I had no hope."

She studied his high-boned features and was grieved. Wolf Killer was surely dying. His looks were the same, a strong and proud Comanche face, and he smelled still of bear grease and horses and earth scents. But the odor of death was with him also.

He lifted his hand, closing his fingers on one braid that lay against her breast. "Is it still the color of the plains grass?"

Katherine smiled, though the ache of tears was in her throat. "It is."

"And does my daughter still have eyes the color of a cloudy sky?"

"As gray as the woodsmoke that streams from this lodge fire," she said softly. "Sleeping Grasshopper is a fine, brave girl of the People."

Wolf Killer nodded, and she touched her fingers gently to his brow, wishing she could have returned to him sooner.

Wolf Killer's grip eased on her braid, and his eyes closed. She moved her hand to his, taking the callused palm in hers. Beside her, Willow keened softly, and Katherine could not reassure her. Wolf Killer still lived, but for how much longer?

Katherine placed Wolf Killer's hand in Willow's and rocked back on her heels to rise. "Does Wolf Killer know of the baby?"

Willow shook her head.

"When he awakens you must tell him of the child you carry, perhaps a fine Comanche warrior."

"He will be pleased," Willow said dully.

"Yes." Katherine looked at Wolf Killer once more. "He will be pleased."

The next morning, Wolf Killer appeared no worse nor any better.

"Stone Gatherer will make good medicine for him," Old Mother told Katherine, seeking to be reassured herself. But Katherine had no faith in the old man, who had retreated to his medicine lodge to fast and read the signs and make medicine for a cure.

Wolf Killer's own medicine was the coyote, and Stone Gatherer used this fact. He had stalked and killed a coyote during the night and scraped the hide, telling everyone that the coyote had lain down before him and died for Wolf Killer. Then he placed the hide over Wolf Killer and began his chanting, the coyote's teeth rattling against the insides of a gourd he shook at measured intervals. And still the fever did not lessen its grip on Wolf Killer.

Katherine held his hand and wished she had real medicine to give Wolf Killer, though she knew he would never take it if he were capable of refusal. For Wolf Killer, nothing good could come of the white man. Katherine recalled how once, in their travels from camp to camp, they had passed an abandoned fort, and Wolf Killer had frowned. "I do not understand these people, Fierce Tongue. They work like ants to build their homes, but their work is for nothing when they leave. Tepees are for many places."

Katherine had given his words serious thought before answering. Often Wolf Killer's words were a shield for a deeper meaning. "When the white man builds he does not plan to leave. He builds strong against the elements, so that when the rains fall hard and the winds sweep the earth it is not all to be done again. They build for permanence." Her own words held a faint warning.

His arm flashed brown in the sunlight as it made a wide arc in the direction of the adobe walls. "The mud houses crumble."

"Not so quickly as our buffalo hide covers wear thin."

"If he builds to stay, why did he leave the

land of the white men where the sun rises in the morning? Why did he come here?" He was angry.

"The land to the east seems small, for the whites are growing in number. These plains are so large, there seems room enough, and they come."

"Room for all white men," Wolf Killer told her harshly. "They wish, now, for the People to leave this place that has been ours for as long as the Old Ones can tell of in their stories. And what will happen when they become more, and this land, also, is too small for them?" There was a sudden, tense silence between them, then Wolf Killer had said softly, "No, Fierce Tongue, there is no room here for them. The People must drive them away before it is too late."

Katherine closed her eyes, thinking back on his anger. No, Wolf Killer would have no part of a white man's medicine.

Old Mother touched Katherine on the shoulder, breaking her reverie. "Take Willow from this place. A son should not see his father this way."

Katherine did not question the old woman's superstition, and Willow did not question Katherine's insistence that they walk to the edge of the canyon, where the walls rose steeply upward in layers of soft-colored clay. But they did not walk any farther than that from the tepee where Wolf Killer lay in such agony. Each was silent with her fear and her grief, but Katherine's sorrow was mixed with guilt. She did not want Wolf Killer to die, but each moment she passed with the Comanche made her realize how far she had come from them in the past year. And she did not know what to do with the realization.

Still, she could not help but believe that this was a better life for Shea, a life where the child would be treasured, not just by her family but by all of the tribe. A life very different than that of the outcast she would live in New Braunfels.

She was pulled abruptly from her brooding by Willow's fingers gripping her wrist. Katherine followed her gaze, and her stomach sank. Slade and his partner rode openly into the camp.

The two men were watched with wary intensity, but it was seen that their rifles were holstered and their hands held only reins. Slade had been right, of course; a troop of cavalry would have been attacked at once, while they were merely surrounded and allowed to come forward.

Katherine knew that Slade had no fear of his quarry fleeing at his approach. He would know that she had come before him and that Rusk, as well as Ford, would have long since fled. She watched from the shelter of a small stand of trees and wondered why he had been so far behind her.

Willow stirred nervously at her side. "I am frightened."

"Do not be afraid." Katherine felt no ill will for Willow's dread of the white men.

"When the soldiers came before they killed." There was real terror in her voice, and her words brought back images Katherine wanted only to forget.

"These are not soldiers," she said sharply, then added more gently, "Besides, Willow, they are only two against all of our warriors. And see, they have kept their weapons away. They are not here to kill or harm."

"All the same, I am going to find Old Mother. Please come, Fierce Tongue; we will be safe together."

"Later." Katherine sighed at Willow's refusal to be reassured. "I will come later."

Watching Willow hurry away, she thought again how suited the girl was to Wolf Killer; quiet and good and obedient. The way Katherine knew she could never be.

She watched as Slade and Jeb ducked into the tepee of Broken Arrow, and her thoughts dismayed her. She wondered if Slade was angry at what she had done. And if he had less respect for a woman who would aid her brother at the expense of the law. But most of all she wondered why she cared.

Dispirited, she gathered more firewood and carried it to Old Mother's little tepee. Not surprisingly, Old Mother was full of gossip about the arrivals. She scorned the two white men to Katherine, seeming to think that she should not take any offense at the remarks.

"These Rangers tell Broken Arrow that their great chief is angry with us. He says it is not good that we deal with these men called outlaws." Old Mother looked up from her cook pot.

Katherine hid a smile, because she could picture the women, straining to hear, huddled near the tepee where the men congregated.

"Broken Arrow said, and also many others said, that we do not care for this great chief's anger. It is no more to us than the wind from a hawk's wing."

"Will these white men be allowed to stay?" Katherine ducked her head over the nuts she was shelling, hoping Old Mother would see her question only as polite interest in her words.

"Broken Arrow will let them stay," she admitted. "But Broken Arrow is a warrior growing old. He has done well, but his time is ending."

It was the first time Katherine had heard this of the band's civil leader, and it shocked her, though she had realized Broken Arrow was aging quickly. But for the warriors to see his power as waning dismayed her. And Katherine knew Old Mother only repeated words she had heard spoken by the men.

Willow entered the tepee and crept close to the fire. "I think Wolf Killer is stronger," she said, but her tone of voice declared it as much wish as fact.

That night, Katherine was summoned to the

tepee of Broken Arrow by his eldest wife. The band's leader sat impassively before the fire, impervious to the heat of the flames. When he did not acknowledge her presence Katherine withdrew to sit in the darkness behind him to wait.

Long minutes passed before the opening of the tepee was darkened by a man's form. Slade came in and sat opposite Broken Arrow in the same manner: legs folded and crossed, back straight, arms relaxed. Katherine did not think he saw her there behind Broken Arrow.

After a brusque greeting from Broken Arrow Slade said in halting Comanche, "You know why I am here."

"I know," Broken Arrow answered. "You would speak more of the words you spoke before."

"The Texans want to make peace with Broken Arrow. I ask you again, what does Broken Arrow say to this?"

"The same thing I said at the council. The Texans want peace too late. We had peace, and they destroyed it."

"Broken Arrow does not remember well. Five years ago, two white girls were stolen with a boy from a ranch in a Comanche raid. The parents were murdered and the ranch was burned. One of those white girls was Katherine Bellamy. You call her Fierce Tongue."

Both Katherine and Broken Arrow had stiffened at mention of her name. Now Broken

Arrow said, "Once all of the Texas prairies belonged to the People. Now the white settlers call them theirs. This is why we raid. To warn the settlers that they come too close and claim too much."

"The raids by Wolf Killer for the last year have been for revenge."

Broken Arrow's eyes glittered as he nodded. "The Texans killed many at Stone Creek. Wolf Killer seeks vengeance."

"More than enough blood has been shed to pay for that which was shed on Stone Creek. Also, it is settlers who are killed, but it was soldiers who killed at Stone Creek. And the soldiers punished their own."

Slade had had difficulty finding the words for all of his speech, and Broken Arrow gestured to Katherine. She saw Slade's frown as his eyes found her. Now she understood. She was to be their interpreter. Quickly, she told Broken Arrow what Slade had said and, without stopping to examine her motives, elaborated slightly in Slade's favor.

When she was done Broken Arrow grunted. "The soldiers have a strange justice. One for their own and another for the People."

"The soldiers of Stone Creek were punished," Slade repeated.

"And what are the words of a Texan worth? Even Rusk, who swears brotherhood and guns, I do not trust."

"There will be no guns for the Comanche,

only a bullet or a hangman's noose for Rusk."

Broken Arrow did not answer, looking insulted.

Slade sighed. "Your dead have been avenged. Many settlers are dead. If you keep on, there will be more trouble; more whites dead, it is true, but also more Comanche. If you stop now, you will be honored among your people for having chosen the way of peace."

Again Katherine had to translate parts of his speech.

"We do not seek peace," Broken Arrow said scornfully. "It is the whites who do so. We will talk no more."

Slade rose slowly and looked first at Broken Arrow, then at Katherine. He left the tepee without saying anything else, and Katherine's heart hurt that he had failed. It would be easier for her here if the Comanche did not war on her people.

Morning found Katherine little more rested than when she had sunk to the softness of her fur pallet the night before. She was at the river with the first pink lines of daylight. It was a cool, misty dawn, dampening her braids with fine beads of moisture. On her knees, she dipped her hands into the cold water, splashing it against her face to drive away a lingering sluggishness. She had walked far, to a point where the creek branched away from the river, to be alone.

She did not hear Slade approach, but when

he placed his hand on her shoulder she knew who was there.

Sinking back on her heels, she turned so that she was facing him. He stooped beside her, resting his weight on one knee and one foot. He stared straight ahead, out over the water, where a faint mist clung to the surface. Katherine waited in silence for him to speak.

"Wolf Killer may die."

She flinched. "I know."

"And if he does, what will you do?"

It was a question she had asked herself many times. And she had no answer for him, just as she had none for herself.

He shifted restlessly, his gaze moving from the flat surface of the river to her. The hard look in his eyes softened slightly, and Katherine found it more difficult to breathe.

"This is no place for you, Katherine Bellamy," he said in a low voice.

She returned his look without flinching, feeling an old pain returning. "There *is* no place for me. Not anymore." She hesitated. "You talked for peace with Broken Arrow—thank you for trying."

"I was following orders," he returned without inflection. When she didn't respond to that he shrugged. "Yeah, I've talked. I even think he's listening. A little. Probably too little—and too late."

"Most of his warriors will not listen to you. You're white, and worse, you're with the army."

"I'm here to speak for the army," he agreed. "If Broken Arrow's warriors will cease their raids, the army promises to stay clear of Comanche lands."

"If Wolf Killer lives, he will never agree to that." She watched him as she spoke, but his expression didn't change. "And how much is that promise worth? If the army had stayed out of Comanche lands to begin with, Wolf Killer and the others would have no reason for their raids."

"Fierce Tongue: They named you aptly."

"So I've been told." Her voice was tart.

Abruptly, he changed the subject. "Your friend Harris set fire to Buck's cabin the night you left."

She caught her breath, her gaze roving over him. There were raw scars on the wrists below the buckskin sleeves, and the hair was singed from the backs of his hands. Her eyes lifted to the grim lines of his face.

"Nobody was killed," he said in answer to her look. "Not in the fire, anyway."

Her breath came again. She had dreaded to ask, thinking of Birdie's generosity. She recalled Harris's smiling face as he put his hands on her. Had he smiled while lighting the fire? It stunned her that he had intended for them to die in that fire. How could anyone be so cold-blooded? She pitied Birdie and Buck, left with nothing by a man who had no cause to harm them.

"Was Harris caught?"

"And hung."

She stared in fascination at his hands. She was certain he had been the one to loop the rope around Harris's neck.

"Is that why you were so far behind me? I wondered."

His eyes met her inquiring look. "I thought you were trapped inside. Jeb sat on me to keep me from going after you."

Incredibly, tears blurred her eyes. Why should he have cared, even risked his life for her?

"Then Buck turned the stock loose in case the fire spread and realized your mare was gone. Wasn't too hard for me to figure out where." To her surprise, he grinned faintly.

"I heard you and your partner talking," she admitted. "You said you expected Broken Arrow to make his winter camp here at Palo Duro. I had to warn my brother."

"And now that you've done that, and he's gone? What now? You're not Comanche, and your name isn't Fierce Tongue. You are Katherine Bellamy, a woman of Texas, but not of the People." He reached one hand out to her. Slowly, she placed her hand in his. Hers was no soft-palmed lady's hand; it was as brown and hardened as his own. "Come with me now," he said. "I'll take you back."

"Back?" She shook her head. "There's nothing for me in New Braunfels but Shea, and I'll soon have her here with me."

"There are more lives in this land of Texas than the one you lived before. More people than those you know."

"Why?" she asked starkly. "Why do you care who I am? Or what I am?"

He looked at her in surprise, his eyes assessing her quickly. A tall, strong-boned, good-looking woman. Sensuous as well as capable. A woman harder to forget than the many who were truly pretty, as she was not. A woman to ride at a man's side, stand behind him in trouble, sleep in his bed—maybe give him sons. "Because I want you," he answered honestly.

She weighed her feelings, the strong pull she felt for this hard man, her mixed emotions for the life she would lead among the Comanche, her love for Shea. Shea.

He read her answer in her face. "Are you happy here?"

The question was unexpected, and she did not know how to respond. "I'm not unhappy," she said at last.

"There's a lot of ground between the two."

"I'll have what I need here," she responded.

His lips thinned to a mocking smile, but his eyes were not cruel. "I hope your needs don't change and leave you wanting, Katherine." Her name sounded curiously soft on his tongue, as if she were another person, a person less harsh than the one she knew she had to be. He unfolded his body and stood above her, and the moment of softness was gone. "And what are you going to do when Broken Arrow uses the rifles Rusk sells him to kill more whites?"

She had no ready answer to that, either. "Are you going after Rusk?" At his nod, she said almost desperately, "If I knew where he was headed, I would tell you, but I had to protect Ford." She suddenly felt as if she was throwing something away, something she should hold on to with both hands.

His shoulders lifted in a shrug. "It's done. I don't fault you for your choice." After a pause he added, "I'm usually in and around Fort Lancaster from time to time. If you need me, you should be able to reach me through the soldiers or the Rangers there. And, by the way, you won't have any more trouble from the white trader, Jack Lawson."

Katherine stared, allowing herself the luxury of relief. "He's gone?" Then the hope faded. "He'll be back. If Wolf Killer dies. He'll be back."

"I don't think so. I paid him for you."

"You what!" Her disbelief turned to horror, as Slade smiled slowly at her.

"I bought you from him." He reached down and touched her face. "I own you, Katherine Bellamy. Remember that."

Then he was moving away from her, and all she could do was stare after him in helpless outrage.

Chapter Twelve

In the first sprinkling snowfall of winter, just as Wolf Killer began to show some signs of recovery, the man named Louis rode alone back into the camp. He slumped over his horse's neck, burning with fever and delirious, a bullet festering in his chest.

Hearing a commotion outside, Katherine stepped out of Wolf Killer's lodge. Wolf Killer had been carried back there only that morning at his own request. The medicine man had not been happy with the move, insisting that the warrior might yet die without his constant skills in attendance. Stone Gatherer had puffed up with vindicated pride when Wolf Killer had again lost consciousness soon after the move.

Now, Stone Gatherer, amid the small crowd that had gathered, stood frowning at the injured man, who swayed in the saddle. The Comanche's gestures spoke as loudly as his words. He would make no effort for this Texan.

"Help me, Old Mother," Katherine said, stepping forward to ease Louis from his saddle. "We will take him to your little tepee." She ignored the medicine man's frown of disapproval.

Looking unhappy, Old Mother grasped the outlaw's legs while Katherine supported his shoulders. She did not want this white man in her tepee. It was not good.

Together, Katherine and Old Mother half carried, half dragged Louis inside and placed him on soft buffalo hides. Katherine cut away his greasy buckskin shirt from the wound and did her best not to gag. As she eased the tanned leather from his chest, the stench of dying flesh struck her nostrils. She looked helplessly at Old Mother, who shrugged.

Katherine pressed her lips together and placed a knife in the edge of the fire. When it was glowing she took a deep breath and looked at the old woman. "Hold his shoulders." Then she opened the wound with the point of the knife. Katherine felt sweat break out on her forehead.

For long minutes Old Mother held the thrashing man while Katherine pressed the edges of the wound until the infected matter ceased to run. Grudgingly, she helped Katherine pack the wound with a poultice of herbs. Just as they finished, Willow peeked into the opening of the tepee.

"Fierce Tongue, Wolf Killer asks for you." Willow's joy and relief lit her every feature.

Katherine smiled at her, but glanced back uncertainly at the injured man. "You will care for him, Old Mother?"

The old woman nodded without enthusiasm. What was one more white man dead? They were more than the grasshoppers in the summer, and as welcome!

Katherine entered Wolf Killer's tepee hesitantly, glancing back to be sure Willow followed. Wolf Killer looked much stronger, his clear eyes indicating that the fever had left him. Katherine sank to her knees at his side.

Wolf Killer studied her for long moments. "It is true. You are here. I thought you were a part of the illness."

"I am no dream born of fever," she answered, touched by his admission and the welcome in his eyes.

"For many months I searched for you and did not find you. Now you are here."

She heard the question he did not ask. "I learned that one man knew where to find you. I followed that man."

"He is not here?"

"No; he looked for my brother. When he found my brother was no longer here he went away."

"But you are still here." He said the words with great satisfaction.

Katherine's feelings were much more mixed as she answered, "Yes, I am still here."

Neither of them mentioned Shea's mother, but Katherine suspected Wolf Killer had grieved upon learning of her death. He had been fond of his frail, red-haired squaw. They spoke of Shea, and Wolf Killer promised, "When the sun is warm again on the mesa she will be with her people once more."

And Katherine smiled and said nothing.

Later in the day, when Katherine returned to his side after checking on Louis, he frowned. "Let the white man die. He is nothing."

"I cannot," Katherine said firmly.

Wolf Killer's attitude was another reminder of the differences between them. The Comanche way was hard, for life was hard. The strong and the healthy survived; the weak and the infirm did not. Food, always scarce, had become even more so with the coming of the white man. Wild game fled the encroaching civilization.

Katherine did not know if she could ever be completely Comanche in her heart, but she could understand even when she did not agree.

Wolf Killer did not argue, but that night when Old Mother told Wolf Killer the man would die, Wolf Killer shrugged. "Then it will be so."

Faced with this indifference, Old Mother was inclined to leave the outlaw to face his demons unaided. Katherine could not.

Old Mother chided her when she spent hours bathing his fevered flesh and listening to his every delirious word.

"So much work and it will be for a dead man."

"He may yet talk in his right mind," Katherine said fiercely. "Then I will not care if he dies or if he does not."

"What do you want to hear so much?"

Katherine paused and looked up. "What happened to my brother," she answered quietly. "This is what I must know."

During the next evening, Louis opened his eyes and looked at Katherine. "Am I dying?" he asked through cracked, fever-blistered lips.

"I don't know," she said, unable to lie to him. "Where is Ford?"

"Camp Colorado, with the others. 'Cept Joe, Rusk, and me. And Joe is dead." His chuckle was obscene. "Coyotes is eating him."

"Where is Rusk, then?"

He shrugged. "He couldn't wait for a wounded companion. He went west, maybe New Mexico. I don't know."

"Tell me what happened." She knew she was being callous to keep him talking, but she could not help herself.

"Damned army. Cavalry patrol. We wasn't even doing anything, but that captain, rot his soul, knew Rusk." A grunt of pain he could no longer suppress was jerked from him. "I killed him, but I reckon he's killed me, too."

"Ford isn't wanted for anything."

Louis's grin was weak. "Bad company."

"Rest," Katherine said automatically, wanting time to think. Had Ford been released when it was realized that he hadn't committed any of the crimes of which the others were guilty? She feared it wasn't likely. As Louis suggested, being in bad company was too often all that it took to brand a man guilty, perhaps to get him hung. Her heart constricted. Had Ford already been judged and convicted? Would those with him attest to his innocence?

Old Mother ducked into the tepee. "Is he dead yet?"

"Cool some broth for him," Katherine said. If it was at all possible, this man would live to take her to Camp Colorado, even if it was at the killing end of his own rifle.

Louis did manage to eat some of the broth and was still conscious when Katherine and Old Mother removed his bandage. Old Mother's nose wrinkled in open distaste at the odor that arose. Katherine nerved herself to meet Louis's eyes. They were closed; beads of sweat trickled down his dark-skinned forehead. He knew.

Old Mother backed out of the tepee. "I will have nothing more to do with this dead man."

Katherine left the bandages off and moved a knife so that its blade lay in the fire. She slipped out of the tepee to find the snow had ceased its soft floating. Stars were visible against the heavens. Soon Louis would slip back into a rest that was half sleep, half delirium. By then, the blade would be hot enough to sear the flesh, to burn away the poison that was slowly killing him. Then he would have a chance; not much of one, but better than none at all.

A woods creature rustled the underbrush nearby, and Katherine closed her eyes, wanting to be stronger than she was, needing someone besides herself who she could count upon. Wolf Killer would supply her physical needs, she knew. He would kill the buffalo so that she might feed and clothe her daughter and herself. If another tribe attacked, he would defend them fiercely and bravely. But Wolf Killer would never have any understanding of the person that she was. And he did not care that this was also a need within her.

She knew he would feel no concern for Ford and would not help her just because she did. He did not care if Louis lived or died and did not care that she cared. Even if he was stronger, now, and completely well, she could not say to him, "Wolf Killer, lay this knife against his flesh, for if you do not, I must." He would, like Old Mother, say, "Let him die."

Wolf Killer was a Comanche, a warrior. He would live his entire life facing death every day. Death held no terror for him, no dread.

He had feeling for her, she knew; perhaps love so far as he was capable of feeling love. Wolf

Killer knew little of true tenderness. Katherine knew if Slade was here, it would be Slade she asked for help. The realization was troubling, but Katherine knew she had to accept herself as she was. It was time she found the strength for that, at least.

She steeled herself to return to the tepee and do what she must. At first glance all was as it had been, but as she came closer, she could see this was not so. The knife still lay in the flames; the contents of the stew kettle still simmered. But the outlaw named Louis breathed no more with that slow, haunting hoarseness. Bright pools of blood had run down from his chest where his hand still clutched the hilt of his knife. She had seen the Arkansas toothpick, as the stiletto blade was called, strapped to his boot, but there had seemed no reason to remove it. She did not touch Louis; there was no doubt of his death. She went to tell Wolf Killer.

"He has poisoned my tepee with his evilness," Old Mother lamented. "I won't live with a bad spirit."

Katherine ignored her and spoke to Wolf Killer. "Louis was shot by soldiers who knew him for a bad man. They took my brother, thinking he is bad also. I must help him."

"No."

She knew he would be inflexible, and she didn't plead. She also knew what he feared. "I was taken from you once, and I returned. I must go again, but I will come back."

"Are you Comanche? Or are you white?"

Katherine looked at him helplessly, not knowing how to answer so that he would understand. "Ford is my brother. Would you leave your brother to die?"

"You are a woman, not a warrior." Wolf Killer, still weak from his injuries, turned to stare into the fire, refusing to look at her. "If you go from me now, you will be no more for me. Your name will not be spoken in this lodge. Sleeping Grasshopper will be the daughter of Willow Dancing."

Willow Dancing gazed at her with sympathy. Wolf Killer would announce to all that though the white girl who had been of his family still lived, the woman of the People called Fierce Tongue was dead. She would be mourned, and in this lodge her name would not be spoken. Even if she returned to the People, she would be like the old ones who were cast away or who threw themselves away if their families were not strong enough to do so.

Katherine shivered at her look, and thought, *someone has stepped on the grave in which Wolf Killer would bury my memory.*

Willow reached out a hand entreatingly. "Do not go, Fierce Tongue."

Tears burned in Katherine's eyes. So quickly had Willow accepted her. "I must." She wanted to say that she would be back, but Wolf Killer wasn't going to make that possible for her. She could not pass the test of her loyalty to his way of life.

Silently, she took a parfleche that Willow or Old Mother had prepared in the fall. Within the rawhide pouch were strips of dried buffalo, layers of fat and dried prickly pear apples between. When there was no food from the land she would eat. Her winter robe, hair side in, would be warm enough for the coldest days ahead.

She turned to look at Old Mother, whose eyes blazed with grief as she held Willow Dancing from moving to embrace her sister. Wolf Killer had spoken; Fierce Tongue was dead. Willow turned away, weeping silently. Wolf Killer glanced up and met her eyes; and then deliberately looked through her. She was dead.

Without another word, Katherine left the lodge. Once more she went to the small tepee of Old Mother. Louis's body held no terrors for her, but she knew Wolf Killer would be furious when he discovered she had taken both rifle and pistol. Controlling a shudder, she even pulled the knife from his chest, wiped it, sheathed it, and transferred the sheath from his boot to her knee-high moccasins. She wrapped the pistol and tucked it inside his saddlebags. His shot pouch she draped over her shoulders. These things had been brought in with the injured man; she didn't know what had become of his saddle.

In the distance a coyote called, and Katherine

thought sadly of Wolf Killer and the choice she had made to stay with the Comanche. That choice was lost to her now. Shaking off regret, she walked swiftly to a tepee along the outer circle of the camp. She called softly to Beaver Talks.

As the young woman stepped from her tepee, her familiar brown face looked beautiful. Katherine knew she was not likely to see her again.

A surprised expression crossed her friend's face at the way Katherine was dressed. "What are you doing, Fierce Tongue?"

"My brother needs me. I must go."

The young woman clucked softly, her braids swinging as she shook her head. "Wolf Killer allows this?"

"No," Katherine admitted sadly. "Wolf Killer says if I do this thing, Fierce Tongue will be as dead."

Beaver Talks took a step backward in horror. "You must not!"

"I cannot turn my back on my brother's need. Wolf Killer knows this."

"Wolf Killer is a proud man," Beaver Talks reminded her. "He has grieved for you. Perhaps he does not mean this."

"It is done," Katherine said quietly. "I shall miss you. You have been a true friend, both to the white captive that I was and the woman of the People that I became. Think of me sometimes, Beaver, and smile, for I will think of you and my heart will rejoice that you live."

"I will think of you, Fierce Tongue." Beaver Talks lifted a hand in farewell, then turned away to hide the tears in her eyes.

Katherine let her own tears fall as she turned her back on one more link with her past.

Sadie was one of the horses kept near the camp. Katherine had not let her run with the herd that was turned out to forage.

The snow was soft and unmarked, a glowing whiteness in the dark of the predawn hours. She could see the pale lift of smoke above several of the tepees as she turned to ride away.

Chapter Thirteen

Wisps of dark auburn hair had slipped free of the neat chignon. Dee fussed nervously with the strands, then laughed at herself. Here she was, a woman far past the blush of youth, and as nervous as a schoolgirl with her first beau. Doyle Shanley had done that for her. Doyle with his easy, laughing ways and his sure touch that set her on fire the way no man ever had. Not even Ford, Senior, all those years ago.

The realization erased her smile of anticipation, and she walked to the window to gaze out across the lands of Ford Bellamy. The winter-dulled fields blurred beneath her gaze as she pictured his tender smile the morning they had parted. Ford hadn't loved her, but he had been grateful to her, and she had done her best by his memory. For twelve years she had tended his lands and his children. Her life had been their life. But Katherine had chosen a new and difficult direction for herself, one in which Dee could neither help nor protect her. And it was time Ford took over this farm.

Deirdre McKenna was free to go on with her life. She was in love with a man who wanted to marry her, and tonight she would tell him yes.

What was between them was becoming too heated, and the reasons for holding those feelings in check seemed less and less important as days drifted by. She hadn't heard from either Ford or Katherine, and she did not intend to spend the remainder of her life waiting to see what others needed of her. This once, she would be selfish.

A smile touched her lips as Doyle's wagon rolled into view just as the last of the day's light began to fade from the rolling hills. Perhaps tonight, after she had consented to be his wife, she wouldn't send him away.

She paused at Shea's room to wake the sleeping child. If she let her nap on into the evening, the baby would miss her supper, then spend a fretful night. Bending over the little bed, she nuzzled her lips against the soft, fragrant skin of Shea's neck. Shea woke with a squeal, grabbing Dee's hair with both hands. Scooping her up with a resigned laugh, Dee knew the strands she had so carefully tucked away were once again tumbling loosely about her face.

"Doy?" Shea questioned.

She had lain down peacefully for her nap only on the promise that Doyle would soon be there to spend the evening with them. Dee smiled, pleased as always with Shea's affection for the man.

"Yes, Doyle is here."

He was waiting for them in the kitchen, having long since abandoned the formality of knocking at the front door and waiting for her to greet him there. He rose from the table and slipped his arm around Dee, but had to abandon that embrace when Shea flung herself from Dee's arms to his. "Whoa, scamp," he said as he caught her.

Shea giggled as she snuggled against his broad chest. "Doy," she chirped.

Doyle beamed at Dee. "And how have my girls been today?"

"Well," Dee said with some asperity, "one of us was very full of mischief, which caused the other not to get much done in the way of work."

The look in Doyle's eyes softened, making Dee feel like someone's treasure. "You work too hard," he told her. "This farm is too much for you."

Dee knew that was true. Ben Yates was getting old, and though Doyle helped all he could, he had his own place to tend. "I keep hoping to see Ford riding over the hills," she admitted. Or Katherine. But she didn't mention Katherine. She longed for her niece but dreaded the day

Katherine might return only to take Shea from her. It was a fear she had to keep to herself. The mere mention of the possibility enraged Doyle.

The pain in her eyes caused Doyle to lean forward and place a swift, hard kiss on her lips. He loved this woman as he had never loved before. Her pain was his pain. Though he knew what thought had brought that look to her eyes, he didn't voice it any more than she. It was the closest they'd ever come to a true fight, the day he'd told Dee that Katherine Bellamy would never take her daughter back to live among the savages. He could still remember the agonized acceptance in her voice as she'd told him, "Shea is not my daughter, Doyle. She is Katherine's. If Katherine comes, I'll not fight her for the child."

And Doyle, who loved Dee too much to hurt her, had said no more. But he wasn't through; not by any means.

For the moment, however, he turned the conversation to something lighter, but no less important to him. "If you would accept my proposal, then I could hire someone to help old Yates without you telling me how improper it is."

To his surprise, Dee stood facing him without any quick and laughing riposte. There was a look in her eyes Doyle didn't recognize as she gazed at him and said, "And if you, Doyle Shanley, would get around to proposing again, I just might accept this time."

Slowly, Doyle placed Shea's feet firmly on the floor, scarcely aware of her murmur of protest. "Deirdre?" he questioned hoarsely.

Tears brightened her eyes, but she did not speak.

Feeling as clumsy as one of his oxen, Doyle placed both hands on her shoulders and drew her close. The warm scent of her was enticing. The touch of her brought him to a painful state of arousal. "Deirdre McKenna, will you be my wife?"

"I will," she responded on a soft sigh of happiness.

To her amazement and Shea's dismay, Doyle responded with a loud shout of triumph that rocked the rafters of the snug little house. Then he kissed Dee lingeringly upon the mouth. Feeling again what his kisses did to her, Dee knew she had made the right decision.

Chapter Fourteen

Not for the first time, the rifle bumped heavily against Sadie's shoulder, causing her to shy. Katherine muttered a curse and brought the mare quickly under control. The rifle had proved awkward to carry from the first mile. With no saddle, Katherine also had no saddle holster, forcing her to grip the rifle with her free hand. She tried shifting the weapon to cradle it in her left arm, but it still felt clumsy.

Studying the offending firearm morosely, Katherine realized it was a single-shot weapon. The pistol, on the other hand, was a revolver, exceedingly valuable and far less unhandy. The rifle was loaded. She would use that one shot to provide a meal; then the rifle would go.

The first streams of daylight edged the ridges ahead, but the aspect of morning did not lighten

Katherine's mood. Though she knew she had to find a way to help Ford, she also knew she had burned her bridges in leaving Wolf Killer. No one in the band would take her in after the war chief had denounced her. Once again, she had chosen her own road without any way of knowing if she did right or wrong. Deep within, however, she acknowledged a sense of relief. What lay behind was clearer than what lay ahead, but she felt in her heart she would not have been happy as Wolf Killer's woman.

When Ford was safe she would have time to think about her future. She was still determined not to raise Shea among the bigots and hypocrites of New Braunfels, but she no longer had any idea where the two of them might find acceptance.

Sadie shied unexpectedly as the swift, bounding lope of a rabbit caught her attention. Glad to abandon her thoughts, Katherine reined Sadie to a stop and lifted the rifle with slow caution.

A short while later, in a grove of pecans along a full creek, she roasted the rabbit over a tiny, warming fire dug shallowly into the ground, then ate every bite. She knew time was a luxury she didn't have to waste, but she needed the warmth of hot food in her belly. The snow of the northern plains was behind her, but the air around her was no less frigid. Even with her buffalo robe, she was cold.

Before she scattered the ashes of the fire she battered the rifle against the frozen earth until it appeared useless. Though she regretted the waste of a weapon, it seemed the best thing. She remounted and rode on.

In the back of her mind Katherine had always known what she had to do. She dared not ride into Camp Colorado dressed as a Comanche. A woman of the People would be fair game to the soldiers, and Katherine remembered too well how they treated Comanche. Squaws who were raped repeatedly and beaten brutally were the lucky ones. Even if she was not mistreated, she had little hope of being taken seriously.

No, she could not be of any help to Ford on her own, but Slade could be. With her jaw set and her heart filled with misgivings, she headed southwest to Fort Lancaster. It was farther—much farther—but she made up for it. She pushed Sadie and she pushed herself. She lived on what little game she could kill and the parfleche of dried meat, prickly pear apples, and buffalo fat. Sadie lived on bark peeled from cottonwood trees and, farther south, on the last tough grass left from summer.

Katherine did not keep track of time or thoughts or feelings. She simply rode—hard— and let her mind wander where it would. Too often, it ended up with Slade, which was disquieting to her. "Better to keep your mind on the problems you have than to make any more," she muttered to herself, causing Sadie's ears to twitch backward.

As she came farther south, the days were less

cold, but she was still grateful for her buffalo robe at night.

Late one evening, she reached what she prayed was Fort Lancaster. She'd never been there, never been much of anyplace, but land in Texas was marked by the placement of forts, and she knew the general direction of most of them.

Katherine was not so foolish as to ride directly into the fort. Her very appearance made her suspect, if not as Katherine Bellamy, white squaw of Wolf Killer, at least as a white renegade. It rained that night, lightly, but still she slept little because of it. Before daylight, she crept toward an outlying homestead. Smoke lifted from the clay-brick chimney, and the aromas of a hearty breakfast tempted the chill morning air and Katherine.

Time passed with unbelievable and agonizing slowness. At last she watched as a man came from the house and walked to the barn, where he yoked his team and started toward a distant field. Katherine could see piles of stone and brush where he worked to clear more land for plowing before the spring. A woman stepped out of the door, egg basket in one hand, swill bucket in the other. The soft light of early dawn muted the blue of her cloak and blurred her features. Katherine could not tell if she was young or old, but her carriage was straight and her walk vigorous.

Waiting while the woman accomplished her

chores, Katherine studied the horizon. She was crouched in a small gully beneath a spreading oak with bare limbs. Beyond the half-cleared field she could see the outline of Fort Lancaster and, beyond that, shallow hills rising gently to touch a clearing sky. The prairie surrounding her was brown and barren, but she could picture it in a few more months when the prairie flowers, bluebonnets, sweet pea, mountain pinks, and daisies would bloom. In those first few days of spring their colors would light the pale prairie grass like a rainbow in a rain-washed sky.

The woman returned with her eggs and empty bucket, and still Katherine waited. Patience was paid when the woman emerged once more, this time with a little girl of seven or eight at her side and a baby in her arms. Katherine watched as they trudged across the fields toward the man. She slipped back to check that Sadie's hobbles were still secure before easing toward the house.

It was a dog-run adobe, two rooms with an open passageway between. Katherine had dreaded entering the strangers' home, invading their private lives. It was a relief to discover that would not be necessary. In the open run hung the wash, probably there from the day before, when clouds had hung threateningly low. Katherine touched them. They were dry.

The only feminine garments were a white linsey blouse and a heavy woolen skirt of dark cranberry. Both were plainly but skillfully made. Katherine took them, thrusting aside her feelings of guilt. This did not look like a poor homestead, and she took nothing that she hadn't a greater need for than the owners. Someday she would find a way to repay their unwitting gift.

Luck held as she returned and unhobbled the mare. Turning Sadie back the way they had come, she cantered her to a freshet at a point where a small thicket provided a natural screen. She tied the mare loosely and then stripped, pretending not to feel the icy air against her skin. Chill bumps covered her blue flesh as she donned the white woman's clothing. The garments felt strange; the modest collar binding, the skirt waist too snug. If the hard ride from the north plains had not lessened her already slender body, she doubted she would have been able to fasten the woolen waistband.

Dressed, she gazed at the freshet longingly. But she was not brave enough to do more than crouch near the edge to wash her hands and face in the stingingly cold water.

She rolled up the dress she and Willow had made and stuffed it into Louis's saddlebag. She had to pull out his one spare pair of breeches and shirt to make room. These she discarded without a qualm. Perhaps they would be found by the man whose wife's clothing she had stolen: a partial payment.

Next she turned her attention to Sadie and

frowned. She could not ride into the fort on an Indian blanket of beaded buffalo hide. Regretfully, she hid it beneath the bushes, along with her parfleche. The beadwork on the blanket had taken many weeks of effort on the part of Old Mother. The parfleche was empty but still a loss. Unfortunately, they would not fit in the saddlebag with her dress and the pistol, and those two were the most needful. Finally satisfied, she remounted and squared her shoulders. It was time, at last, to brave the soldiers of Fort Lancaster, in search of Slade.

The fort sentry stared as if he disbelieved his eyes as Katherine, moccasined legs dangling, rode her mare bareback toward the gate. The stockade was earthen ramparts and uneven posts lashed together. The gate stood open.

Katherine slipped from Sadie's back and lifted her hand in greeting. She walked past him, unchallenged. The fort within was adobe. At her right shoulder were the barracks. Across from them, the parade ground stretching between, were the officers' quarters. She walked toward these, instinctively choosing the door outside which an infantryman stood at ease. He looked even younger than Ford. At her approach, he snapped to attention, and she had to hide her amusement at this effort to impress. Some of her trepidation began to ease.

"Is there someone who could take my mare?" she asked.

He was staring at her braids, and Katherine

cursed her own stupidity. She could do nothing about her moccasins, but she certainly could have loosened her hair.

"Private." She made her voice a gentle nudge.

"Yes, ma'am!" He gestured to one of the regulars, who had wandered conspicuously near to appraise this novelty. "Take this lady's horse, Avers."

The man loped forward, grinning at Katherine as he took the reins from her fingers. She smiled back, ignoring the first private's look of disgust for such indiscipline.

She approached and read the nameplate on the door. "Is the colonel in?"

"Yes, ma'am."

"Please ask if I could have a moment with him."

He turned and rapped briskly, entering at the command.

The door was closed behind him, so Katherine could hear nothing of what was said. She shivered in the wind, which swept across the parade ground. With each passing moment she grew more uncomfortable with the staring eyes of passersby focused on her. What would she do if she encountered the woman whose clothing she wore so flagrantly? The possibility almost unnerved her, which was laughable in the face of all she had already been through.

The door opened once more, and the private waved her in.

She tried not to glance down at her moccasins as she walked through the doorway.

The fort's commanding officer was standing. With a faint smile of welcome, he beckoned her to a chair and did not sit until she had done so. He was a man of indeterminate age; the hardships of west Texas roughened a man until his years could never be told by his appearance. Katherine cared only that his eyes neither judged nor condemned her for her own appearance.

"May I or the U.S. Army be of assistance to you, madam?" His speech was educated, though his voice was not polished.

"I am looking for a man named Slade. I was told to look for him here."

He shook his head regretfully, and her heart sank. "I believe Captain Harding requested his service on a Ranger expedition into the Chisos area of the Rio Grande. You will have to speak with Captain Harding for further details. The Rangers are under his jurisdiction."

"May I see the captain now? My business is urgent."

The colonel rose and opened the door. "Private Chase?"

"Yes, sir." The young man's voice was all crisp perfection.

"Escort Miss . . ." he paused, "escort this young lady to Captain Harding's office."

"At once, Colonel." Private Chase saluted smartly and stepped back for Katherine.

She still felt an inclination to smile at his enthusiasm, and suspected he had not been in the army long. Perhaps he had come straight from the military academy. A little part of her hoped he would not soon become as disillusioned as she with the world he had chosen. It was not all honor and glory.

Harding was not in his office; they found him in his quarters. Private Chase left her with the same stiff formality he had maintained during their brisk walk across the diagonal length of the hard-packed surface of the parade ground.

Gilbert Andrew Harding betrayed no surprise at having a handsome young woman ushered into his presence, even one with braided hair and moccasins on her feet. He accepted her introduction by the private and accepted also that he was given no name by which to address her. He was older than the colonel, and equally willing to help. He was, however, more informal, and his quick gaze more assessing.

"Please sit down, ma'am." He lifted a decanter from a narrow serving board. "Would you care for a drink? I can offer something as mild as sherry."

"No, thank you, Captain." Katherine sat stiffly on the edge of the rawhide-bottomed chair. The position was far from comfortable. "I am looking for Slade. The colonel said you might be of help in that."

"Is your business with Slade personal—or with his profession?"

She hesitated. "With Slade." Although she did not want the man to get the wrong idea, she also did not want him offering a substitute for Slade to assist her.

"I see." He turned on his feet, thinking swiftly and seeming to reach a satisfactory conclusion as he turned back to her. "The colonel may have told you that Slade is absent from the fort at present. But he's due back any day." Deep in thought, he stroked his thick gray beard, then added more briskly, "I'll see that you are given a place to sleep until his return. You'll have privacy, of course, but I'm afraid I cannot offer much in the way of comfort."

Katherine smiled. "I wouldn't know what to do with comfort." She got to her feet, hesitated, and asked, "Is Jeb here?" She had to force herself to use the name familiarly, as if he was known to her as more than a voice from beyond a dividing wall.

"Jeb Welles? Yes, he's here, or," he amended, "he will be by nightfall. He's on patrol." He waved her back to her chair. "Make yourself at ease. I'll speak to the quartermaster myself about your accommodations."

Katherine sat only until he closed the door behind him. Then she jumped to her feet in a flurry of nerves. She paced the few steps afforded by the width of the room. It was confining, this room, little more than an entry hall for the bedroom beyond. She felt stifled.

Captain Harding returned with a seasoned

veteran of Texas to take her in charge. He had all the authority but none of the dignity of his commanding officer.

Katherine thanked the captain for his efforts and turned to the old ranger, who looked her up and down and said, "I reckon I ain't going to be bored the next couple days while I'm looking out for you. Come on, then; let's get you settled."

Katherine did not take his words for a compliment.

He held the door open for her, and she preceded him out into the winter cold. This man, Kettle, as he told her to call him, was both more openly curious than Harding and more willing to voice that curiosity. He was also much more blunt.

"Will Jeb expect you to share his quarters?"

"It is Mr. Slade that I've come to find," she said, undisturbed by his suggestion. She'd long since learned not to care what others thought of her.

"That'd be even easier to fix. Slade ain't under regular army or even regular Ranger discipline. Ain't under any discipline I can see."

She stopped in the middle of the parade ground, the wind whipping at her skirts, and faced him squarely. "You mistake the matter, Sergeant Kettle. The only interest I have in Mr. Slade is a business exchange."

"Yes, ma'am." The sergeant wasn't smiling,

but the impression was the same. He didn't believe her.

She shrugged and walked on.

The sergeant led her to her quarters. She didn't know who had been ousted for her convenience. Whoever it was, she did not believe he would miss the tiny cubicle or be any less comfortable wherever he might be placed. The cot was narrow, the room windowless. In the full heat of summer it would be unbearable. For now, it was chill but not miserable. The smooth adobe walls were bare save for a single hook above a small chest. Lid open, interior bare, the chest had obviously been cleared for her use. On the floor next to it were her saddlebags.

"Will it suit you?"

She turned to find the sergeant watching her as if he expected some complaint and was delighted to confound him. "It will suit me very well, Sergeant. Thank you."

There was the barest hint of approval in his eyes as he said, "I'll be bringing you something to eat when it's served up. You won't be wanting to eat in the hall with the men."

"I wouldn't mind," she said almost defiantly; and then wondered what had happened to her fear of soldiers.

"It wouldn't do." He was emphatic and, she suspected, a bit disconcerted too.

"Perhaps, then, you would care to bring your own dinner and keep me company."

He was almost as surprised at receiving the invitation as she was at issuing it. "I might just do that," he replied gruffly.

He did, and proved a great entertainment to her, for he had a fascination with human nature combined with a propensity for gossip. The people of the fort and their problems were nothing to her, but Kettle's way of telling about them succeeded very well in taking her mind from her own problems. Captain Harding was branded a woman-scorner, which surprised Katherine, for he had seemed so respectful during their brief interview. Perhaps his views on women were influenced by the colonel's wife, whom Kettle described scathingly. She commiserated with the colonel by the time Kettle was done telling of the woman.

"She won't make a home for him, because she hates Texas and wants him to request a transfer. Says Texas killed her baby, but more like the woman's own milk poisoned it. She's a damned good cook, though. Too bad she keeps the colonel so off his feed he can't enjoy none of it."

Katherine saw no need to discourage this commentary. Kettle was enjoying himself, knowing she would soon be gone, probably never to see any of them again. And she was enjoying the company, as well as the opportunity to learn more about the fort and its ways. If Slade didn't show—and even if he did—some of the information could be as useful as it was entertaining.

"Can you believe it," Kettle asked, "the colonel often eats this slop just so he won't have to go home to his wife."

"This isn't so bad," Katherine protested. Nor was it.

Kettle snorted. "It's plain to see you're used to a lot worse than what's dished up here. 'Course, the first time I laid eyes on you, I didn't reckon you to be holding yourself above others."

Katherine's eyes narrowed in amusement for she knew just what it was he had thought. "What you mean," she said, "is that I'm no lady."

There was no disconcerting the sergeant on that score. He grinned at her. "I never took to ladies much."

She was sorry when the hour grew late and Kettle had to take his leave. As he gathered their dishes, she asked, "Shouldn't I have had word of Mr. Welles by now?"

"If his patrol came in, which it probably didn't. You'll hear sure enough when it does."

She stopped him at the door. "I'd like to ride in the morning. Would you tell the stabler for me?" After spending days on the trail, she didn't particularly care to ride, but she wanted even less to be left to stare at the four walls of this tiny room until either Jeb Welles or Slade put in an appearance.

"Can't go alone. We're too near the Comanche Trail here. It ain't safe."

"I came in alone," she reminded him, wondering what his reaction would be if he knew just how little cause she had to fear their proximity to the Comanche Trail.

His gaze touched her braids and fell to her moccasins. Then he looked her squarely in the eye. "Yeah, but you're now under the protection of the Texas Rangers."

She closed the door behind Kettle, looked for a bolt, and, finding none, realized that a Ranger or army regular would have little use to lock his door. She went to bed with an easy mind, not fearing for her safety. Being "under the protection of the Texas Rangers" had its advantages. Uncomfortable as the cot proved, she slept at once and very deeply through the night.

Kettle was at her door at daylight with the information that a horse had been saddled for him, as well as her mare, and that Jeb's patrol had not yet returned. He did not seem at all concerned about the latter, and the only comment he made on riding with her was, "I'd just as soon play nursemaid to a female as a bunch of raw recruits."

She ate the light breakfast he brought for her and wondered if she was expected to remain a recluse for the length of her stay here. Kettle was standing outside her door when she emerged. He walked with her to the stables.

In half an hour's time, she was racing Sadie over the level ground, far outdistancing Kettle's gelding, and circling back to laugh at his dour expression. She felt strangely lighthearted but refused to search her soul for the reason behind the mood.

On their return to the fort, she rode more sedately at Kettle's side, once again enjoying his comments on some of the officers, their wives, and the lives they lived here on the edge of danger.

The afternoon proved dull and eventless, broken only by the small, daily ceremony of the lowering of the colors. It was a sweet evening despite the cold, the sky glowing with the orange blaze that was the setting sun. The flag's colors flashed with the roll of the drum and the vibrating thunder of the evening gun.

Watching and listening, Katherine felt a poignant loneliness. She rubbed the gooseflesh on her arms and walked slowly back to her room. She didn't belong here, but then she didn't really belong anywhere. Thoughts of home teased her, but so much had changed. Or had only she changed?

The evening stretched before her, a lonely time in which she tried not to wonder what her future held.

Jeb Welles came to her room that night. He entered the door she opened to his sharp knocking. Reeking of several days' travel, he dismissed his filth without embarrassment.

"I couldn't believe it when the captain said you had dared to come here looking for Slade." Piercing hazel eyes challenged her.

She stiffened as much at that look as at his tone of voice. "You knew who I was?"

"Harding was very descriptive." His laugh held no amusement. "Yeah, I knew." A damned fine-looking woman, Harding had said, and the very phrasing of the words had spoken of Katherine Bellamy as Buck and Birdie had described her to Jeb. The kind of woman who didn't back down from a stare, or a challenge. The kind of woman who could haunt a man's dreams, distract him from his work—and get him killed.

Katherine motioned him farther into the room, hiding her reaction to his instant antagonism toward her. Her eyes assessed him with the same cool calculation as his were studying her. His heavily bearded face seemed pleasant enough, but his hazel eyes were cold. He was taller than Slade, and more heavily framed. Slade was compactly muscular; Jeb Welles was hewn from oak.

"You aren't as pretty as I thought you'd be, Katherine Bellamy." Jeb sought a reaction from her, a means of measuring the person she was.

Her gray eyes chilled with anger. "And you are not as pleasant as your voice once led me to believe, Mr. Welles."

"Of course, Slade never said much about your

looks," he went on, ignoring both her comment and her furious expression, "never said much about you at all. I just figured it had to take some woman to send him rampaging back into a burning cabin." She was silent, and he stopped baiting her abruptly. "What do you want here?"

"That is my business and Slade's. Not yours."

"You asked after me," he reminded her curtly.

"But I did not send for you," she answered, just as shortly.

"Why don't you go on back to your Comanche warrior? You got nothing for Slade." Nothing but trouble—or danger.

"Do you generally arrange Mr. Slade's relationships for him?" Katherine felt her temper flare. What right had this man to presume? What right had he to make assumptions?

Jeb's eyes narrowed. "You might be sorry not to take my advice, Miss Bellamy." At her scornful look he shrugged and turned away. He paused with his hand on the door. "The captain would be damned interested to know your name."

It was her turn to sneer at the empty threat. "If you think he hasn't already guessed, you've less respect for your commanding officer's perception than I."

He left the room without another word. To her surprise, Katherine realized she felt no real animosity for Jeb Welles, despite her anger.

Intuition told her his concern was for his friend and partner; she had sympathy for that. A true friendship, one that dared, was a rarity and not to be despised. Jeb Welles would be a worthy ally, but she did not think he would ever befriend her.

Whatever he was, whatever he felt, she could not let him interfere in her efforts to save her brother. Ford needed her help, and she needed Slade.

She felt surprise and some caution when it was Jeb rather than Kettle who waited for her when she went to the stables to ride the next morning. He was bathed and cleanly clothed in a loose linsey shirt and leather leggings. He was also clean-shaven, revealing good looks she would not have suspected.

"I see you found some water somewhere, Mr. Welles." Instinct warned her it was far smarter to strike first than to wait for him to begin the sparring. If he ever gained the advantage, she suspected he would go for the jugular. Still, she could not completely dislike him.

A stabler handed him the reins of a saddled horse and snapped a salute. "Your horse, Lieutenant."

"Thank you, Private." Jeb ran a hand lightly over the horse's nose and gave a nod of approval.

Katherine accepted Sadie's reins and mounted with the aid of the private's cupped hands. She had not realized Jeb's rank. She felt his eyes on her and looked up. He was smiling and, unexpectedly for both of them, she returned his smile.

"Lieutenant," she said with a nod, as if greeting him for the first time.

"Jeb will do," he corrected. "Shall we go?"

It was a pleasant ride, though it lacked Sergeant Kettle's entertaining monologue. An early comer to midwest Texas, Kettle had a comment or comparison for even the most commonplace scenery. Jeb preferred to ride in silence, and Katherine was more than willing to oblige.

It was only as they started back toward the fort that Jeb opened a conversation. Katherine soon wished he hadn't.

"Are you going back to Wolf Killer after you've taken care of this business you have with Slade?"

Katherine glanced sideways at him, but he wasn't looking at her. His gaze was fixed on the horizon.

"I don't think that is any of your business," she said at last, careful to keep her tone neutral. She preferred that he not realize how truly vulnerable her position was.

"You know what Slade is going to think when he hears you've come after him." Jeb knew. Without Slade's having said a word, Jeb knew.

She glanced at his profile. "Probably that I'm a pain in the ass," she said, hoping to shock him into silence.

"Liar," he returned softly. "You know Slade wants you."

Katherine drew rein, forcing Jeb to stop his own horse. She waited until he met her gaze before she answered. "Believe me, Jeb Welles, I know all about the lusts of *white* men—particularly soldiers—for Comanche women. Even white squaws."

His skin darkened as he recalled her past, the things she had seen and survived. Not a cruel man by nature, Jeb regretted what he'd reminded her of, even unwittingly.

She took pity on him. "Look, Jeb, I'll make myself clear to Mr. Slade. He won't mistake my reasons for being here."

Jeb started his horse forward, leaving her to follow. "Slade's got some peculiarities," he said over his shoulder. "Sometimes he sees what he ain't been shown and hears what he ain't been told."

"I don't know what to say to you," she said honestly, unable to discern his meaning.

"It doesn't matter." And Jeb had the feeling it truly did not matter; that it was too late for any warnings from him. If Katherine were a different kind of woman, perhaps it wouldn't matter. But if she were a softer woman, and less brave, she wouldn't be here, and Jeb wouldn't be talking to her like this. No, unfortunately, Katherine Bellamy was the kind of woman to ride straight into trouble, taking any man who cared for her with her. And Slade cared.

The next morning, Kettle was waiting for her once more. Jeb was nowhere to be seen, and she did not ask after him. He came to her room that night.

"I'm going out again come daybreak. I expect you'll be gone before I get back."

She felt a small pang of regret that they could not have learned to know one another. Perhaps she had been wrong. Perhaps, given time, they could have been allies.

There was a strangely intense look in Jeb's hazel eyes. "If you've got a job for Slade, you'd better be sure what pay he'll expect."

"I can take care of myself."

"I ain't worried about you."

She drew back and laughed. "Are you always so honest, Jeb Welles?"

"Not when it's a hindrance."

She sobered. "I'm not going to play any games with Slade. He'll know where I stand."

"I hope he believes you."

There was that warning again—that Slade might choose to make up his own mind concerning her motives. Why was this man so protective of a lawman as tough as Slade?

"I can do nothing about what he will or won't accept," she said with some asperity.

Jeb grinned. "I think I know now why Slade would walk over some damned likely looking girls to get to you."

Before she could respond he surprised her still further by reaching for her and pulling

205

her close against him. His lips were hard and questing—questioning. She did not pull away, even responded a little. When he released her she stepped back, not trying to examine what she felt at that moment.

"You'd better go, Jeb," she said slowly. "I wanted to be your friend."

"I could never be your friend. And I'd rather stay." There was no doubt of his meaning.

"I'm sorry." And she was, but there was too much in her past for what he suggested. Too many memories. But it wasn't Wolf Killer who got in the way of what she might have been able to feel for this man. It was Slade.

He grinned wryly. "I'm a damned sight sorrier."

A day later, Slade rode into Fort Lancaster.

Chapter Fifteen

Katherine saw the expedition riding in from the east. She and Kettle had been about to start back toward the fort when they halted to watch the fast-approaching, low-lying cloud of dust. When she spied Slade's buckskin her heart began a faster beat. Her voice was a little shaky as she requested Kettle to intercept and send him to her.

Whatever Slade's reaction to her presence might be, she was sure she would not want the curious eyes of his companions as witnesses to it.

Kettle frowned and rubbed his bristly jaw. "I don't know about that. He's supposed to report in first thing to the captain."

Reluctantly, Katherine pulled her gaze from the riders, who had begun to be distinguishable, one from the other. "Why don't you let that be his decision? Please."

With a snort, Kettle turned his horse toward the group of riders and kicked him to a gallop. Katherine suspected he was mumbling under his breath about the peculiarities of women. Then he was forgotten as she realized anew that, within mere minutes, she would be facing Slade once more.

She slid from her saddle and looped Sadie's reins to a pecan sapling. She felt more tense than even she had anticipated. After she had ridden so hard to get here, wasted precious hours waiting for him, would Slade refuse to help her? If so, what then? And what of the things Jeb had said? If Slade desired her, would that be a help or a hindrance? And what of her feelings? She dared not even examine, much less define them.

Not all of her fear was that Slade might turn his back on her need. Mixed with it was dread that he would look at her with hot and hungry eyes—and fear that he would not. Wolf Killer was behind her, but what lay ahead? Was there any future for her anywhere?

The wind, almost constant through the winter days, pressed her skirt against her long, slender legs. She had grown accustomed to the feel of the stolen homespun blouse and cranberry dyed skirt. Over them both she wore a heavy coat Kettle had found for her. For the first time in a long time, she wondered how she looked.

Hearing hoofbeats behind her, she turned. Slade jerked his horse to a halt and leapt from his saddle. His jaw was set in grim lines, but perhaps it was only weariness that made it appear so.

"What the hell are you doing here?"

No, not weariness. It was not quite the greeting she had hoped to receive, and Katherine recoiled. Slade stepped toward her, and she lifted a hand defensively. Remembering Jeb's warning, wanting no misunderstanding between them, she said quickly, "I need your help, Mr. Slade."

He stopped abruptly. The *mister* was as effective a douse as she had intended it should be.

"You need my help?" he repeated blankly.

She nodded warily. Would some emotion, only half guessed by her, make him refuse? Had she been foolish to come? Foolish to expect him to help her? She had been the one, after all, to warn his quarry to flight.

"What is it you want, Katherine Bellamy?" He'd spent days trying not to think about her, trying not to picture her with a Comanche warrior thrusting into her. And even that had been preferable to the thought that she might have been in danger if Wolf Killer died. Deliberately, he turned his mind to the fact that she had obviously survived any dangers. Not only survived, but found her way here, where she could torment him in actuality rather than merely in memory.

His calm was not reassuring. She found herself watching his lips. They were compressed. Indeed, his entire face was a mask of uncompromise.

"Are you still looking for Rusk?" She could see the question caught him by surprise. His uncertainty seemed to place her on surer ground.

"Between times," he said at last. "I got called off by something Harding considered more urgent." And, almost, this time he had not heeded the call. The knowledge that Rusk was likely within reach, the desire for revenge, for repayment of old debts, had very nearly been stronger than a reminder of responsibilities and loyalties.

Katherine wondered at the emotions flickering in the depths of his dark eyes, so brown they were almost the black of a rain-soaked forest. She had to force herself to speak into the silence that followed his answer. "Then your work will be easier. He's the only one left of his band. The rest are dead—or held at Camp Colorado."

His eyes narrowed. "I hadn't heard."

"You've been gone," she reminded him quietly.

Or, Slade thought, Harding hadn't wanted him to hear. He'd deal with that possibility later. For now, there was Katherine. "What has this to do with the help you need?"

She licked her lips in a resurgence of nerves. "Ford was with them."

"I expect he ain't one of the ones that got killed," Slade said callously, fighting the protective instinct that rose in him at her distress, "or you wouldn't need me."

Katherine glared. "No, he isn't dead, though I can see it would matter little to you if he were."

"Why should it?" he asked reasonably.

She turned away from him. "It shouldn't, and I've obviously made a mistake. You've no reason to help me," she said.

"You're wrong."

She turned back at the quiet pronouncement, and her heart thudded at the look in his eyes. Then she knew she was mistaken in thinking she saw tenderness there as he added, "If you want to hire my services, that's reason enough."

"Are you for hire, Mr. Slade?"

He shrugged. "For the U.S. Army, the Rangers—and maybe for you. If the price is right."

"I haven't gold."

"I don't want gold. Not from you." He stepped closer, and his forest dark eyes held fire but no light.

Her own trembling angered her, and she said sharply, "I am not for sale, Mr. Slade, or for trade!"

"Then you'd better think of a damned good substitute, or you and your brother are out of luck." There was absolutely no mercy in his expression.

Without thinking, she drew back her arm to slap him. He caught it deftly, twisting until she cried out in pain.

He eased the pressure. "Don't make that mistake again, Katherine Fierce Tongue."

"Don't call me that!" She spat the words at him. "I think Jeb's warnings were for the wrong person. I should have been warned against you instead of away from you."

"And why should you and Jeb have anything to say to each other?" He was furious.

"Why should we not?" she retorted.

Somehow the confrontation had gotten out of hand. Katherine knew she was no longer in control, if ever she had been. In that moment, she was a woman faced with a jealous man, a man hungry for her. And she hungered for him even as she denied the quick flare of knowledge within her. The situation bested her. She didn't know what to do, what to say.

She didn't stop the hand that lifted to touch his face, a face dusty and rough with a beard several days old. Her touch was light, exploring, and a thrill went through her as his own hand slid up her arm to her shoulder. It didn't seem wrong to Katherine to be pressed against him. It didn't seem wrong, even, to feel his other hand slide under the looseness of her blouse, upward across the rippling of her ribs to breasts that remained full and firm despite her thinness.

They fit comfortably together. Her head

rested on his shoulder as they stood hip to hip, thigh to thigh. The empty landscape seemed adequate shelter as Katherine tipped her head back for his kiss. His callused fingertips caressed the tender tip of one breast while his tongue plunged into her mouth, leaving her weak and gasping.

Her own fingers gripped his shoulders, and she fought not to succumb completely to his desire. There was danger here. She could taste it in his kiss, feel it in his touch. With the last of her strength, she pushed away from him. "Stop," she said clearly, praying he would, knowing she was incapable of stopping herself if he did not.

His hand eased from under her blouse, and he held her at arm's length. "You're beautiful."

She stared at him. She knew her hair was in tangles around her face. And that face would be no different now than her last glance into the mirror that morning. Eyes too strained. Features too sharp.

"No," she said, "I'm not."

Slade smiled at her, only a touch of his old derision in that smile. "Now, what is it you want me to do?"

The abrupt change was almost too much for her. How could anyone swing from passion to business in a heartbeat? What kind of person did that take? But Katherine knew the answer to that; it took a hard person. And Slade was as hard as they came.

"You'll really help me?" she asked on an uneven breath. She found it difficult to turn her mind from the touch of his hand against her bare breast.

"Did you forget?" He watched her steadily. "I own you. And I take care of what is mine. Now," he repeated with quiet patience, as if he didn't know how his words would infuriate her, "what is it you want me to do?"

She had to force herself not to give in to that fury, though she felt the heat of it flare within her. When Ford was safe, then she could lash out at Slade with all the anger and frustration she felt. "It's obvious, isn't it?" she said with an effort. "I can't go into Camp Colorado and demand Ford's release."

"Why not?"

The color flooded her face, then receded. "The soldiers. I haven't forgotten Stone Creek." Her voice was so low, Slade had to strain to hear her.

"You came here," he reminded her.

"And placed myself under your protection," she said bitterly. "At Camp Colorado I'd be nothing but the sister of an imprisoned man."

Slade squatted before her, deciding to ignore for now her belief that all of the military were like those she had encountered at the Stone Creek massacre. "You'd better tell me all you know."

"It isn't much," she admitted, dropping gracefully to sit cross-legged before him. "When

Louis reached us he was dying. He told me only that Ford had been taken with the others. Only Rusk escaped. And Louis, of course. Oh, and a man named Joe, but he died or was killed on the way."

"That would be Joe Hamill," Slade said thoughtfully, his mind already racing ahead, envisioning Rusk once more within his grasp. "What was the charge for Ford and the rest?"

Katherine shrugged. "I don't think there was one. If he is to be trusted, Louis said simply that Rusk had been recognized, that they were not doing anything illegal at the time. The soldiers opened fire, and Ford was taken because he was with them."

"I'll help you, Katherine Bellamy. What will you pay me?"

She felt a singing relief. He wasn't going to set the price at something she could only give freely—or not at all. "I've money in New Braunfels. Nothing with me. But you'll be paid, I swear."

"I once asked for your influence with Wolf Killer. What of that? Are you still unwilling?" The name brought the man, a third presence, there with them.

"I no longer have any." She kept her chin high, meeting his look squarely. "As far as Wolf Killer is concerned, I no longer exist."

Slade tilted his head, studying her quizzically. "Will he trade for rifles with Rusk?"

"I think so," she said with a sigh of defeat.

That brought a frown to his face. He got to his feet and pulled her up. "You had better sleep well tonight. It's a long ride to Camp Colorado."

He snapped his fingers, and the buckskin moved toward him. There was a scowl of concentration on his forehead that told Katherine he was no longer thinking about her. She mounted Sadie, wondering at her inner peace. Nothing was changed, nothing resolved, but her confidence in Slade bolstered her.

They rode back to the fort, and Slade insisted she accompany him to Captain Harding's office. Katherine moved quietly to a chair in a corner, grateful the captain's gaze did no more than skim over her before concentrating on Slade, who took a place at a small table opposite the officer.

Captain Harding betrayed no surprise at being told Slade would go with Katherine. Nor did he seem irritated at losing, if only for a time, the services of a valuable man.

Katherine surmised he was only too aware that he had no real hold on Slade.

He said only, "Try not to be gone more than a month. Remember, we are to have a meeting with the Mexicans. They had a rough September, and they're already worried about the one ahead."

September. The Comanche's Mexican Moon. Katherine felt a chill. In that month Wolf Killer raided. Thinking of the children brought back

216

to the camp by Wolf Killer and his braves, Katherine did not hear Slade's reply, but the anger in Harding's voice drew her attention sharply.

"Damn it, Slade! I know we have as much trouble from the border as we do from the Indians, but this could be the start of a truce along the boundaries if it's handled right." Harding rubbed his mustache irritably.

"I'm not a politician," Slade retorted curtly.

Harding cursed fluently, adding, "Just you be back here."

"I might," Slade returned, "but it might be that I won't."

That was as good as the Ranger captain could get from him. It wasn't enough, and he clearly wasn't satisfied, but he was helpless. He was always returned to the fact that Slade was a free agent: He could work when and where he would.

That night, Katherine lay in the little cubicle allotted to her and wondered if Slade would come. And what she would do if he did. She fell asleep still wondering.

Slade came for her at dawn. He didn't seem surprised to find her awake, dressed, and waiting for him.

Slade was unprepared for the fierce surge of feeling that flooded him at the sight of her. She looked too small, too defenseless in her homespun clothing and borrowed coat. God knew, Katherine Bellamy was anything but defenseless.

Coloring beneath his stare, Katherine touched her hair self-consciously. It was neatly braided once more. Between her braids and moccasins, she knew her appearance was incongruous.

"You have circles under your eyes," Slade said abruptly.

Katherine glared in exasperation. The man never did or said the expected. Ignoring his comment, she lifted her chin and said, "I'm hungry."

To her surprise, Slade smiled. "I am too."

They left as soon as they had finished the food Kettle brought to them. Katherine refused the saddle the stabler wanted to fasten to Sadie, shocking him and amusing Slade.

"Take it, Katie. It'll make the going easier."

She glared at him, most of her irritation for the intimate version of her name—and for the way the use of it made her feel. "I want nothing to do with the property of the U.S. Army." But deep down she knew her bitter hatred for the soldiers was being tempered by the slow acceptance of truths she had long denied.

When Slade stood his ground she stood back and let the stabler saddle her mare. Grudgingly, she fastened the saddlebags and caught Slade's stare. "They were Louis's. I have his pistol too."

He nodded, swung into his saddle, and led

the way. As usual, his packhorse followed on its lead.

For miles Katherine stared more at Slade's broad shoulders than at the terrain through which they passed. It was difficult not to let her mind drift to the way it had felt to have his hand at her breast, his tongue thrusting deep into her mouth. But thinking about it brought a heavy ache deep within her that was almost painful.

When it grew dark they stopped. Katherine built a fire, spitted the game Slade had killed for their supper, and watched the flames in silence. She knew too well that Slade watched her. She thought of the time he had taunted her for being a good squaw. He did not taunt her now. After they had eaten she cleaned their plates with handfuls of grass, then washed herself sparingly from her canteen. When there was nothing left to be done she stood with her face lifted to the heavens, her arms wrapped around herself. The night was cold and alive with stars. She heard Slade behind her but did not turn.

His arms slipped around her, cradling her upper body. "Will you lay with me?" he asked softly.

Katherine turned in his arms, lifting her face to him for answer. With a husky groan, Slade lowered his lips to hers. This was a gentle kiss, his lips brushing the tender flesh of hers again and again. Katherine slid her arms around him, pressing her fingers into the hard muscles of his back, exploring the valleys and ridges of his torso.

It took a visible effort for Slade to step away from her, lifting one hand in silent invitation. Katherine reached out and took the hand he held out to her.

She barely felt the cold as she eased her coat from her shoulders and slid into the bedroll beside him. Need warmed her, her need and his.

A shiver rippled over her when his fingers moved to unbutton her blouse. A thought crept unbidden through her mind that this moment was to have been Wolf Killer's. But there followed a memory immediately after of the night he had taken Jeane Pearson, Little Feather as she was known by then, for wife. It had not occurred to the Comanche that the girl would wish for privacy, that she would feel embarrassed to have her virginity taken in the tepee where Old Mother and Katherine lay on their piles of furs. Nor had it occurred to Wolf Killer that she would crave tenderness. And he had not known—nor would he have cared— that every move of the act had been torture for Katherine, who had dreamed of that moment for herself. Afterward, Jeane had wept, so silently that Wolf Killer did not waken to hear. But Katherine did, and had wept with her.

No, Wolf Killer had not shown his bride the tenderness that Slade conveyed with

every touch as he bared Katherine's body
to his questing fingers. Filled with hunger,
Katherine gave no further thought to the
past or to the man she had once thought
she wanted. She thought only of Slade as she
pressed her fingers into the crisp fur covering
his chest.

Slade murmured to her, words of need and
hunger, while he touched, caressed, and kissed
her burning flesh. He touched the dampness
of her until she writhed against his fingers,
whimpering with raw desire. When he entered
her the whimper became one of pain, but the
pain was brief. Katherine clung to him, arms
embracing him, lips moving over the slightly
salt taste of his flesh. Tears blurred her sight,
but it was, of course, only the stars shining
down into her eyes. She could love this man;
but she put the thought away from her, for he
was not of her world. He was a wanderer.

Abruptly, his slow thrusts quickened, driving
all thought from her mind. She felt no sadness, no empty longing, none of the pain that
had been with her so long she thought it a
part of her. She felt only a driving urgency
of pure physical need. Aching for release, it
was given her. She felt Slade's own pulsing
trembling and drew him to her until his storm,
too, had passed.

When he could, Slade rolled to one side and
pulled Katherine with him. He felt her tears
against his bare chest and wondered if they

were real or another of her lies. He stared at the stars sprinkled like tiny crystals across the sky. "Tell me, Katherine Bellamy, how did the mother of Wolf Killer's baby come to be a virgin?"

Chapter Sixteen

Ford tossed his reins over his horse's head and dismounted in one quick movement. His heart swelled at the sight of the whitewashed house with Aunt Dee's yellow curtains swaying in the front room. She always changed the curtains with the seasons. Yellow was her favorite, for it signified spring.

With a light step, Ford started for the house. The decision to come here first, rather than to town to see Elizabeth, had been a difficult one. But he owed so much to Aunt Dee. He needed to tell her that Katherine was safe with the Comanche, and happier now than she had been in a long time.

The front door opened slowly at his approach, and not Aunt Dee but Elizabeth stepped out onto the porch. Her smile warmed him more surely than the sweet sunshine warming his back and shoulders. Her dark hair looked almost blue in the morning light, shimmering with each step as she rushed toward him. Her lips were as red and inviting as he remembered, her eyes as blue.

Elizabeth held open her arms for him. . . .

Cold sweat drenched Ford as his body jerked to wakefulness. There was nothing but the pitch black of the stockade roof above him, and hard as he tried, he could not bring back the dream. Fear gripped him, fear so strong and icy that his teeth chattered. He was going to die here, and he'd never see Elizabeth again. Or he was going to go crazy.

Maybe he already was.

Sensing that Ford was awake by the fact that he had ceased the violent thrashing that accompanied his dreams every night, the other man in the crude cell with him rolled over on his hard pallet. "Rusk will come for us."

"You're a fool if you believe that." Ford's voice sounded dead and dry, even to his own ears. He could hear the hopelessness. "If he made it to safety, Rusk won't look back, won't even think twice. We'll rot in here if it takes his efforts to get us out."

The sound of a rat scurrying across the packed earth floor followed his bitter speech. For a moment he regretted saying the words that had echoed in his head for days now. Saying them made them real. Besides, he knew Emile didn't really believe his own bravado either. He just wanted to make Ford feel a little better about their chances. "I'm sorry, Emile."

Emile sighed. When he spoke again there was a plaintive edge of fear to his question. "Do you think they will hang us?"

It was a question Ford had asked himself many times. He didn't answer now.

After a long silence Emile asked another question, one he asked at least once a day, hoping against hope that the answer would change. "Do you think Louis made it?"

Louis was Emile's brother, and no, Ford didn't think Louis had survived the bullet both he and Emile had seen Louis take solidly in the chest. But the troops were riding after Ford and Emile, and Louis, wounded, had taken a different route. To ride after Louis, even to go to his aid, would have ensured his capture as well.

Finally, Ford said, "If he did, it's because you played sitting duck for those soldiers, drawing them away from him." He didn't really know that Emile was noble enough to have done so deliberately, but he knew saying so would ease Emile's mind.

The rattle of doors at the other end of the row of cells told them of the changing of their guards. It would be almost dawn, Ford reckoned. That was how he marked time these days, by the four-hour shifts of the guards.

"You ever done anything worth hanging for?"

Ford finally asked, dreading the answer but needing to know.

"I killed a man once down along the border," Emile admitted in a low, scared voice. "You?"

"No." Ford wondered if this would be the day they were taken from their cell and asked to face their crimes. Whatever those were. "But I wonder if anyone here will believe that."

Chapter Seventeen

Slade was furious with Katherine, and Katherine was furious with herself. How could she have been so stupid? All those months of guarding her secret wasted with one careless, mindless moment of hunger. Slade now held a power over her she could afford no one to have, and there was nothing she could do about it.

She glared at him across the campfire at daybreak, feeling the chill of early winter through her coat. Slade, his usual taciturn self, might never have asked that question, might never have held her to his side through the long hours of the night, refusing to allow her to leave his bedroll. All of his anger was contained behind an implacable mask, but Katherine was not deceived. She knew the anger was there, simmering and waiting.

Which only served to fuel her own. How dare he feel betrayed? Her life was her own—and Shea's life depended on her. How could she trust anyone with knowledge that would place the child of her heart in danger?

Standing, Katherine moved away from the fire, carrying her tin cup with her. The warmth emanating from the coffee did not dispel the early morning cold, but it helped.

"Saddle up," Slade told her in his no-nonsense tone. There might never have been a moment of passion or tenderness between them.

Katherine shot him a look of sheer venom, but he had already turned his attention to destroying every trace of their campfire.

They rode in silence throughout the day, Katherine following Slade and keeping far enough back from him that she could not see the slant of his jaw as his gaze continually scanned the horizon. When they made camp that evening she again prepared their meal, keeping her distance. But she could feel his eyes on her. Feel his thoughts.

Slade was growing exasperated with what he felt was sullenness on her part and stupidity on his own. He had hated the thought of her in Wolf Killer's arms, had been plagued by visions of the warrior's brown body plunging into Katherine's. Now that he was free of those visions he was angry with her. And he knew the cause of the anger. He had believed, had wanted to believe, that Katherine had learned to trust in him. He'd been convinced of that when she had come to Fort Lancaster looking for him.

He knew her terror of the soldiers, yet she had placed her faith in Slade—that he would let no one and nothing harm her. She trusted him with her life and with her brother's. But she had not trusted him with her secret. It was stupid to feel hurt over that—but he did.

"What would you have had me do?"

Katherine's fierce, low tones broke into his thoughts, and he glanced up from the stick he was whittling to where she crouched, tending the fire. She wasn't looking at him, and all he could see was the top of her head. Without answering, he continued to watch her, and at last she lifted her face. There were tears on her cheeks.

"Would you have had me hand her to the first soldier who tried to rip her from my arms? To the one who chased me down and wanted to bash her head against the stones in the creek?"

There was a despondency in her voice that tore at his heart. Katherine Bellamy had been through far more than most women who neared the end of their lives. And she had withstood it well.

"Why did you keep up the lie after you were safe?"

"I didn't *feel* safe!" she said bitterly. "Every soldier I looked at might have been one who murdered my people. I could see bloodstains on their hands, as if they'd never been washed. I could recall every smile as they struck with bayonets or clubs. And even if I had trusted them not to kill Shea, they would have taken her from me."

Slade watched her steadily. Her tears had dried and her eyes were alive with the courage that had kept herself and Shea from death.

"Even before the soldiers came Shea had begun to think of me as her mother. Little Feather wasn't strong enough to take care of her. She'd never recovered from Shea's birth. The night the soldiers attacked she was already near death. I don't know if it was her illness or the soldiers that killed her."

"Little Feather?" Slade tried to recall the little girl's looks when he'd seen her that day in town. He'd have sworn she was a half-breed, which was why it had never occurred to him that she was not Katherine's daughter.

"Jeane Pearson," Katherine answered quietly. "Jeane was known as Little Feather."

Slade nodded. "Your family knows?"

Katherine shook her head. "Not at first. I was too afraid they wouldn't be able to accept Shea unless they thought she was mine. And I couldn't risk anyone taking her from me. But Ford learned the truth when he was with the Comanche."

"He'll keep your secret?"

Katherine met Slade's eyes and nodded. Her

question remained unspoken: would Slade?

He didn't try to stop her from spreading her own bedroll. Katherine could feel every stick and stone beneath it as she stretched her weary limbs. And she could feel the cold that seeped into her very bones.

Just as her eyes were drifting closed, Slade spoke. "I reckon I would have done the same."

A peace crept over her, and she slept.

Slade peered through the deluge at the Brazos River and muttered a curse. He'd been afraid of this since morning, when they'd risen to a sky filled with sparse, drifting clouds. His glum forebodings had increased with the steady warming of the air around them. And each hour had seen an increase in the clouds until they darkened the sky.

Slade looked at Katherine and almost smiled. Beneath the battered hat he'd shoved on her head she was completely sodden. He lifted his voice over the solid roar of the downpour. "Dismount and wait here. I'll look for some kind of shelter."

As she moved to obey, he thrust his reins into her hands and set off through the veiling sheets of rain. Within moments, Katherine was alone, isolated in a fury of nature. The horses were skittish and hard to hold. She had little time to be uneasy; it took all her concentration to keep Sadie and the buckskin under firm control. She was almost startled when Slade returned.

231

He did not try to communicate with words. He simply took his reins and motioned for her to follow on foot.

It wasn't a cabin or even a tepee, but a halfhearted combination of the two that he had found. Two walls were crudely fit logs; the third was hides stretched to complete the triangle. The roof was both logs and hides, and appeared fairly sound.

They pulled the saddles from the horses and stowed them within the shelter. When Katherine would have hobbled Sadie, Slade stopped her. The mare would be safer in the storm with her legs free, and neither she nor the packhorse would leave the buckskin. And the buckskin wouldn't leave Slade.

An unexpected flash of lightning illuminated Katherine and Slade momentarily as they stood beneath the shelter, looking at one another. Slade's hat dripped water onto his soaked leather jacket. An expression of annoyance was fixed on his face. "Wood's too damned wet to build a fire."

Despite her own discomfort, Katherine smiled at his look and leaned forward to wipe the water from his brow—and found herself caught up in a savage embrace. She responded instantly, feeling her nipples tauten and thrust against her blouse. Slade pulled her coat from her shoulders, but it was Katherine's own hands that unfastened her blouse, baring her breasts to his touch. His hands touched her with fire, and she knew a frustration that her own questing fingers found only his rough clothing.

Slade chuckled deep in his throat as she attacked his shirt, but he didn't help her. He just stood there with narrowed eyes, watching what his hands did to the dark crests of her breasts.

"Damn you," she muttered when she finally had his shirt hanging open. But she didn't hear any chuckles when her attack moved to the fastening of his pants: only a moan deep in his throat. When her hand slipped low to caress the flat of his belly the moan turned to a low growl of hunger, and Katherine found herself pressed deep into their bedroll.

She parted her legs to receive him, closing her eyes against the dark, fierce hunger in his.

"Look at me," he commanded hoarsely.

And she did, her gaze clinging to his, just as her hands clung helplessly to his shoulders. She wanted to torture, as he tortured, but all she could do was gasp beneath the feelings that built hotter and deeper within her at his every move. Her release from those feelings was so explosive, she scarcely realized, or cared, that his own came but a heartbeat later.

Slade did not release his hold on Katherine but eased to his side, taking her with him. She felt so damned good against him, soft and trusting, the way she never was when she had all her defenses about her. For this moment, at least, she was completely his, completely dependent upon him. The feeling was better than anything he'd known in a long time.

Through that night and all of the next day they waited out a series of storms. Lightning terrified the horses and thunder deafened them, while Slade and Katherine loved, slept, and loved again. And talked.

Katherine lay on her stomach, watching the drops of rain beat against the sodden earth. Slade's hand rubbed circular motions between her shoulder blades. "How long have you worked with the Rangers?"

"A while."

A half sigh, half chuckle escaped Katherine. She supposed it just wasn't in Slade to volunteer information. "How long have you been looking for Elzy Rusk?"

To her surprise, Slade's hand stilled. She felt the change in him and wished she'd known not to ask that particular question.

"Ten years ago I hunted for him the better part of a year—'til it was reported a bounty hunter had killed him. I was sorry I'd missed my chance. A year ago he was heard of down along the border, and I started hunting again."

It was the first Slade had allowed her a glimpse of himself, of what drove him. Katherine both dreaded and needed to know more. "Why are you after Rusk?" she asked softly, wondering if he would answer, or if his protective curtain would drop once more.

234

"In 'forty-five or 'forty-six, Zack Taylor rode in to Corpus Christi to guard the border against the Mexicans. At sixteen, I was too green to realize we were doing more taking than defending. I'd only been married and on my own for a few months and was all fired up with the notion of defending my home."

Katherine lay very still, hearing the derision in his voice for the boy he had been.

"So I rode down into Mexico with Taylor, leaving a pregnant wife with a farm to take care of. A farm I was going to help 'make safe.' I got letters from Maggie as often as she could find a way to get them to me. She kept the farm going without me and managed to have a son without me there too."

Slade's eyes were fixed on the saplings that braced the stretched rawhide roof above them. "An injured man showed up at the door one day, and Maggie was too tenderhearted to turn him away. She took care of him, and in payment he raped her. And then he forced her to leave with him—and he made her leave our baby behind. Alone. Neighbors found him two or three days later, starving, too weak to cry anymore. Too weak to survive. He was seven months old."

"Slade . . ." Katherine's voice was no more than a sigh of horror. She knew he didn't hear her speak.

"When I got home a few months later there was a letter from Maggie waiting for me at the mercantile. She'd left it in the hotel room where she hung herself after Rusk gave her to the owner to pay for his board."

A sickness filled Katherine as Slade's voice died away and she realized the magnitude of what she'd done in warning Rusk away. If she could so easily hear the hungry cries of the baby, the horrified pleas of Maggie as she realized her son was being left to die, what must Slade have suffered over the years? "I'm sorry," she whispered. "Oh God, I'm sorry."

When Slade didn't answer she shifted so that her head lay against his chest. To her relief, his arms came up to hold her. She wanted desperately to heal his hurt. "I've always thought Maggie is such a pretty name. What was she like?"

Slade closed his eyes, picturing his wife as he'd seen her last, framed in the doorway of their home, one hand resting on the gentle curve of her stomach where their child grew. She'd been so proud to be carrying his baby. "Maggie was . . . sharp like spice." *And sweet like wine.* "Always laughing or talking or cussing me for some fool thing." *But never quiet—never solemn.*

He knew it would have taken a lot for Maggie to break to the point of giving up—of taking her own life. She must have been half-crazed by the time she knotted that sheet around her neck. Maybe with the sound of her son's frightened cries still ringing in her ears.

Katherine kept still, realizing he had forgotten her very existence.

"She was a pretty thing with bright red hair and the bluest eyes." Slade opened his eyes and looked at Katherine, his own eyes bleak. "I left her. Pregnant, alone, and helpless against men like Rusk."

Without realizing what he did or why, Slade drew Katherine close, holding her protectively against his side. "Your brother made a mistake taking up with Rusk."

"I know. But Ford was frightened by the shooting. And he panicked." Katherine pressed closer, wishing she could erase Slade's painful memories, leaving only the good things. But she couldn't even do that for herself. The past seemed always there. "What will you do when Rusk is dead?" She had told herself she wouldn't ask that question, but it seemed almost to have asked itself.

Slade didn't answer right away. He wasn't sure he knew the answer. Although he'd imagined many times the moment when Rusk finally faced him, imagined making Rusk suffer as Maggie had suffered, he'd never pictured himself walking away afterward. Or where he would be headed.

For just a moment Slade recalled an image he'd once carried of himself striding across fertile fields, a son or daughter close on his heels, a woman watching them from a shaded porch. But the woman wasn't Maggie. He looked at

Katherine, trying to match her to the woman on the porch. But Katherine Bellamy was as much a misfit as he was. *Could* they build some semblance of a normal life between them? Did he want to try?

After a moment Katherine realized he wasn't going to answer her question. Maybe he couldn't. But there was a hungry look in his eyes that she was beginning to recognize, that sparked an answering hunger in her. She forgot her question and lifted her lips to his.

The next morning they crossed the Brazos. The sky had faired and was blue in the sun's light, but the river current was swift after the storm. Leading the packhorse, Slade went first, admonishing Katherine, "Forget your reins. Just hold on to that mare's mane and let her take you across on her own."

Katherine gave him a look of disgust. "I've crossed every river in Texas."

Slade shrugged and headed the buckskin into the water.

Katherine followed wordlessly. When the ground dropped from beneath Sadie's feet she felt the mare's brief panic. The pull of the water was stronger than Katherine had expected. Instinctively, she dropped the reins and clung to Sadie with one hand, the other grasping her saddlebags. Glancing up, she saw Slade reach the bank. He was upstream from her, which meant Sadie was losing her struggle with the current. Katherine began talking to the mare, urging her on, reassuring her.

Dimly, she heard Slade's warning shout, turned, and felt the spinning, driven log strike painfully against her shoulder. She lost her grasp on Sadie, fingers raking over slick hair as she was pulled sideways. She went under, choked, and surfaced. The muddy water she had swallowed made her gag. Her arms felt leaden, her legs icily numb. She did not want to drown in this filthy yellow river. The thought made her angry: She would not drown.

Forced by her determination, her tired muscles began to pull against the water, seeking shore. Trash swept over her, and she pushed it away or let it cling, indifferent. Something heavy struck the surface of the water in front of her. She grasped for it automatically, her fingers closing on Slade's rope, her body sagging in sudden relief.

Slade's hands grasped her arms and he yanked her from the sucking water. She felt sticks, briars, and bushes claw at her exposed legs.

"You damned little fool!" He caught her hard against him.

The pressure upon her middle was too much. She tried to push away from him, feeling sweat mix with the river water on her clammy skin, but Slade held her firmly while she vomited. When she was empty of her breakfast, the waters of the Brazos, and her fear, Slade wiped her face with the soaked hem of his shirt. Then he simply held her, and nothing had ever felt so good or so safe as his arms around her.

"Sadie?" she asked at last.

"That damned horse is fine."

He made no recriminations about the saddlebags she had tried to preserve and lost in the end, nearly losing herself with them. He built a fire, stripped her, and dried her with his own spare shirt, pulled from the packhorse's burden. When she was warmed he set about cooking another breakfast of salt meat and fried meal. He handed her a plate with a straight face, and for once she was glad of his ability to conceal his thoughts. She had no desire to know what Slade was thinking at that moment.

Chapter Eighteen

A gray light seeped through the cell, but it didn't wake Ford. He'd been awake for hours. Sleep was more and more elusive. His body craved exercise, and the few minutes they were allowed morning and evening were not enough to satisfy that craving.

He didn't move when he heard the guard clatter at the door.

"You've got fifteen minutes to eat," the man growled, as he did every morning. But then he added, "Captain's got a little heavy labor for you this morning."

Ford sat reluctantly, not feeling particularly cooperative but interested in the notion of getting out of the tiny cell. He glanced across at Emile. "Better get up, friend." They'd been really careful not to reveal their names. That

241

had been Emile's idea, and it had seemed a smart one to Ford.

Emile didn't move, and Ford couldn't blame him. There was nothing particularly appetizing about the food brought to them every morning. Of course, it was better than some Ford had been forced to eat while riding with Rusk. The bread was as hard as the mattress he slept on, but at least it didn't have weevils crawling through it.

"Get your friend up, mister. I want to see both of you awake."

Ford shrugged and leaned across to nudge Emile with the tip of his fingers. "Come on. I ain't going to whisper sweet words in your ear to get you up. And our buddy with the gun sure as hell ain't."

To Ford's surprise, Emile still did not move. Leaving his bunk, Ford crossed the few steps between them and punched Emile's shoulder. When there was still no response he leaned closer with a faint stirring of alarm. But Emile was breathing. His face looked rigid, however, not relaxed in sleep.

"Something's wrong with him," Ford said without looking away from Emile's face. "You'd better get help."

"Bullshit! He's just lazy and don't like the idea of a little work." Still cursing, the guard slid the key in the lock, motioning with his shiny new carbine for Ford to back away.

In that half second, while the man's attention

was on Ford, Emile rose smoothly from the bed and, in the same motion, pressed a gleaming blade against his throat. The guard stilled, his eyes bulging in fear as he felt the bite of the knife. For a heartbeat, Ford stood frozen.

Emile grinned at him. "Take the rifle."

Ford just looked at him. "This is a damn-fool idea."

"Take his rifle, friend, or I'll be forced to cut his throat. I do not care much one way or the other."

Ford believed him. Emile was as relaxed as if he was lounging around the campfire, slicing ticks in half. Ford had no doubt he would slice this man's throat with as little hesitation. Slowly, Ford reached for the rifle, seeing the relief in the guard's eyes.

"Now," Emile said, still in pleasant tones, "gag him and tie his hands. Then we will leave this place. I do not like it here any longer."

Ford did as he was told, trying to decide if he would be better off letting Emile lock him in the cell or breaking out with him. So far, he'd done nothing wrong. But was anybody here going to believe him? Even if he didn't try to ride out with Emile, he might well end up hanging just because he'd been caught with Rusk.

"How the hell do you expect to get past the gate?" Ford asked as he finished gagging the man, who was almost eager to put his hands behind him to be tied. The guard seemed not to doubt he would feel the slice of that wicked blade if he was not safely bound and gagged. Ford didn't doubt it either. There was a hard look in Emile's eyes, one Ford had seen in Rusk's and Louis's on occasions he didn't care to recall.

Emile grinned. "We have been here many weeks, *amigo*. We are forgotten by all but this guard and maybe the captain. And this fort sees many travelers. We will not look as if we expect to be stopped, and so we will not be stopped."

It proved not quite so easy as that. The stabler knew who had horses with him and who did not. Ford clubbed him from behind when he grew belligerent, just to keep Emile from knifing the man. He was beginning to doubt that Emile had killed only one man— or that he felt any remorse for it. But Ford was committed, now, to escaping with him, and he was going to do it without bloodshed, if possible.

Once they were mounted, leaving the fort was as easy as Emile had been confident it would be. They approached the gate with two packhorses piled high with goods. Ford knew they appeared to be the traders, who were going to be furious at the loss of their horses and trade goods. Ford's heart was thundering, and he felt a sickness in the pit of his stomach as Emile hailed the gate. Emile ridiculed the sentry for not recognizing him after only a few days in the fort. "I am not so much cleaner than I was when I came!" Emile shouted to him.

The sentry grinned in agreement and waved them on.

As Ford followed close behind Emile, his back muscles tensed against the bullet he expected, for surely the guard who had brought their breakfast had been missed by now.

Emile nudged his horse to a trot and Ford did the same. Still there was no sound of alarm from behind.

Ford drew his first good breath when they eased to a gallop. Within minutes they disappeared into the safety of the tall grasses that covered the sloping hills surrounding the fort.

Emile grinned over his shoulder at Ford when they could no longer see the walls of the stockade behind them. "Now, my friend, we are safe."

Ford didn't feel safe, however, and suspected he wouldn't for a long time to come.

Keeping the sun at their backs, they traveled hard, not stopping until long past midday to dig into the saddlepacks. Ford was the first to find food, a rancid dried venison. He handed Emile a strip and took one for himself.

Emile glanced around them as he chewed. "I think we will start north here. Maybe look for Rusk back with the Comanche."

Slowly, Ford shook his head. "This is where we part, Emile. I'm going south. I'm going home."

Chapter Nineteen

Katherine studied the bare yard surrounding the log cabin homestead within sight of Camp Colorado and wondered why Slade had stopped here. There was no sign of life except a cur yapping at the horses' heels. Slade motioned for Katherine to remain astride before he dismounted and dropped the buckskin's reins to the ground. He was forced to nudge the dog out of his way before walking up to the crudely built cabin.

The door was ajar, but Katherine could not see into the dim interior. Peering through the door, Slade called out, and almost immediately was surrounded by a parcel of redheaded children whose locks ranged from fox fur to autumn gold. They were grubby but wore a look of health as they swarmed from the rear of the cabin around the outside. Katherine counted five, then six, as a woman came to the door, babe in one arm, ladle in her free hand. Her apron was clean, and her russet hair was neatly braided and bound.

Katherine heard every word Slade said to her.

"'Afternoon, ma'am. Your man at home?"

"Will be soon."

"I have business at the fort and was thinking to leave my wife someplace she would be more comfortable."

Biting her tongue, Katherine seethed in silence. How dare he? He hadn't even taken the time to ask how she would feel about being left behind! And she damned sure didn't like it!

The woman looked beyond him to Katherine and smiled. "I can't say how comfortable she'd be here, but she'd be mighty welcome."

"Maybe you'd rather wait 'til your mister was here before saying," Slade suggested.

"No need. His answer'd be the same."

"You're sure?"

"Certain sure."

Slade walked back to Katherine and helped her down. Her glare made no impression on him whatsoever.

At the woman's instructions, Slade took Katherine's mare and the packhorse around to the back while Katherine walked inside with the woman. She was bound on all sides by children. Once inside, their mother shooed them out again and turned to Katherine.

"I'm Eileen Cullen and pleased to have you here."

"Irish?" Katherine asked in pleasure.

"Couldn't be more." Eileen Cullen grinned back at her.

"My mother's maiden name was McKenna. I'm Katherine . . . Slade." She choked on the last word.

When Slade came back in Eileen had returned to her cooking, and Katherine held the infant. The baby's name was Bevin, and she made Katherine ache for Shea. Slade beckoned Katherine to the door and she went, still holding the baby.

"Are you crazy?" were her first words. "You can't leave me here."

"I reckon I'd be more crazy to take you with me. I don't know what I'm riding into. Hell, I might have to fight my way out with that brother of yours. And I sure as hell don't want to have to fight every soldier in that fort over you."

She gritted her teeth before reminding him, "I spent days at Fort Lancaster!" Even in her anger, she spoke quietly, aware of the baby sleeping peacefully in her arms and the mother behind her.

The look Slade gave her was infuriating, his answer humiliating. "The men at Fort Lancaster thought you were my property. That made you safe. But this isn't Fort Lancaster."

He saw her slitted eyes and angry color and bent close, putting his mouth on hers. From a distance it looked like a kiss, but it wasn't. He growled against her lips, "You settle here, or I ride back the way I came."

She pulled back and hissed, "We made a deal."

He shrugged, and she knew he would do as he threatened. She felt Eileen Cullen staring as if she sensed something amiss, and she forced a smile. "Hurry back."

Slade's look mocked her as he nodded.

She stood glaring at his back as he walked out the door.

Eileen came up behind her. "You must not have been married long to be so sorry to have him gone for a day or two. I sometimes think it'd be better for me if Adam was gone from time to time," she said with a laugh, touching her sleeping baby lightly. "I have too many young'uns already."

Katherine smiled but did not answer as she laid the baby in a cradle that stood in one corner of the room. As she helped Eileen with dinner, she talked to her about Shea, letting the other woman believe the little girl was hers and Slade's.

"It must be terrible to have to be away from her."

"It is," Katherine admitted, "and I hope it won't be for much longer." But when she was reunited with Shea, Slade would be gone. Back to Fort Lancaster, back to his traveling ways. She wished the thought didn't hurt, but it did.

"You're real lucky you have folks you can trust to leave your little girl with. There's no one around here that I could depend on, as far as I know. No family or anything."

Katherine thought of Old Mother, who had loved her Sleeping Grasshopper; of Aunt Dee, who probably lived in daily dread that Katherine was returning to take the baby away from her. "Real lucky," she answered, wondering what Eileen Cullen would say if she knew the truth.

Adam Cullen returned from his fields when the last light of day was fading. Katherine had met each of his children, though she was not certain she would remember all of their names with any accuracy. She watched as they clambered over their father; watched, too, as his face lit up with a smile. He had merry eyes and a ready laugh, and she liked him even before they exchanged their first words.

"This is Katherine Slade, Adam," Eileen said, eager for him to meet the girl who had lightened the work of another tedious day. "Her husband had important business at the fort, and he didn't want her to be uncomfortable."

Adam held out a large, stained hand to Katherine, which she clasped without hesitation. "I'm glad for my Eileen to have some company. It's a lonely place for her sometimes."

His wife reproved him gently. "Now, how could I be lonely with all of my children around me, Adam Cullen?"

Nonetheless, Katherine suspected it was so. She also suspected the woman would never admit to it, for fear of giving pain to the man who spent his days working to provide her with security. Their marriage was clearly a warm and loving one, and Katherine wondered if Slade and Maggie would have been like this if they'd ever had the chance. Slade might have been different if he could have come home to his wife and baby. Maybe he would never have gotten that hard, deadly look in his eyes. And Katherine would never have known him.

Adam was speaking to her again, and she pulled her thoughts back. "Whatever the reason you're here, 'tis glad we are to have you for a while, Mrs. Slade. Your husband was wise. I would not want a wife of mine for many days at the fort, with the sort of gypsies that pass through it."

Over a meal of food harvested with his own hands, Adam and his wife made Katherine feel as much at home as if she'd known them for the greater part of her life. After a blessing was asked on the food she watched the children pass plate after plate from oldest to youngest, no one eating until all had been served. At a nod from their father, however, they displayed a very healthy set of appetites.

When Katherine complimented the meal, to

her amusement, it was Adam who took credit for it.

"It is such good soil here," he said earnestly, "rich and black. All that a man could hope to find. If you and your husband are thinking to settle around here, you'll find you could not do better."

"No," she said quickly, "we . . . we don't plan to stay."

She could see that Adam was as curious as his wife, but that neither would press her for more than her vague answer. They were a couple used to tending their own business and allowing others to tend theirs. She was grateful, for she didn't know what she could have told them without being rude if they had pressed for more information than she could give.

That night she slept downstairs with the children, laughing with them before they settled for sleep in a room made cozy with a warm fire. Later, however, the muffled sounds from the loft made her lonely. She thought of Slade and shifted restlessly. Damn him anyway. But her anger was less than her fear. When they parted company for good would she be lonely for Slade for the rest of her life?

"They escaped?" Slade stared at the fort's commander. This was the one circumstance he hadn't anticipated. "How the hell did they do that?"

The officer flushed. He was new to his post and suspected he wouldn't last long at this rate. "One of their guards was . . . lax. He was overtaken by force three days ago."

"And the gate?" Slade asked, still incredulous.

"The two disarmed the stabler and stole horses and goods belonging to some traders. The sentry at the gate saw no reason to question them." At the look on Slade's face he tugged at his collar. "Our experience is in fighting Indians, not outlaws." A thought occurred to him. "How did you know they were here, anyway?"

"I've been following Rusk for months, and I'm always one jump behind him." This time the disgust in Slade's voice was for himself.

"We didn't have Rusk," the post commander admitted. "Just two of his men, and I'm not completely sure of their names. I suspect the younger was a kid named Ford Bellamy. Word went out some time ago that he's the newest addition to that band."

Slade stilled. He'd described Emile and several of the others to a fare-thee-well but deliberately omitted any description of Ford Bellamy. "It couldn't have been Bellamy," Slade said finally, lying without compunction. "He parted company with them weeks ago, fortunately before he could get involved in anything illegal."

The commander didn't argue. "Well, whoever

they are, they're gone, and we were not successful in recapturing them." To tell the truth, he
hadn't tried too hard. As he'd said, the main
charge of this fort was to guard the area against
Indians. Within his ranks were some of the best
Indian fighters in Texas. There wasn't much of
interest to outlaws in the soil-rich, property-
poor holdings of the settlers. As a consequence,
outlaws weren't of much interest to the soldiers
at the fort.

Slade rose to his feet, then waited as the
commander followed suit.

"I'll have someone show you to your quarters."

For a moment Slade almost considered riding back to Katherine. But it was hours past
dark. The family she was with had probably
long since gone to bed.

He followed a corporal who led him along
the edge of the parade grounds and into a low-
roofed building. He glanced around the room
he was shown and nodded to the young man
waiting for his reaction. "Thank you, Corporal.
I'll need nothing further."

As he settled his long frame on the hard cot,
he wondered where the unfortunate officer he'd
ousted would rest for the night. Then he closed
his eyes and slept.

Elzy Rusk crept slowly toward the cabin. He
couldn't believe his good luck. That bastard
Slade had been making his life miserable for

years, and he'd just ridden out and left a golden opportunity for Rusk to return the favor.

Not that he didn't deserve a little break in his bad luck. He'd been hanging around this place for two days, trying to figure a way into the fort without being recognized. When he finally managed that feat he found out it was all for nothing. That damned Emile had escaped without him. He should have followed his first instinct, which was to leave every one of them behind. They were a stupid bunch, after all, or they would not have been killed or captured. What did he need with stupid men? But, then, he'd told himself, he was used to their presence, and they were loyal. So he'd turned back finally and trailed Louis to the Palo Duro, where he'd gotten a very cool reception thanks to that damned white squaw. She had enraged Wolf Killer by running after her damn-fool brother. And Wolf Killer held great influence over the other braves. Louis was dead, and Rusk had found no welcome there.

It had been harder to track Emile to Camp Colorado, but he'd managed. He wouldn't have bothered for the Bellamy kid, but Emile had been with him a long time. He trusted Emile, needed him.

And now Emile, too, was gone.

By the merest stroke of fate, his path had crossed Slade's and the Bellamy girl's that morning. He hadn't even recognized them at first. He'd just followed, needing money and needing a woman. Then he'd realized who it was he was trailing. He didn't want to tangle with Slade, but he'd relish any opportunity to get the lawman off his trail for good. It was proving more and more difficult lately to elude the man.

When Slade had led the way toward the log cabin Rusk had faded into the tall prairie grass nearby and waited. The hardest decision had been whether to go after Slade or take the girl. The girl had won out. She was worth money, after all. And somehow he suspected that what he would do with her would cause Slade more grief than dying. And he would make sure Slade knew. Eventually, Slade would catch up to him, and Rusk would kill him then.

Even in her sleep, Katherine had been listening for Slade's return. She was not surprised to hear the creak of leather in the yard, followed by a light rap on the door. The sounds from the loft had long since stilled, and the children were all asleep. Katherine eased from her warm cocoon, shivering slightly as she moved to unbar the door.

She stepped out and pulled it closed behind her. "Slade?"

Bright moonlight revealed her mistake. Elzy Rusk held his horse and Sadie by the reins—and he was laughing at her silently.

She crossed her arms against the cold and waited, saying nothing.

"Mount up, missy. We've got a ways to go."

"I'm not going anywhere with you." She said the words quietly, without any of the fear she couldn't help but feel. Slade was too far away. Adam Cullen and his family, too vulnerable.

"Unless you want to bring trouble to this family—to all those little ones sleeping so soundly inside the cabin—you'll come with me." He shrugged. "I would not care to kill children, but I will if I have to."

Katherine's shoulders slumped in defeat. She forgot any thought she had of waking Adam. Nor could she risk waking one of the children to leave word for Slade. "I'll have to go back in to get dressed."

Rusk thought about whether she would try to escape or rouse the man of the house to aid her. Then he nodded for her to go ahead. It would make no difference. He would kill them all if need be.

Chapter Twenty

Ford sat astride his horse, staring at the farmhouse for a long time, watching as the lowering of the sun deepened the shadows in the yard. When he'd ridden away early summer had gentled the hills with soft carpets of wildflowers. Winter had replaced those flowers with windswept grass, withered and browned. Those changes were natural, as inevitable as the spinning of the earth.

If Ford had known what other changes he would face on his return, he'd never have taken the jaunt. At the time, it had seemed like a harmless adventure. The things he'd seen and done had made him a man, but the cost had been high. Katherine was gone. Shea would be soon. And Aunt Dee? Well, he could tell by the line of clothes drying in the back yard that some change had come here as well. Those men's pants flapping in the brisk wind weren't his.

He lifted his reins and clucked to his horse, which stepped forward eagerly, smelling the barnyard odors that beckoned of feed and a warm stall.

Dee met him halfway across the yard, running and laughing, so that he had to dismount to keep her from flinging herself up into the saddle with him. With his heart full of feelings he hadn't sorted through, Ford held her close to his chest. He knew when her laughter turned to tears.

"It's all right now, Aunt Dee," he murmured helplessly. He pressed his hand against her hair, seeing the first hint of gray there. "Don't cry. Everything's fine." But it wasn't, and he knew it. And she knew also.

Dee drew away, wiping her hands across her cheeks. "Thank God you're safe, Ford." She felt the familiar lump in her throat. "Katherine . . . ?"

"Is fine." Ford hoped it was true. He worried about all the things that could happen to her. But it was her life, her choice.

A man stepped out on the porch behind her, and Ford looked into the welcoming eyes of Doyle Shanley. Shea nestled against his chest, her arms circling his neck.

"Welcome home, son. Your aunt's been mighty worried."

Ford nodded gravely. "Yes, sir, and I'm sorry for that. I've done some ignorant things lately."

Unexpectedly, Doyle grinned. "Better now than later, when you've got a wife and little ones who would be thinking you've taken leave of your senses." He stepped down to slip one arm around Dee's shoulders.

Ford smiled when Shea reached out one hand to pat Dee's cheek. "Mama smile," she demanded.

"Yes, sweeting, Aunt Dee is going to smile now."

Silently, Ford noted that Katherine's daughter had called another woman mother, and he noted, also, the gentle correcting. He felt a quick concern for Katherine. She'd suffered so many hardships, so much pain. She didn't need another—he wasn't sure how much more she could take.

With an easy movement, Doyle transferred Shea to Dee's arm and reached for the reins to Ford's horse. "Go in with your aunt, son. I'll take care of your horse."

Ford smiled, grateful to Doyle for a private reunion with his aunt. Moments later, he lounged at the table, holding Shea, who clearly did not remember him but had decided he was friend rather than foe. Dee bustled about the kitchen, as she had a thousand other times, preparing the evening meal. Her wedding band glinted with each quick movement of her hand.

"When did you two get married?"

Dee smiled brilliantly. "Just two weeks ago. Elizabeth was our witness."

Ford knew she had brought the name up deliberately. But he didn't bite. "You're happy?" It wasn't really a question that needed asking. Dee's happiness was evident from the sparkle in her dark almond eyes to the soft flush of color on her cheeks.

"Aye. I'm very happy." She hesitated. "But I'll worry until you and Katherine are safely settled."

"I hope I'm settled now," Ford said feelingly. It would be a sheer miracle if the United States Army wasn't trailing him. That worry would be with him for a long time to come. He dreaded what he had to say next, knowing it would diminish the happy glow in his aunt's eyes. "I'm afraid Katherine's pretty much settled too."

Even though he wanted that to be true, wanted Katherine settled and happy, he wished things were different. Nor could he help feeling worried about his sister. What if Wolf Killer had not yet returned? Or had changed his mind about wanting Katherine? The thought that Katherine might be in need or in danger gnawed at him.

Dee moved slowly to sit across from Ford. "What about Shea?"

They stared into each other's eyes, Dee's anxious, Ford's reluctant, so caught up in their feelings that neither heard Doyle open the outside door.

"She'll not take the child," he said from the doorway.

"Doyle." The soft word was a plea and a warning.

Ford got the idea this discussion wasn't new.

"I'm perfectly willing for her to come back here and have the mothering of Shea, but I don't mean for any murdering redskin to have the raising of her." Doyle bristled from his massive shoulders to his strong jaw.

"Do you forget that Shea is the child of a 'murdering redskin'? That's her heritage." Ford fought the quick anger that rose in him. It was clear to him that Doyle's stand was born of love for the little girl.

"If you were any other man, I'd make you eat those words. Your aunt and I have fought hard to have Shea accepted in this town these past few weeks."

There was a tormented look in Doyle's eyes that struck a chord of sympathy in Ford—but Katherine was his sister. "Shea is Katherine's daughter, Doyle. Not yours and not Aunt Dee's. If Katherine comes for her," Ford said evenly, "I'll not let you or anyone else stand in her way."

"Will you face down a gun to do it?" Doyle's sandy freckles blazed with his anger.

"Doyle!" Dee was as shocked as she was angry. "You'll not threaten the boy."

Shea whimpered, distressed by the angry tones around her. She reached her arms to

Dee who took her, hushing her soothingly.

Ford sighed. This wasn't the reunion he'd anticipated. "Don't bring bad blood into this family, Doyle Shanley. There's never been any before. Shea will go with her mother when the time comes. I'll see to that."

"Do you know what you're saying, boy?"

"Yeah. I'm saying you can't take a little girl away from her mother just because you think you can do better for her." If Ford had ever considered revealing Katherine's secret—that Shea was *not* her daughter—he knew that was impossible now. For everyone's sake.

Dee touched her husband's arm. "He's right, Doyle. And I can't let you do anything about it."

Doyle's shoulders slumped in defeat. His eyes met Dee's. "How would we bear it?"

Tears filled her eyes, but all she could do was shake her head mutely. She did not have the answer to that.

Two days later, Ford garnered enough courage to make his first trip into New Braunfels. It was going to take that courage for him to face Elizabeth.

Dee stood in the doorway to his room after he'd bathed and scrubbed his hair. He grinned at her as he buttoned his shirt, but she could tell he was nervous. She smiled at him, and for just a moment she saw his father, so heartbreakingly handsome. Ford was his image now.

"Reckon Elizabeth will have forgotten me?" Ford tried to speak lightly, as if it wouldn't matter if she had. But he could tell by Dee's eyes that he hadn't succeeded.

Forget him? When Dee herself could recall details of his father as clearly as if it was yesterday that she'd last seen him? "No, Ford," she said softly, "Elizabeth will not have forgotten." She blinked tears from her eyes and smiled at him. "Give her my love."

Ford cleared his throat. "I will. Right after I give her mine."

Then he picked up his hat, dusting at it ruefully. At least he had an excuse to ride into town. His hat needed replacing; he'd practically worn holes in the crown.

"Do I look okay?"

Dee straightened his vest lovingly, touching the collar that was already lying flat and neat. "You look just fine, Ford. Just fine."

She walked him downstairs, glancing in at Shea, who played quietly in the front room; and then followed him out onto the porch. "Shall I expect you back for supper?"

Ford smiled ruefully. "I hope not."

Doyle paused in chopping wood and whistled at Ford's spruced appearance. "Courting?"

"I aim to try," Ford admitted. The two men had made an uneasy truce, their love for Dee and Shea a bond that could not be ignored.

With a smile, Doyle leaned against the handle of his ax. "The trick is," he said sagely, "to make them think they're the ones doing the courting." He winked at Ford. "Worked with your aunt."

"Doyle Shanley," Dee warned laughingly, "if you keep on, you'll need to be following Ford into town for *your* supper!"

"Now, sweetheart, I'm just trying to help the boy."

Still chuckling, Ford headed for the barn, leaving the two of them to their flirting, for that's what it was. He needed to remember they were still newlyweds and make sure he gave them their privacy. Hopefully, he'd soon be so busy doing some flirting of his own, they'd have all the solitude any couple could want.

A warm afternoon sun beat against Ford's back as he rode into New Braunfels. Some days, it seemed as if winter barely even touched Texas. On others, a cold norther would come whipping through, sending everyone scurrying for cover.

While no one could call the little town bustling, it seemed busy enough for an afternoon in the middle of the week. Riding past the neat white church, Ford wondered if he and Elizabeth would be standing on the steps one day, surrounded by their wedding guests. The thought brought a funny feeling to the middle of his stomach. Lately, he'd given a lot of thought to marriage. But always with Elizabeth. If she wanted nothing more to do with him, he didn't think he'd ever find another woman he could spend his life with.

Farther down the road, the smithy rang with the task of shaping a horseshoe. Ford stopped in front of the stable next door. Evan Burch met him out front.

"Ford! How long you been back? Did Katherine come back with you?" For a moment, Evan could hear Katherine's chiding voice ringing in his ears. He'd taken her warning to heart, and no words of his had ever caused townsfolk to think less of Ford Bellamy. Unfortunately, most couldn't have thought less of Katherine herself if they'd tried. Somehow it didn't seem fair to Evan that a young girl could be kidnapped by Indians, held captive for two years, and come back a criminal instead of a victim.

For just a moment Ford hesitated uncomfortably. Then he stepped down from the saddle and answered as easily as he could manage. "No. We got separated. Aunt Dee and I are hoping to see her soon."

Evan scratched his rough-shaven jaw, then reached for the reins Ford held out to him. "Don't seem safe for her to be roamin' the countryside alone."

Although Ford knew the truth would come out sooner or later, he decided he'd rather it be later. "Oh, she wasn't alone. She caught up with that Ranger she was following. Take care of my horse a few hours, will you, Evan?" He turned to stroll away before Evan could think of any more questions he needed to have answered.

"Goin' to see Elizabeth?" Evan called the question to his back.

Ford paused and glanced over his shoulder. "Any reason I shouldn't?" Like a gentleman friend? Or a husband? He couldn't have spoken those questions aloud to anyone.

Evan grinned. "None I know of. Give her my regards."

"Sure will, Evan." But Evan Burch and his regards were gone from Ford's mind before Elizabeth's house was even in sight.

Long moments passed while Ford stood in the street, unashamedly staring at her front door, trying to gather enough courage to approach it. After all, he'd been gone a long time. And he hadn't asked her to wait for him when he'd come to say good-bye last spring. A loose, drifting lifestyle had appealed to him back then. He hadn't wanted to tie himself down. But he'd traveled a lot of miles. He'd seen a man die, and he knew what it was like to bed a whore. He now knew what lonely meant. And what home meant.

Being tied to one spot was a whole lot more appealing than it had seemed back then. When he'd said good-bye he'd known the words Elizabeth had wanted to hear from him. He just hadn't wanted to say them. Now he wondered if she had changed her mind. Maybe she didn't feel the same—or maybe she felt that way about someone else.

Taking a deep breath, Ford swept his hat from his head and walked up her front steps. Before he could think about it long enough to falter he lifted his hand and rapped sharply against the doorframe.

For six long months Elizabeth Kern had told herself to forget Ford Bellamy. That last day they'd spoken, when he'd come to tell her he was leaving on a cattle drive, she'd seen the truth in his eyes. She was losing him. Not to another woman—Ford cared about no one but her. But she was losing him to something far more exciting than a small farm in New Braunfels.

She'd always expected to see him again. After all, his family was here. He'd be back at least long enough to say good-bye for good. But she'd seen the eagerness in his eyes to be gone, and she hadn't made any effort to cling. She had been so careful not to let him see a tear. But standing in her upstairs bedroom, looking down on Ford as he stared at her house, she was afraid she couldn't be that brave again. This time, she knew, good-bye would be for a lot longer. And she would have to let her dreams go with him. She was too practical to waste her life yearning for a man who would always be gone.

While her thoughts were far away, Ford disappeared from sight. For a moment she thought perhaps she had simply dreamed he was standing there. It wouldn't be the first time. But when her mother knocked at her door and called her name softly she knew it wasn't a dream.

"Come in," she answered softly.

Martha Kern opened the door and stepped in. Her eyes softened as her gaze touched her daughter, then took in the curtains drawn away from the window. Elizabeth had already seen him then. It was there in the touch of color against suddenly pale cheeks. And in the sparkle of hope Elizabeth could not quite keep from her blue eyes. "Ford's here to see you, Elizabeth."

Self-consciously, Elizabeth lifted one hand to smooth her hair. The other clutched nervously at her skirts. "I . . . tell him I'll be right down."

Martha nodded, giving her daughter a reassuring smile that she suspected was scarcely seen.

For long moments, Elizabeth stood with her gaze fixed on the door her mother had closed behind her. She had thought to take a few minutes to brush her hair, which tended to escape from the neat coils in which she attempted to capture it each morning. And she had thought she would perhaps exchange her gown for something less plain. In the end, she did neither.

Nor was she successful in using those few minutes to calm her racing pulse. Finally, giving up the effort, she opened the door and left the safety of her room. The room that had heard all of her dreams and seen all of her fears as those dreams gave way to reality in the long months just passed.

Elizabeth took so long, Ford began to think she did not mean to see him at all, but at last he heard the door open in the hallway above. He stood in the door of the parlor where her mother had tried to put him at his ease and waited for Elizabeth to descend. His first glimpse was of the tiny ruffle at the hem of her gown and her neat shoes peeping beneath it as she took one careful step at a time.

Wryly, Ford recalled the dreams in which Elizabeth had raced precipitously toward him. His first glimpse of her face caught him off guard. To his dismay, she looked almost frightened, her face pale and strained. She tried to smile at him as she reached the last step, but it was a sad little smile. Ford's heart dropped to his toes. This was not the heartfelt welcome he'd hoped to find. "Elizabeth," he said gently. She had never looked more beautiful. His hand ached to touch the wisps of hair that had escaped their confines, ached to caress the soft cheek they framed.

"Hello, Ford." She felt better after speaking. Her voice, at least, was in control. "When did you get back?"

"Day before yesterday." He smiled ruefully. "Found lots of changes."

"You've been gone a long time," she reminded him. But not long enough for her to have gotten over the effect he had on her. If anything, it was more potent. His hard muscles had turned to whipcord, lean and rippling beneath his clothing. The sun had bronzed his skin and turned the rich copper of his hair to dark fire.

"Yeah." Too long, he guessed.

"Would you care to sit down?"

Ford almost groaned out loud at her polite little voice as she gestured to the stiff sofa that was her mother's pride. "I'd rather sit on the porch, if you don't mind. I'm not much used to being indoors, and it's warm outside."

"Of course." Elizabeth felt herself color as she led the way through the front door to the porch swing where she and Ford had courted during the long spring evenings before he'd left. He'd kissed her there for the first time—and the last.

For the first little while they sat in silence while Ford kept the swing gently moving by pushing the toe of one boot against an uneven board. It was Elizabeth who broke that silence. "I guess your life has been pretty exciting lately." And all she had to offer in its place were picnics after church on Sunday and rare Saturday-night socials.

"It seemed that way at first," Ford admitted. "And I was glad for the opportunity to see more than that farm where I've lived all my life, but I reckon what I've seen will last me a long time." Maybe someday he'd tell her all the things he knew Aunt Dee would rather not hear. He hoped he'd have the chance.

Elizabeth heard the words but was afraid to believe. She glanced cautiously sideways, wishing she could see the expression in his dark eyes. But he was staring out at the street that passed by the house. Deep inside, was he longing even now to be gone along that road that led out of town? "New Braunfels will probably seem very quiet to you now."

Ford grinned ruefully. "Suits me. The most excitement I care to experience for a while is the good reverend when he preaches on hell and damnation." And maybe the excitement of a wedding. Casually, Ford slipped one hand into his vest pocket, touching the tiny object there as if it were a talisman. "I've missed you, Elizabeth."

Afraid to hope, Elizabeth squeezed her eyes against the ready tears. She had to catch a ragged breath before she could answer. "I've missed you, too, Ford. I was afraid you wouldn't come back." She opened her eyes and turned to look at him, letting him see the brilliance of tears, letting him see her heart. "And I'm afraid you won't stay."

Ford wished it was dark, wished he could pull her into his arms. He ached to feel her pressed against his body. She was all sweet softness. "I'm not going anywhere, Elizabeth. And I'm hoping not to get any farther away from you than your folks force me to when they get tired of having me underfoot." Slowly, he

Susan Tanner

pulled his hand from his pocket, the ring with it. "This was my mother's. I'd like for you to wear it. And the gold band that comes with it."

Elizabeth stared at the sparkle of tiny diamonds and even tinier emeralds in the sunlight and let her tears fall. She didn't care that it was broad daylight. With a sound that was half laughter and half groan of pure pleasure, Ford was forced to put both arms around her to keep the swing from overturning as she flung herself at his broad chest.

Chapter Twenty-one

"You ain't asked where I'm taking you."

At the gibe, Katherine glanced dispassionately at the outline of Rusk's back in the predawn shadows. They were traveling south. She had deduced that much from the placement of the stars in the heavens, but she had no intention of letting him know she had discerned even that little.

"Ain't you the least curious?" In the brief silence that followed, the slow, steady hoofbeats sounded very loud. "I ain't going to do anything to hurt you, you know."

Katherine didn't answer that either. Whatever his plans for her were, she knew she wasn't going to like them. She thought of Maggie, forced to leave with the cries of her baby ringing in her ears, doubtlessly dying with those same sounds haunting her memory. Obviously disgruntled, Rusk fell silent, leaving Katherine with her thoughts once more. And her thoughts were of Slade. Would he return to the Cullens' when daylight came? Would he find their tracks? Would he bother to look?

Surely, she told herself, he would realize that she'd never willingly ride away without knowing what had happened to Ford. But she couldn't quite convince herself that he would care enough to follow. Unless he knew it was Rusk who had taken her.

The first faint glimmers of a cold dawn streaked the horizon when Rusk reined his horse to a stop and dismounted. He looked at Katherine, who remained astride. "Get down, girl."

By his expression, Rusk was becoming irritated with her continued silence. That realization afforded the only satisfaction she could find at the moment. Still without comment, she glanced down at her hands, tied loosely together.

Rusk followed the look. "That ain't stoppin' you. You can step down with your hands tied."

She managed, but it was awkward. In her mind she pictured herself with a gun trained on Rusk, the outlaw pleading for mercy. She would enjoy making him beg.

"Yeah, I reckon you'd love for me to slice through that rope." His teeth, white and even, flashed in a smile, but his eyes were coldly glittering. "I don't know why that brother of yours bragged on you so much. You ain't such a spitfire by what I can see."

Katherine lifted her chin and gave him a cool look. "If you're lucky," she said evenly, "I'll find a way to kill you before Slade catches up with us. You'll suffer less if I do it." Maybe.

A gleam of satisfaction in his eyes made her regret the words, especially when he said, "I was right, then. He *will* come after you." He'd have him then—Slade, at his mercy. The thought was a satisfying one.

"No, it's you he'll be after." She lifted her hands to anchor her hair as the wind whipped it against her face.

To her surprise, Rusk turned away with a snarl. "I suggest you stretch your legs and take care of whatever's necessary. We ain't stopping long."

For just a moment Katherine sagged with relief. She hadn't realized just how much she feared the possibility of rape. Not that she considered herself safe now, by any means. But it did feel like a reprieve. For the moment, at least, Rusk showed no indication of that kind of interest in her. She closed her eyes briefly and said a prayer that Slade was indeed following them for whatever reasons; then she moved to the minimum shelter afforded by a lone boulder and the scraggly bushes that had grown up around it.

*　　*　　*

Slade rode into the Cullens' yard at daybreak. As he dismounted, a seeming multitude of children filed into the yard and surrounded him. He met the solemn look of one elfin-faced girl with silky red hair and pale green eyes and knew something was wrong. He lifted his gaze to her father, just stepping out the door.

"You'd be Mr. Slade." Adam Cullen extended his hand, his pleasant face creased by an anxious frown.

Slade grew very still. "Where's Katherine?" He couldn't think of a single reason why she wouldn't be here waiting for him. But he knew that she wasn't.

"Truth to tell, I was hoping you'd ridden up during the night and left with her. But I didn't think you had," Cullen admitted. "She was gone when we got up an hour or so ago."

"Her horse?" Slade's mind raced over possibilities.

"Gone." Cullen shrugged helplessly. "I don't know what to tell you. The door was bolted from the inside when we went to bed. The younguns' didn't hear anything." He glanced at the tallest, who shook her head in confirmation.

Of all the reasons Slade could imagine that Katherine would leave, none of them included that it would be willingly. He was certain of that for one reason only: She wouldn't have left without knowing that her brother was safe. It

278

occurred to him that Wolf Killer could have had her followed from the moment she had left the band, and Slade's blood ran cold at the thought. Indians had some particularly nasty ways of dealing with errant wives, especially unfaithful ones. He'd seen the scarred and mutilated faces of some of those unlucky women.

Leaving the buckskin gelding ground-tied, he turned abruptly toward the barn, only half aware of Adam Cullen falling into step behind him.

"I checked out here," Cullen told him. "There was no sign of a struggle. Not in the barn or in the yard."

Slade looked at the stall where Sadie had been bedded, then studied the neat hallway and the ground leading away from the barn. He found what he was looking for just at the edge of the clearing. Where the ground was not so well trampled by children's feet there were several clear tracks. After identifying those belonging to Katherine's mare he studied those of the other horse. Relief blended with a deepening confusion. The other horse was shod. And neither animal had left in any particular hurry.

He straightened and looked into Cullen's worried face. "I'll be riding out now."

Adam thought of his Eileen, sitting inside and rocking the baby and fretting over what might have happened to her newfound friend. "I could ride with you a ways. Just in case you need a hand."

Slade tipped the brim of his hat away from his eyes and stared into the distance. "Thanks, but that won't be necessary." He glanced toward the house. "Tell your missus we appreciate the hospitality."

He whistled sharply, and the buckskin trotted over to him. Swinging up into the saddle, he nodded to Cullen, then turned the gelding toward the south.

The sun climbed in the sky, and Rusk turned their path in a southwesterly direction, following a trail made by deer hoofs and Indian moccasins. And all the while he talked to her. "You ain't much of a squaw woman. I expect Wolf Killer's new wife would have found a way to slit my throat by now."

Katherine thought of the timid Willow Dancing. She would have to be careful or she would fall into the trap of thinking Elzy Rusk a fool. That he had succeeded in eluding Slade thus far was proof that he was not.

"I reckon Wolf Killer don't think you're much of a squaw either, seeing as how he's announced your 'death.' Tell me, now, how does it feel to be a walking dead woman?"

"Probably about the way it feels to be a walking dead man—so why don't *you* tell *me*?" She smiled as he hunched his shoulders at her words. For all his bravado, he was intimidated by the thought of Slade coming after him. Although she couldn't resist baiting him, she wondered what would happen to her if Slade *didn't* come. If her fate wasn't already sealed, her goading of Rusk was surely taking care of that for her.

Rusk halted again at midday, handing her another piece of the dried beef they'd had for breakfast. To her relief he left her alone, and they rode in silence for the remainder of that day. She much preferred being ignored to being baited.

He killed a rabbit for their supper, and Katherine prepared it because she was hungry. Rusk divided it evenly to her vague surprise. He took a bite and grinned. "You're a good cook." He watched her while they ate. "I half thought you'd be scared out of your wits by now and showing it. Should have known, though, any woman what can live with that devil, Wolf Killer, wouldn't be afraid of anything." As he spoke, he tossed the last bone into the bushes. He scowled when she didn't answer and began carving at a stick with his greasy knife. "The army's going to catch your brother and hang him." He looked up from his whittling.

So much for a respite, Katherine thought. She met his gaze without flinching. "If they do, you won't be around to see it. Slade's going to finish you off. He's tired of hunting you, and he's ready to end it."

Rusk's reaction to her words was almost frightening. He threw the knife he was holding into a tree just past their campfire, so close

Katherine could hear it quivering from the impact.

"The son of a bitch. Why the hell doesn't he chase somebody else? Hell, there's higher bounty on a hundred other poor bastards."

Katherine glared at him in disgust. "But none of those others cost him his wife—and his son."

"What? What the hell are you talking about?" The edge of anger was still in Rusk's voice, but there was also a faint confusion. Or disbelief.

"Maggie Slade and her baby." Katherine said the words slowly, prodding his memory. "Both dead because of you."

"I ain't ever killed a woman. Not a white woman," he added defensively, deepening Katherine's anger and disgust. "And I've for sure never killed a kid."

"No, Maggie took her own life after you raped her and left her for others to rape. After you forced her to leave her baby boy alone in a house to starve to death."

Slowly, the dark color faded from Rusk's face. "That was Slade's wife?" he asked hoarsely.

Katherine nodded, scarcely able to believe he hadn't known. Slade had been hunting for Rusk all this time, and the man had never known why.

"Shit." Rusk stared into the fire. "Shit." He had only a bare memory of the girl. He couldn't recall the color of her hair, but he could still hear her screams when he'd dragged her from that house. The baby had been crying. The girl had been begging. He had been drunk.

He looked up at Katherine, almost pleading. "I thought somebody would find that kid in a day or two. There was people in and out of that damned house the whole time I was there. I had to pretend to be a hell of a lot worse off than I really was." Realization was slowly sinking into his brain. That was why Slade was impossible to shake for more than a few days, or weeks at the most. The man wasn't out for money; he was out for blood. "Why the shit did she kill herself? I didn't hurt her. I didn't beat her or anything."

Katherine thought of all that Maggie had suffered. She thought of the agony she would feel if it had been Shea who was left to starve in a house all alone, and the little sympathy she felt for him died. "You're a bastard and a fool. And you're as good as dead."

"Get up. We're riding." Rusk jumped to his feet and began kicking dirt into the fire.

"We've been riding all day! I've got to rest," Katherine protested.

"Yeah? Well, you'll just have to do your resting in the saddle. We're getting out of here." He cursed as he fumbled when saddling their horses, but he didn't untie Katherine's hands to let her help. When he led her horse over to her he glared into her eyes. "You're lucky. I could travel faster without you, but I'll need money. And you're worth something anyway."

Katherine's blood chilled as she climbed into

283

the saddle. She knew as well as Rusk that it would take too long to contact her family and arrange for a ransom. And he couldn't be sure anyone *would* ransom her. He had to be planning to sell her, and nothing good came to mind with the realization.

As they rode through the dark, she tried to think as he would be thinking. There weren't many safe places for a man on the run. Mexico, maybe. And they were headed that way.

Comancheros. The thought came to her with terrifying certainty. The traders from Santa Fe. She had never been to the Valley of Tears, but she had heard tales. That was the place, one of the many appointed trading spots, where captives were taken to be sold, traded, and, very rarely, ransomed. It was a place where there was no law. Only treachery, and the beginning of much suffering.

Courage flowed back to her, along with determination. If she would be free, it had to be soon. Herself against Rusk. She couldn't know if Slade would catch up to them in time, and she could never hope to escape the Comancheros.

Dark gave way to morning light, and the shadows gave way to grassy plains. Rusk pushed them harder after sunrise, as if the daylight made him more vulnerable. And Katherine supposed it did. She wondered if Slade was truly somewhere behind them, and she wondered what he was thinking as he followed, if he realized it was Rusk he tracked. Did thoughts of Maggie haunt him now that his quarry was so close? Did he try to visualize how his son would have looked if he'd not been left to die?

If Katherine closed her eyes, she could easily see a young boy in Slade's likeness. He'd be eleven or twelve now, long and leggy, growing swiftly to a young man. Katherine could picture him with his father's dark hair and eyes, standing at his mother's side. But, somehow, in her mind, the woman he stood beside, his young arm slipped around her waist, was not Maggie. It was Katherine.

Katherine opened her eyes abruptly. Those thoughts were dangerous. At least for her. Whatever Slade might have been if Maggie had lived, he was something different now. He was a lawman living on the barest edge of the law he was sworn to uphold. And he was a wanderer, with no roots and no dreams to tie him to a future. She could not conceive of him settling into the quiet life of New Braunfels. Nor could she imagine herself dragging Shea from one outpost to another. Even if he wanted her, and she couldn't picture that either.

If she was growing increasingly weary, at least she knew Rusk was, too. He had let his horse drop to a slow walk, and from time to time he swayed in the saddle. "If you don't rest, he's going to catch up with you anyway." Her throat was parched, and her voice sounded hoarse in the quiet that surrounded them.

"Shut up and ride," Rusk growled at her. The eyes he turned her way were red-rimmed with exhaustion.

Katherine knew she couldn't possibly look any better. She sure didn't feel any better than he looked. If she'd known the reaction her revelation would cause in Rusk, she would never have told him why Slade was so determined to find him. Rusk was running for his life now, and she began to fear he would push her beyond what her body could endure. What would he do when she could no longer ride? Was the gold she could bring worth the risk of keeping her with him? Of keeping her alive?

By nightfall she was swaying in her saddle, and even Rusk couldn't go any farther. Grudgingly, he made camp and watched Katherine by the light of the small fire he'd allowed her. They ate cornmeal she had boiled to mush and flavored with salted pork. He watched her, but he didn't say anything, and neither did she. There was accusation in his stare, as if she had brought all this down upon him, as if his own actions had no part in Slade's hunting him down to kill him. And they both knew Slade would kill him. There would be no jail cell for Elzy Rusk. Afterward she slept, uncaring if he did or not.

Slade pushed his hat back and wiped at his forehead. It was damned warm for November. At least he thought it was still November. He found it hard to keep up with time when he was on the trail. Besides, time didn't mean that much to a man in his position; a meeting with army officers in one camp, a rendezvous with Rangers at another. If he was late or didn't make it, there was no one to worry, no one to care. He didn't pay heed to holidays, never knew when his birthday passed, although he always felt sad when he realized it was Maggie's or his son's. Which was another real good reason not to keep up with the passage of days. Memories hurt. He didn't want to know when his and Maggie's wedding day rolled around each year. He didn't want to know that this was the day she had been born or had died.

All he knew was the changing of the seasons and the beginning and ending of each day. That was enough.

Of course, he didn't want to care about anybody either. For a long time he hadn't, at least not significantly. There was a kinship of sorts between Rangers, and he cared as much about keeping his partner alive as he did about looking after himself. For years that had been the only caring he'd done, and it had been enough. But that had changed somewhere along the way these past few weeks, and he wasn't sure where. And he wasn't sure he liked it.

Katherine was there. Embedded. Thoughts of her teased him through the day, tormented him through the night. Thoughts of her in danger tortured him.

And she was in danger. He knew it, gut deep. Alternating between the terror that he wouldn't reach her in time and the rage at whoever had spirited her away, his mind twisted over possibilities. The one hope he'd had—that somehow Ford Bellamy had found her—faded when the path he followed turned toward the west and continued that way. Whoever had her wasn't taking her south to New Braunfels, but west. To Mexico.

Filled with resolve, he kept his buckskin to a ground-eating trot, noting almost dispassionately that the two horses ahead of him alternated between a hard gallop and an exhausted walk. Someone was running from him or from something unknown. But they couldn't run far enough or fast enough that he couldn't follow.

Chapter Twenty-two

Elizabeth slipped her hand into Ford's, savoring the warm thrill of having him next to her, of knowing he would always be there. She'd never get enough of looking at him, of touching him. He looked so handsome in his best clothes. His clean-shaven jaw just begged for her touch. Elizabeth blushed at her own thoughts, glad they were hers alone. Of all things to be thinking while she sat listening to the Sunday service.

Ford squeezed her fingers, and she saw him smile, though he kept his eyes upon the preacher. Elizabeth blushed again. She'd just bet Ford Bellamy knew her mind wasn't on the Gospel of Luke this morning!

Moments later, the sermon concluded, they rose to leave. Ford put his arm around her waist, an intimate gesture afforded only to married couples or those engaged to be. Elizabeth smiled at him as she moved into the aisle.

Dee stepped out of the pew ahead of them, followed by Doyle, who carried Shea in his arms. Elizabeth was always amazed at how good Shea was in church, never chattering or disrupting. And she was always amazed at how determined Doyle remained to have Shea accepted by those equally determined not to accept her.

One of those was Mrs. Addis, who stopped Elizabeth and Ford at the front steps of the church. "I've begun a quilt for you, my dear," she told Elizabeth, "for your wedding. Please stop by one day this week, and tell me if you like the colors. I'm so proud to see you and Ford getting married."

To Elizabeth's discomfort, Doyle had stepped up beside them, still holding Shea. "Ford's aunt and I are proudest of all, Mrs. Addis. Proud that Ford had the good sense to grab our Elizabeth here before she got away."

The woman's eyes were fixed on Shea as if the child were a viper. "Indeed, yes," she said a bit hurriedly, edging away. Her naturally pursed features looked even more pinched than usual.

"I've been meaning to ask you," Doyle continued, ignoring the woman's attempts to flee, "if you would make up a couple of those pretty lace collars like you're always wearing for my

Dee. And not mention it to her, if you please."

Mrs. Addis's handiwork was her one vanity, and in her preening she forgot she didn't want to be quite so close to "the little savage," as she thought of Katherine Bellamy's child. "Well, I suppose I could do that. Are they to be gifts?" From time to time folk did ask her to make presents for their wives and daughters and sweethearts. After all, none of the other women in town could match her skill in lace-making.

"Yes, ma'am. It'll be Dee's birthday in a few weeks. I'd like them matching," Doyle continued easily, "one for Dee, and one for our Shea."

Mrs. Addis recoiled visibly, and Elizabeth stiffened in outrage, ready to pounce if the woman said one insulting thing within the little girl's hearing.

Feeling the anger run through her body, Ford moved his hand from Elizabeth's waist to her shoulder, ready to keep her from flying at the woman, though he knew he'd never be able to silence her tongue. He didn't know that he wanted to. He'd about had enough of the Mrs. Addises of this town. They had cost him his sister, and likely would cost him his niece, as well. Still, he didn't think he wanted his fiancée brawling in front of the church.

But Doyle was prepared for the woman's reaction. He didn't give her an opportunity to draw a good breath before he said, "I tell you, Mrs. Addis, it's a trial for us to think of what this child might have suffered, and a blessing to consider what she has been spared. Why, she and her mother might never have been rescued, and those murdering redskins could have had the raising of this sweet little girl."

Doyle fought an urge to wink at Elizabeth. "It's thankful we are," he continued right along, "that she can be raised among good Christians like yourself. Such a shining example she'll have in learning to be godlike and generous."

Mrs. Addis looked at him suspiciously, and Elizabeth almost choked.

"Well," Mrs. Addis began dubiously, "I don't suppose I've ever looked at it quite from that point of view before. But aren't you the teeniest bit fearful? I mean, how can you be sure she won't grow up to feel like her . . . her father? She might well hate all white people."

"Mrs. Addis," Doyle said softly, "I don't think people hate without reason. They hate from fear or from pain. I'm praying that the people of this town never give this sweet child a moment's pain, never give her anything to fear or to hate." He smiled. "And I'm sure with you setting the example, no one ever will. You're respected and followed in this town. If you accept our Shea, no one else will dare not to."

This time it was Ford who choked, then grunted as Elizabeth jabbed her elbow in his side.

Dee, who had been talking to Elizabeth's mother when she realized Doyle and Shea were not at her side, hurried to join them. An anxious frown touched her forehead, and she had to force herself not to take Shea from Doyle's arms. All of her protective instincts combined with her love for Shea rose up at the sight of Mrs. Addis standing so close to the little girl.

But Mrs. Addis was actually smiling. "Why, Dee, so good to see you and your little family. I must be going now. The reverend is joining my sister and myself for dinner today, you know. But," she beamed at Doyle, "perhaps you and your husband and . . . and the child could stop by for tea one afternoon very soon."

Dee's mouth dropped open, and she could only nod as Doyle answered, "I'm sure we'd love to, Mrs. Addis."

"You young people come too," Mrs. Addis told Ford and Elizabeth before hurrying away to her buggy.

Doyle looked at Dee and placed one finger under her chin to gently close her mouth.

Chapter Twenty-three

Katherine woke feeling as if her shoulder had been pulled out of its socket. Rusk still refused to untie her hands, so there was no possible way for her to lie comfortably. Twisting until she lay on her back, she gazed upward at a soft night filled with a shower of bright stars. Nearby, Rusk snored.

Did Slade look up at those same stars and wonder where she was? It was both comforting and disturbing to think he might be awake at this moment, seeing the same heavens she saw, thinking of her as she was thinking of him. She had to keep believing he would follow and that he would reach her in time. She had not yet found a way to escape Rusk.

She had hoped that by now the outlaw would have grown more comfortable with her, that he would unbind her hands, leaving her free to attempt an escape. She thought of the knife Louis had thrust into his own chest and wished she had one as deadly to bury in Rusk's. A rock, such as the one she had used to strike Ugly Jack, wouldn't do. Rusk was too tense, too fearful. She'd never get close enough. He'd never let her have enough time. But if her hands were free, and if she had a knife . . .

Disgust touched her at the direction her thoughts had taken. If! *If* did her no good at all. They were getting closer and closer to the lands of the Comancheros. She had to escape. She had to.

Already the stars above her were beginning to pale as dawn touched the sky. Soon it would be daylight, and Rusk would drag her ever closer to the Valley of Tears.

Desperation brought Katherine as quietly and quickly to her feet as her bound hands would allow. This might be the last chance she would get. She flinched at the soft sounds her movements made in the tall grass. Holding her breath, she inched closer to the saddlebags heaped near Rusk's head. If she could just get inside them before he awoke.

"What th—!"

She knew a sharp despair when she heard Rusk's furious growl behind her. He jerked her backward by the hair, and she stumbled to her knees.

"Bitch!" he spat, still holding her hair, dragging her upward with his painful grasp.

Turning to face him, she straightened her shoulders proudly. Cowering before him would not save her—and even if it would, she suspected she could not bring herself to do so.

That pride, evident in her imperiously lifted chin, made Rusk furious. "Bitch," he repeated, striking her cheek with the back of his hand.

Tears of pain filled Katherine's eyes, and she bit her lip until she tasted blood trying to keep them from falling. But still she would not cringe or beg.

The violence of his own action excited Rusk, and he knew suddenly how to bring her low. No woman had any pride when her legs were spread to a man, especially when they were spread unwillingly.

Katherine felt a chill run through her veins as Rusk's expression changed. She had seen that look before, knew what it portended, even before his hand dropped to fumble with the fastening of his pants.

"If you touch me," she said in a low voice, "I'll find a way to kill you. I swear it."

Rusk smiled cruelly, certain he would hear her beg before too much longer. She wouldn't be so proud then.

A single rifle shot blasted the silence around them. Rusk released his grip, whirling toward his bedroll and coming up with his own rifle. His gaze found Katherine where he had left her; and then searched the dim shadows of the receding night.

Though her heart was pounding, Katherine watched him with less fear than she would have thought possible. She didn't fear Rusk, and she didn't fear whoever watched them through the darkness. She did not want to die, but she could face death more easily than Rusk's violation of her body. And if she was going to die, at least she could think of Shea safe with Aunt Dee. Curiously enough, her mind would not stay with Shea. It drifted instead to thoughts of Slade—and to regret for what might have been if they were different people with different lives.

"Go for it, Rusk."

That voice took her breath away, and she strained to see in the faint light of dawn. The tears she had not allowed Rusk to see rolled slowly down her cheeks, amazing her. Until this moment she had not realized how very desperately she had wanted to hear Slade's voice again.

"That you, Slade?" Rusk's voice was quiet, unemotional, no more revealing than Slade's. "I knew you were coming after me."

For a heartbeat in time his words hung in the cool dawn air, unanswered. Katherine realized she held her breath, waiting.

"I wasn't coming for you, Rusk. Not this time. You're just in the way."

Katherine saw Rusk's eyes move to her

involuntarily in realization. The satisfaction she might have felt in that moment was overshadowed by her joy and her fear. Rusk made his living with his gun, just as Slade did. One would live and one would die. She would rather face a thousand degradations from Rusk than lose Slade to his bullet.

Silently, Rusk cursed his luck. He knew he had made his second mistake with Slade, and this one was going to cost him his life.

Slade had come up on their camp in the night while it was still too dark for him to do more than identify two separate bedrolls. Until the moment Katherine had left hers, easing her way across the campsite, he had not been completely sure she traveled unwillingly. The sight of her bound hands inflamed him. Her stealth convinced him she was making a bid for escape. When Rusk had struck her Slade had almost gone over the edge.

He'd hunkered down, taking deep breaths, until he was under control again. But anyone who knew him would have known he was deadly just by the look in his eye. The shot he'd fired had been aimed high. When he killed Rusk, Slade wanted him to know who had pulled the trigger. And why.

He watched approvingly as Katherine calmly backed away from Rusk, placing herself out of a desperate man's reach. All three of them knew Rusk was fated to die today. He could smell the knowledge in Rusk, the fear.

Rusk's voice as he spoke confirmed that fear. "I didn't hurt her, Slade. Ask her. I haven't touched her."

"She's mine, Rusk. If I'd known it was you that had her, I'd have ridden harder and killed you sooner. This is the second time you've taken something that belongs to me. It's a pity I can only kill you once."

"I didn't mean for your wife to die," Rusk said. "She didn't have to kill herself. And the kid—that was an accident. I'd never hurt a kid."

Katherine clenched her hands until her fingernails bit into her flesh. She knew what those words were doing to Slade, and she hurt for him. She wanted to tell Rusk to shut up, but she didn't want to distract Slade's attention, not even for a moment.

"Rusk," Slade said softly, "lift that rifle and die like a man."

Katherine wondered if Rusk could see any better than she. She prayed that he couldn't, that not even a hint of Slade's form caught his eye. Because she could not see Slade, she kept her gaze on Rusk. Much as she despised the man, she had to admire his control as he lifted his rifle without a tremor. Still he hesitated.

"Now, Rusk."

Almost immediately, two shots sounded, one barely before the other. Rusk stood looking into the shadows, and Katherine's heart stopped beating. Then Rusk's knees slowly buckled, and he pitched forward.

Katherine sank to the ground, trembling with reaction and relief. Rusk's death meant little to her, less than even she would have thought. Slade reached her, and she closed her eyes, leaning into his embrace. His callused hand caressed the cheek where Rusk had struck her.

"I'm sorry I let that bastard get his hands on you, Katherine. I'm sorry."

Katherine touched her fingers to his lips. "Hush. It isn't your fault, and I'm not hurt. Not really." She'd never tell Slade what Rusk had in mind for her.

Effortlessly, Slade scooped her up and carried her to the bedroll. He cursed Rusk again as he cut the rawhide strips binding her hands. When he pulled her close to his chest she slipped her arms around him, straining to get closer than clothing allowed. Her heart ached that he had cared enough to come for her, not even knowing it was Rusk who had her.

Perhaps because she had been prepared to die, had—for one heart-stopping moment—believed it inevitable, life seemed infinitely sweet and precious. Though she and Slade could not have tomorrow, they could have this one moment. She needed the closeness, the touch of another human. Of Slade.

Her breath quickened when he slid his hands under her blouse, cupping her breasts, caressing the fullness and the taut nipples. Her own hands pressed hard against his muscled shoulders, her fingers digging into the ridges.

More gently than she would have believed him capable, Slade undressed her, tucking her into the bedroll, before he removed his own clothes and joined her.

He touched her, and the wet, warm feel of her moved him past the boundary of his control. As he entered her, he pressed his lips to the hollow at the base of her throat and whispered her name.

Katherine felt tears sting her eyes at the depth of her feelings. By morning she knew those same feelings would terrify her. For now, she was caught up in the beauty of them.

And then the tenderness of the moment was lost to the rising urgency of their need. Slade's thrusts quickened, and she moved to meet them, needing the hard length of him to sate the fury he had ignited.

As the first spasm caught her, she called his name.

The soft sounds she made as her burning need was met sent Slade over the edge to his own release.

Above them, the first faint streaks of dawn were fingering outward. Slade caressed Katherine's bare shoulder, and she reveled in the gentle touch. She had seen so little that was gentle in him. She suspected there was not much left after all that life had dealt him. Her hand was on his chest, and she felt the steady rise and fall of his breathing.

"How did you know where to find me?"

"Tracks." His voice sounded as if he was smiling. "You let him catch you by surprise at the Cullens, didn't you?"

She wished she could see his face. His smiles were so rare. "Yes," she admitted. "I wasn't expecting him. When he knocked at the door I thought it was you. And Ford."

Slade sighed. "It appears that brother of yours is as resourceful as you are. He didn't need rescuing. He escaped with Emile."

"Are they looking for him?" Katherine dreaded to hear that her brother was a hunted man.

"No. Your brother had sense enough not to tell them who he was, and I lied," Slade said easily. "I told the officer at the fort that the man with Emile couldn't have been Ford, that I'd sent him safely home weeks ago."

"He believed you?"

"Yeah. Mostly because he wanted to. And there wasn't much danger to Ford from that direction anyway. The post commander barely has enough men to defend the fort, much less chase after outlaws."

"So Ford's gone home," she said softly.

"And what about you, Katherine Fierce Tongue? Will you go home, or do you want me to take you back to Wolf Killer?" His hand stilled on her shoulder as he waited for her answer.

Katherine felt a small, swift pain that he had not offered her a third alternative. But deep inside she hadn't really expected it; not from a man like Slade. "No," she answered finally. "As far as Wolf Killer is concerned, I am truly dead. My name will never again be spoken in his lodge."

"Do you still love him?" Slade asked the question roughly, angry that he couldn't keep himself from asking it at all.

"I don't love Wolf Killer. I guess I never really did. I don't understand everything I felt for him after Jeane and I were taken captive. At first I hated him. I hated them all."

Slade said nothing, not wanting to interrupt the flow of her words.

"It was Jeane's sixteenth birthday. There was going to be a party, and it was the first time Aunt Dee had ever let me stay away from home." Katherine stared up at the sky, seeing a different, long-ago daybreak. She twisted an edge of the bedroll between two fingers. "It happened right at dawn. We had just woke up, and we were lying there talking, about the party, about boys." Her mouth twisted wryly. "It was the first time I ever heard that sound."

"The Comanche?"

"War cries." Her fingers opened, and the bedroll settled against the ground. "By the time Jeane and I got downstairs, Mr. Pearson had gone outside. We—we saw him later. Mrs. Pearson was in the front room. There were Indians there. And blood everywhere. Her nightdress should have been white." She shuddered.

"They took you and Jeane," Slade prompted to move her past those memories.

"And Davey." Katherine almost smiled. "Davey was a bear cub, that one, always fighting with the other boys. Usually winning. He was adopted almost at once, and he was treated well. Eventually, I think he would have forgotten most of the pain and accepted his Comanche family as completely as they accepted him."

"And you?"

She did not answer for a minute. "If it had been Aunt Dee killed, or Ford, I think I never would have been able to put it from my mind. Sooner or later they would have been forced to kill me too. As it was, I gave them a lot more trouble than anyone in the tribe except Wolf Killer and maybe Old Mother thought I was worth. It was Old Mother who finally got to me. She was hard and she was a tyrant, but she liked me for some reason. She respected my stubbornness, even though she was determined to break it. And she did to some extent. I learned to live as a Comanche, and I learned to accept where I was and what my life was to be."

"You never tried to run away?"

"I had no faith, whatsoever, in my ability to find my way to anywhere, much less home. And then there was Jeane and Davey. I couldn't take them, and I couldn't leave them. Especially Jeane. She was so helpless. I don't think she ever quite got over her parents' death. She never seemed—quite right, afterward."

"And then there was Wolf Killer." Slade couldn't stop himself from bringing her thoughts full circle. He had to know how she felt, then and now.

"And then there was Wolf Killer," Katherine agreed. "He protected me from those who would have treated me like a true prisoner. I always knew I could be tortured and killed. I was grateful to Wolf Killer, and I was very young. He was a great warrior, and he cared what happened to me. After a time my gratitude turned to admiration. To a girl's infatuation. I mistook that for love. And then the soldiers came."

Hearing her pain, Slade touched her face. "You'll learn to forget."

But Katherine knew she never would. Each time she looked into her daughter's face, she would remember. She did not tell Slade that. He did not need to know.

"I am not a Comanche," she said finally. "You were right about that. I don't know where Shea or I belong, but there must be a place, maybe not in Texas, where she and I could start over with no one judging or condemning—not even me."

Daylight separated them, for it revealed with brutal clarity the staring, dead eyes of Elzy Rusk. His face held a stiff look of dismay. Slade's bullet had taken his lungs.

Katherine dressed in haste, then occupied herself in preparing breakfast from Slade's pack. She wasn't hungry, but she had to keep busy, keep from watching as Slade deepened a natural hollow in the slope of the creek bank nearby. She could not help turning to look as he dragged the body to the opening and arranged it; and then concealed it with rocks and dirt and brush. He took Rusk's saddle and discarded it, along with his saddlebags, into the brush. He did not even look into the bags.

"It's ready," Katherine called to him softly, watching as he scrubbed his hands with sand and water. "Come eat."

Hunkered before the fire, Slade ate what she had prepared. When he finished he looked at her gravely. "It's time we got started. We have a lot of traveling to do."

Katherine wondered what he was thinking, how he would feel at their parting, but she couldn't ask.

Of all the people in her life, Katherine had never felt as close to anyone as she did to this man she knew only by his last name. Yet she didn't know him at all. As they traveled she let

307

the buckskin set the pace and fixed her eyes on Slade's back. She wondered what he would do with the rest of his life, where he would go when he tired of being a Texas Ranger. If he ever did. When she could stand her own thoughts no longer she broke the silence.

"Were you born in Texas?"

"Far as I know."

She frowned. That was a typical Slade response. "Why wouldn't you know for sure?"

He glanced back at her. "My folks came from Louisiana. I can only remember Texas. I never thought to ask before they died if I came with them, happened along the way, or after they got here."

"How old were you when they died?"

Another look back. "Thirteen, maybe fourteen. It was a long time ago."

"What did you do then?"

"I survived."

She fell silent at the brief answer, and he sighed, turning his buckskin aside to let her move up beside him. "Why all the questions?"

"I don't know. I guess because I don't know anything about you, and maybe I'll never get the chance."

"You know more than most. More than anyone since Maggie."

There was a sadness to his voice that struck deep into her heart. "I don't know the important things," she answered softly. "What your dreams are. Where you want life to take you."

Slade was silent for a long time. His stare was fixed on the thick wheat grass that stretched around them. "I don't guess I've got any dreams. Not anymore. My one aim was to kill Rusk for what he did to Maggie and my son." He half smiled. "I ended up killing him for what he tried to do to you instead."

Startled, Katherine looked at him, but he didn't move his gaze from the horizon.

"As for where life's going to take me—" He shrugged. "None of us knows that for certain."

"Some of us try to shape our own destiny," Katherine suggested softly.

"And that's when the gods laugh at us."

Slade fell silent, and Katherine asked no more questions.

"I need to stop at Fort Lancaster before we go on," Slade told her that evening, "to report Rusk's death."

They sat in front of the campfire. Slade's arm was around her shoulders, resting as easily as if they had sat this way every night of their lives.

Katherine nodded. She didn't really want to go back there, but she understood. Her feelings were so mixed. In a hurry to return to Shea, she dreaded the moment New Braunfels came into sight, for that would signal her parting from Slade. She wondered again if he would ever change, ever settle. If he would ever even want to.

She could feel him watching her by the

firelight, and she wished she could be beautiful for him; not sunburned and weather-roughened but soft as she had once been. Soft and fresh and innocent. She could not wish her past away, for she would never regret Shea, but she wished that so much of it did not show in her face.

He leaned to kiss her, and she moved to meet him. She desired him so much, the power of it was overwhelming. Just at his kiss, her nipples swelled and hardened, and when he reached to cup one breast liquid heat engulfed her.

Slade pulled away from her slightly. "Undress." His voice was heavy.

She rose gracefully to her feet and her hand went to the buttons on her blouse. His eyes followed. His desire was so apparent, she grew flushed as her fingers slowly unbuttoned the blouse. With each movement, a deeper strip of flesh was revealed.

When the last button was opened he pulled her down until she knelt before him. He drew the edges of the blouse aside and touched the tip of one breast. Lightly, caressingly; then harder. Watching him touch her, she burned. When his lips followed his fingers she gasped; then she curled her fingers into the hair at the back of his neck. It was cool from the night air.

His lips trailed upward to her collar, and at last he slipped the blouse from her shoulders. He removed her skirt. And his kisses did not stop. When she lay open to his gaze and the soft warmth of the fire he continued to torment her, lifting his head away from her time and again to look at her, to look at his effect on her.

When she was writhing and could stand no more he placed her hand against him, and she moaned, "Please, Slade. Now."

"Yes." He undressed and came to her. "Now."

It was so easy for her to be at peace when he made love to her. She had only to think about him, to feel his desire for her. There were no other thoughts, no other feelings. She did not have to think of who she was and what lay behind and ahead. She could forget everything but each movement of his body. And her release to the pleasure was all-consuming.

From a distance, Jeb Welles waited. Slade was lucky it was him that had come upon them and not some damned band of renegades. Or Indians. Just from what Jeb felt in watching, he knew what would happen if it had been anyone else. Few men would hesitate to kill Slade for what he had in his arms at that moment.

Chapter Twenty-four

Slade held Katherine until she drifted to sleep; then he carefully eased her from his arms. Shivering with gooseflesh, he dressed before turning his attention to the dying fire. After a few false starts winter was coming on. The air was sweet and clean and cold.

"You can come ahead now," he called softly to the waiting darkness.

Jeb chuckled as he led his horse into the camp. His square face wore the beard he grew when he was on the trail. "How did you know I was there?" he asked without surprise.

"Didn't know it was you. Just knew it was a friend."

Hobbling his horse, Jeb moved to the fire to join Slade. "Yeah, but how?" He held his hands toward the warmth.

"Horse." Slade nodded toward the buckskin, who had nickered some time ago. And Slade had heard. He'd learned long ago never to be so lost in the depths of sleep or the throes of passion as to court death.

"Should have guessed," Jeb grunted. "That damned horse is half human."

Slade eased back against a tree trunk, glancing at Katherine, who continued to sleep peacefully. "Should have," he agreed. He and Jeb had ridden together a lot of years, and Slade hadn't gotten them killed yet. "How'd you find me?"

"By looking." Jeb grinned. He could be as taciturn as Slade, but it didn't come naturally. The truth was, he hadn't really started looking yet; he'd just lucked out running into Slade this way.

"Why were you looking?" Slade asked agreeably.

Jeb looked at Katherine, and his grin faded. "Wolf Killer."

For just a moment Slade hesitated; then he asked, "Want some coffee?"

To Katherine, it took an agonizingly long time for Slade to boil water and allow the coffee to settle at the bottom of the pot. Only men—maybe only Slade—could leave such a comment hanging while he made coffee. Her agony came both from the waiting and from keeping up her pretense of sleep. She had been awake from the moment Slade had called out

314

into the darkness, but as soon as she recognized Jeb's voice she knew she preferred to avoid conversation with him. Her reticence was for a variety of reasons, not the least of which was her presence in the single bedroll spread before the fire.

When she realized from their brief conversation that he had been there for some time she was even less willing to face him. If he'd been near enough for the buckskin to know he was there, he had been near enough to hear and see more than she cared to think about.

Her crimson blush had been driven from her face by the mention of Wolf Killer. She was no longer warm with embarrassment but icy cold with dread.

Slade poured Jeb a tin cup full of coffee and passed it to him before pouring his own. The hot liquid sent spirals of steam into the air.

"What are you doing out here with the girl?" Jeb watched the fire curling around two small logs.

"Taking her home."

After a moment, when Slade didn't say anything further, Jeb looked at him. He didn't comment on the fact that they were halfway across Texas from both New Braunfels and Camp Colorado, which was where Slade and the girl had last been headed.

"Then what?"

"Nosy son of a bitch, ain't you?" The words

carried no animosity. Jeb was always nosy. Slade was used to it; even looked forward to it when they'd been working separately for a long while.

Jeb thought of all the miles they had traveled together. The times one or the other had almost gotten killed—and would have without the other being there. And Jeb thought of how he had felt when he had yielded to an impulse to kiss Katherine Bellamy, how much he'd like to again.

"You're thinking of leaving the Rangers, aren't you?"

Slade didn't answer. Not even to remind Jeb that he wasn't under any commitment to the Rangers. Or to anyone else, for that matter.

"There ain't a farm tool in the world that will fit your hand," Jeb said flatly.

"It did before." Slade thought of Maggie, how good it had made him feel to come home to her each evening. Lately, though, each time he tried to think of Maggie, images of Katherine stole her place. He could even picture Katherine standing on the porch of the little house he'd built for Maggie, her hand resting against the door frame as she called him in to eat.

"That was before. The only thing that will fit it now is a gun. You can't raise a family on a gun, Slade."

"Now who the hell said anything about raising a family." Slade had begun to feel cornered. The things Jeb wanted to drag out into the open were only half-formed thoughts, born more of feeling than reason.

"She's got a kid."

"Drop it," Slade finally growled.

Jeb sighed. He'd gone too far, and he'd known he was doing it. He wasn't sure why he had pursued the subject, but he was sure it was a futile effort. Now was clearly a good time for a change of conversation. "Did you get her brother out of Camp Colorado?"

"Didn't have to. He'd escaped by the time I got there."

Jeb gave a low whistle. "Do any damage on the way out?"

"Guard with a sore head. That's about it. With a little luck the stupid kid headed for home."

"Maybe he's learned enough not to want to join forces with Elzy Rusk a second time."

"Rusk is dead."

Slade spoke the words as casually as he might have announced that the moon was shining. Jeb was not deceived.

He watched Slade watching Katherine. The firelight touched her sleeping face with a soft glow. "So it's over," Jeb said.

The vendetta against Rusk, Jeb realized glumly, was the one sure thing that had held Slade to his work with the Texas Rangers. That, and an inborn need for the savage thrill born of danger. Could any woman sate that need? Jeb knew that in his own case a woman like

Katherine Bellamy definitely could. He wasn't so sure about Slade.

"Yeah. It's over." Slade placed his tin cup carefully beside the fire. "Now tell me about Wolf Killer."

"He's left the canyon, heading south with a small band of braves—and a white man."

Slade's eyes narrowed. "There's at least one of Rusk's gang left."

"Could be him. Whoever it is, he's as savage as any of Wolf Killer's braves. They've attacked two homesteads and killed three people."

"Damn it. Comanche don't raid in the wintertime!"

"Maybe not," Jeb said shortly, "but this Comanche is doing just that. The question is, why. What set him off?"

Slade's gaze followed Jeb's to Katherine, and he shook his head. "She says he doesn't want her anymore."

Jeb wasn't sure he believed that. "But what about the little girl? His daughter?"

Slade flinched. He hadn't thought of that. "Son of a bitch."

"Exactly," Jeb agreed wryly.

"Well, if this white man is the same one of Rusk's band who escaped from Camp Colorado with Ford Bellamy, chances are he knows where to find Ford—and the little girl. Son of a bitch," he said again. "You got a plan?"

"Harding sent word I was to find you and

meet a company of Rangers at the Waco settlement. Then we find Wolf Killer."

Beside him, Slade sensed as much as saw Katherine's shiver and knew she was awake and listening. He suspected she had been for some time.

Katherine bit her tongue on a moan as she heard Jeb's words. Wolf Killer looking for his daughter? Katherine's blood felt like ice as she recalled the things Wolf Killer had said to her in his anger. "Your name will not be spoken in this lodge. Sleeping Grasshopper will be the daughter of Willow Dancing."

She scarcely heard the remainder of the conversation between Slade and Jeb as her tortured thoughts led her to images of Dee and Ford lying in pools of blood. Of Shea in the hands of a father determined to destroy all white men. Of Shea in the hands of the soldiers, who would surely one day defeat Wolf Killer.

When Slade finally crept into the bedroll with her, leaving Jeb to think what he pleased, he pulled Katherine into his arms.

She stifled a sob as she pressed her face to his throat. "Don't let Wolf Killer take my daughter, Slade. Stop him. Dear God, please stop him."

It took Jeb less than a day to have his say with Katherine. She knew he was just waiting for the opportunity. It was there in his hazel eyes each time their glances met, which was far too frequently for her comfort. Katherine hadn't a doubt that she wasn't going to like anything he had to say. She could recall every word, every nuance of the conversation between the two men when they had thought her sleeping. Jeb perceived her as a threat to Slade's way of life.

Katherine knew Jeb Welles was wrong. Slade had no intention of settling down for her sake. She just wished Slade had said so right out. It would make things easier now with Jeb. No doubt sheer perversity had prevented Slade from doing just that. He didn't like anyone questioning his actions or his intentions. That had been plain enough to her, at least when he was evading Jeb's questions. Too bad for her it hadn't been as plain to Jeb. Now she had to endure whatever he thought he needed to say to her on the subject.

His chance came when they made early camp, and Slade decided to investigate a curl of smoke against the distant horizon. The strands of gray drifting against the sky looked innocent enough, but there was no sense in taking chances.

"Want me to ride with you?" Jeb offered.

"No need. I'm not planning to go in close." Slade walked to where Katherine stood beside her mare. He stood looking down at her and then touched her chin lightly. "Think you can find anything left in these packs to feed us?" He had not bothered with the packhorse when he left the Cullens. He'd known he needed to travel fast, hard, and light.

She smiled. "Not much in ours. We're lucky Jeb arrived when he did." But she didn't feel lucky, both for the other man's presence and the news he had brought. It had been painful lying in Slade's arms the previous night, unable to experience more than his arms wrapped tenderly around her, knowing how soon they would be parted.

She longed to move into his arms now but had to content herself with a smile. Jeb was watching. He seemed always to be watching.

Slade swung into his saddle, giving her one brief wave of his hand. She watched him until he disappeared from sight; then she turned to find Jeb watching her. "Go ahead," she said dryly, "might as well get it out before you choke on it."

Jeb grinned, and she relaxed as she recalled how easy he was to like even though she hated the part of Slade's life he represented. Even though he thought little enough of her.

"What makes you think I've got anything to say?" Jeb asked innocently and began to remove the saddle from his horse's back.

Katherine turned her own attention to Sadie's trappings. "You're just about puffed up with it," she retorted. "That's what makes me think it."

"You're one hell of a woman, Katherine Bellamy." Jeb lifted the saddle from his horse with one easy motion. Placing it on the ground at his feet, he removed a strip of rawhide to hobble the horse.

"But?" she prompted.

"Life's been hard as hell on Slade."

Katherine's eyes narrowed as she straightened from hobbling Sadie. "You think it hasn't been hard on me?" she asked incredulously.

Jeb didn't answer that. He just stood there looking at her. "Slade tell you about Maggie?"

"Yes." Katherine couldn't be angry. Jeb cared about the man he'd ridden with for so long, and he couldn't help that he thought Katherine was bad for Slade. Likely he was right. The realization didn't make her feel any better.

"I've seen men like Slade before," Jeb said quietly. "Something happens—like Maggie—and something inside of them dies. There's nothing left to start over with. He doesn't have what you're looking for, but by the time you realize it he will have turned his back on the only life he knows. You'll leave him, and he won't have anything left to hold him up."

Suddenly Katherine was furious, the rage running through her veins keeping her from the despair of knowing Jeb could be right. "How do you know what I'm looking for, damn it? I don't even know myself. I'm tired of you warning me away from Slade. I'm tired of the past getting in the way of the future. My past and Slade's."

Jeb felt a tightening in his loins as he watched the play of emotions across her face. Dusty and travel-worn, Katherine was more tempting than any soft, perfumed lady of the night. With an effort, he focused on her words and knew she was right. It was not his place to arrange Slade's fate or hers.

The rage left Katherine as quickly as it had come. "I don't think for one minute that Slade is defeated—not by Maggie's death or anything else. But he'll make his own choices. We all do."

She turned away, leaving him standing and staring after her.

When Slade returned she had a fire burning low. The aroma of salt meat and beans boiling lessened the chill of the night air. Jeb sat some distance away, whittling patiently on a small piece of wood. Katherine looked up as Slade approached, smiling a welcome but leaving the questions to Jeb.

"Trouble?"

Slade shook his head. "Wagonload of settlers who got separated from their wagon train when one of them became ill. Santa Fe bound, but they're as lost as a flock of tame geese." He hunkered down tiredly beside Jeb.

Jeb frowned. "It's too late in the year for them to get much farther."

"I gave them directions to Fort Davis and told 'em to stay put until spring."

"Reckon they will?" Abandoning his carving, Jeb flicked his knife into the ground.

"Who knows? But they'd better. They've got three younguns with them." He looked over at Katherine. She was listening gravely, and he wondered if her thoughts were on her own little girl.

That night he held her close. This night or the next or the night after that could be their last together. Their parting was inevitable, and it would be painful. He couldn't help but believe that Jeb was right; their worlds were too distant. Maybe once he could have been a father. He knew he had been a good husband to Maggie until that one last day when he'd rode out and left her all alone. Still, the thought of never holding Katherine again, of never again sinking his rigid flesh into her sweet body was agony.

The direction of his thoughts wreaked as much havoc with his body as with his mind. He felt the hardening between his legs and caught Katherine's hand in his. Gently, he pressed that hand down between them, hearing the breath catch quietly in her throat as she felt his fullness.

He nuzzled the curve of her neck, smiling as she moaned. His free hand slipped into her blouse and found the already taut nipple. Shifting slightly, he slid his tongue into the warmth of her ear.

She jerked. "Stop." The word was no more than an agonized whisper.

In answer, he withdrew his tongue, then plunged again.

"Bastard," she whispered hoarsely. But her fingers gently caressed the hard length of him.

Abandoning the teasing that was torturing him as much as it was her, he wrapped both arms tightly around her. "God, I want you."

Katherine snuggled against him, savoring the scent and the feel of him. If they spent too many more nights with Jeb Welles lying within hearing distance, they'd both go crazy.

It was Slade's decision to abandon Harding's plan. They would have to travel northeast to reach Waco. At any point, Wolf Killer and his braves were likely to bypass them to the west of their route northward. "How many warriors ride with Wolf Killer?" he asked Jeb.

Jeb shrugged. "Half a dozen. Maybe less now. Harding thought at least one, maybe two had been killed in the attacks. You thinking to take them on, just the two of us?"

"That worry you?"

The irrepressible grin tugged at the corners of Jeb's mouth. "Nope. Just wondering."

"It worries me."

Both men turned in their saddles to look at Katherine, who rode between them. She had been completely silent for the past half hour, while they discussed various possibilities.

She looked back, first at one, then the other. "You think you're invincible. That you can take on anyone, anywhere, anytime." She glared at Slade in exasperation. "You're human. Humans can die. They can be killed."

Slade snorted and looked across at Jeb. "Little lacking in faith, ain't she?"

Stung, Katherine returned, "This isn't a joke, Slade."

"No, Katie, it isn't, and I know you're worried, but I've been matching wits with Indians and outlaws for more years than a man should have to. If I ever start to doubt myself, I'll quit—or maybe be killed, like you say." His voice was soft as he added, "But until that day I don't want you worrying about how I'll make out in a fight. Okay?"

Uncomfortable with the feelings he sensed between the two of them, Jeb looked away. Could be he was wrong about what was left inside Slade, after all. He sure sounded like a man who could start over.

Katherine nodded at Slade's words, fighting tears. How was she not to worry? How could she not be afraid? So many times she'd listened to the warriors after a battle. Listened as they bragged at how close they had come to death and escaped, as they boasted of comrades who had faced their death with glorious courage. Comanche warriors did not mind dying if they could do so with pride, in battle. And Wolf Killer was the fiercest Comanche of all. No one knew that better than she.

Nor could she be happy with the other side of the coin. She ached to think of Wolf Killer wounded and dying. He was a part of her life. He lived within her soul. If not for Wolf Killer, she would have died as horribly as other captives she had heard tales of during her captivity. She had lived because of Wolf Killer; she did not want him to die because of her.

The next morning Slade roused them early. A still sleepy Katherine prepared their breakfast; and then cleaned up afterward while Jeb and Slade broke camp.

"We're about a day's ride from Austin," Slade said. "We'll see if anyone's available there to give us a hand."

Jeb paused in tying his bedroll behind his saddle. "You going to ride in and ask for volunteers to hunt Wolf Killer?" His look spoke volumes on what he thought Slade's chances of success were.

Slade wasn't too busy burying their fire not to see Katherine's hands grow still as she saddled Sadie. "Well," he answered grimly, "it might be their own families they're protecting. There's no way to know where Wolf Killer will strike on his way to New Braunfels."

That was true enough, Jeb admitted to himself. He didn't say it out loud. He, too, could see the effect each mention of Wolf Killer had on Katherine as the hours passed. Was she worried for her daughter, for Slade—or for the Indian?

They hadn't traveled very far into the morning when the gray puffs Katherine had taken for clouds took on the unmistakable characteristics of smoke. Heavy smoke.

Slade's lips thinned as he studied the horizon. "Looks like we might not make it to Austin, after all."

Katherine didn't speak. She couldn't. The weight of her dread was a heavy knot in her throat beyond which no words could pass.

A scowl marred Slade's forehead as he studied their surroundings. The only protection to be seen was a thin line of trees that followed a creek a few hundred yards to their left. He turned to Katherine. "Take your mare and wait at that creek. If we're not back by dark, follow it as far as you can. It should lead you to something."

"I'm going with you," Katherine said flatly.

"Hell, no, you're not!" Slade made no effort to keep the savagery from his voice. A muscle jumped in his jaw. "Worrying about you would sure as hell get me killed!"

White-faced, Katherine stared at him. "Don't you dare get killed, damn you!" Her voice broke. "Don't you dare!" She wheeled Sadie toward the creek, unable to say more past the lump that arose in her throat. By the time she reached the first silver-leafed tree there were tears rolling down her cheeks. Only from the shelter of the trees did she turn to watch as Slade and Jeb rode from sight.

Chapter Twenty-five

Katherine's resolve to obey Slade lasted all of five minutes. By the end of that five minutes, however, her palms were icy and her heart was pounding. Terror had her in full grip.

She knew she couldn't just stand there in the shade of those trees and wait, and she knew she'd never be able to start riding away from there at dark if Slade didn't come back. If he and Jeb didn't return, she'd have to ride after them. If she was going to do that anyway, she reasoned, the time to go was now—when she might be of some assistance.

Filled with dread, she began riding toward those dark drifts of smoke rising against the morning sky. Sadie seemed almost to be tracking the buckskin and Jeb's horse, for she picked her way carefully through the tall brush, walking at an angle now and again, but always moving toward that dreadful smoke. Katherine did not urge her to anything faster than a walk, though she suspected reality could not be worse than her imagination.

She was wrong. When she reached the clearing, dying flames licked at what was left of a homestead and beyond that a barn, burning slowly to the ground. The acrid smoke was choking. Sadie danced nervously at the crackling of the flames, but Katherine paid her little heed as she slid from her back. The horror around her had her full attention.

A brave sat cross-legged on the ground, holding his stomach in place, chanting his death song. Several bodies were scattered around him. A man, a woman, a teenage girl with her skirts above her head, her bloodied legs spread awkwardly. Some distance away, a toddler lay pinned to the ground by a spear. Katherine had thought she was inured to the hideous forms of death. She was not.

But it was the living that drew her terrified gaze now. Outlined against the scene of destruction, Slade and Ugly Jack Lawson circled one another with grim intent. Each brandished a wicked length of steel. Each appeared determined to slash the other to ribbons, and judging by the amount of blood visible, each appeared to have succeeded to some degree. Beyond them, astride a stocky pony, Wolf Killer watched impassively. At his side were two braves.

It wasn't difficult for Katherine to guess that Slade and Jeb had ridden up while Ugly Jack was raping the girl, who was surely already dead or dying at the time. Nor was it difficult for her to guess why Ugly Jack would be willing to help Wolf Killer find his daughter. Even if Wolf Killer offered him nothing, he would do it for vengeance. Katherine had not forgotten his fury that she had bested him.

"What the hell are you doing here?" Jeb asked between gritted teeth.

Katherine turned to look at him, eyes blazing that he was a safe distance from the combatants, but her initial response died in her throat. Jeb remained astride. The rifle he held in one arm was aimed at Wolf Killer's chest. The other arm was pressed against his side. Blood seeped from the mangled sleeve above the elbow. Slowly, Katherine pulled her rifle from the saddle holster, turning her attention to the braves beyond Wolf Killer.

"You knew I couldn't stay and wait, not knowing," she said tiredly. She glanced at him briefly before fixing her gaze once more on the watching Comanche braves. "You're going to have to shoot Ugly Jack. Slade's lost too much blood."

"If I shoot him, we're going to have three Indians riding down on top of us in no time flat," Jeb answered. "Are you going to be ready for that?"

"I'd damn well better be," she said flatly; then she hesitated. "But, Jeb . . . ?"

"Yeah?"

"You'll have to take Wolf Killer. I can't."

Jeb's face was gray and pinched with pain, but he managed a sympathetic smile. "I know, Kate," he said gently. "It'll be all right." Then, "You ready?"

Katherine sighted her rifle while Jeb swung his toward the two dueling with knives. "I'm ready. You just be damned sure it's Jack you hit."

Her fingers began to sweat on the rifle as she waited for Jeb to have a clear shot at Ugly Jack. Though she was ready for the blast of his rifle, when it came, she jerked at the sound. She didn't spare a glance to see if Ugly Jack dropped in his tracks.

Wolf Killer and his braves proved Jeb right. With his shot, their gouging heels drove their horses forward while their blood-curdling cries filled the air. Wolf Killer and one brave rode toward Katherine and Jeb, but Katherine aimed at the other brave, who veered in Slade's direction. She didn't so much as flinch when she squeezed the trigger. The warrior dropped from his horse, and Katherine fumbled to reload her rifle.

She heard Jeb screaming at her to ride, but it was too late. She knew that. She couldn't leave Slade or Jeb. They would kill or they would die together. There was no escape for any of them.

Lifting her rifle once more, she realized it was indeed too late. The remaining brave was now only a few feet away, his lance lifted high. His face twisted in a grimace of hatred as he rode toward her. Hatred for her, for all white men. Katherine felt her skin tingle as she waited for him to send that lance straight through her body, ripping flesh and bone and muscle.

Even as she watched, his chest exploded, the bullet from Slade's rifle exiting his body just below the breastbone. Her eyes lifted to Slade, watching ashen-faced as the Indian slumped against his horse's neck before slipping to the ground. The horse thundered away.

As if freed from a spell, Katherine looked around. Jeb was still in his saddle, but his wound bled profusely. The brave she had shot lay as still as the one Slade had killed. But her gaze did not linger on any of them as it searched for Wolf Killer.

He lay facedown in the dust, arms outflung. His lance lay just beyond the grasp of his fingers. The feathers adorning his war lance moved slowly in the winter wind. Katherine started toward him on numbed legs, hearing yet not hearing Slade calling to her in warning. Even if Wolf Killer should rise and take up his spear against her, she knew she could not stop herself from going to him. But Wolf Killer did not move.

Images of Wolf Killer touched her mind. Threatening, as he warned her against attempts to escape. Laughing, as he taught her to wield a bow and arrow. Fiercely proud as he lifted his infant daughter to the heavens. Then, much later, hungry with longing for her. So many moments, so much a part of her life.

Katherine sank to the dust beside him, gently rolling him toward her. His face looked so peaceful. Grief-stricken, she brushed a heavy lock of black hair from his face, willing him to open his eyes. But he did not, and her heart ached with the beauty and the strength that was ended by his death.

She felt Slade's hands on her shoulders, lifting her up, cradling her against his chest. And Katherine cried.

Chapter Twenty-six

Jeb grinned at Katherine from his bed. "I reckon you're ready to be out of here."

She nodded, looking around the neat room. There was a picture of an English hunt scene over Jeb's head. It looked as out of place as Jeb did lying against white sheets. "I reckon I am," she agreed. "Do you have everything you need?" Jeb had almost died of an infection from the wound in his arm. When the doctor had given up hope Katherine had not, though there were times she had come close to despair.

"Well, if I don't, that sweet little gal who helps her mama run this place fetches it for me right off." Jeb smiled almost angelically as he answered her question. At times he found himself saying just about anything to lighten the haunted look in Katherine's eyes. Her grief was still very much a visible part of her.

Katherine wasn't fooled in the least, but she played along. "You just watch yourself around that 'sweet little gal,'" she retorted, "unless you want to wind up married to her. Her mama looks well able to take care of her own."

"Might not be so bad," Jeb returned with the devil's own gleam in his eye, adding, "as long as there's no chance of settling down with you. If there were, I wouldn't give that gal a second look." There was a hint of seriousness in his playful tone.

Katherine tried to smile at his words, but her heart was still so heavy from what lay behind her—as well as what lay ahead. "You don't want to settle down with anyone, Jeb Welles, and you know it."

"I expect you're right." He shifted restlessly. "Not if it's anything like being confined to this room for a week." He'd been stuck in worse places than Austin, but he sure as hell had never *felt* any worse.

"You were lucky, Jeb," Katherine told him, meaning it. "You could have lost your arm. You almost did. Besides, you couldn't possibly remember much of this past week."

Jeb couldn't argue with that, nor did he care to think about the fact that he'd been practically helpless for an entire week. "Where's Slade?"

"Probably gambling or flirting with loose

women," Katherine responded lightly. Actually, Slade spent most of every day with the Rangers stationed in Austin, but it seemed cruel to remind Jeb of the life that waited beyond this room. Although he was healing rapidly, he had yet to regain his full strength. It would be several days more before he was ready to ride out. "Speaking of which," Katherine drew a deck of cards from her pocket and grinned, "are you ready to lose gracefully once more?"

"Damned if I should have taught you this game," Jeb grumbled good-naturedly. He drew himself up farther in the bed while Katherine placed the tray on his lap.

She tossed the cards on the tray. "Deal."

By the time Slade returned Katherine had beat Jeb three times at poker. He'd been so egotistical about teaching her the game, she'd never told him that Ford had taught her long ago.

While Slade was still teasing Jeb about his lack of skill, the pretty young girl who kept Jeb so entertained brought his lunch.

Slade looked at Katherine. "Are you ready to eat? It makes me pure sick to watch such a nice girl pampering this renegade."

Jeb protested, and the girl blushed.

Katherine smiled at Slade and nodded. Deep inside, she knew if he'd just asked her to jump off the roof of the building, she'd smile and nod. That scared her, but not as much as it once would have.

The boardinghouse was well run and extremely respectable. The woman who ran it assumed the two of them were married. Slade helped her with that assumption, while Katherine said nothing either way.

Halfway through a meal of baked chicken and several vegetable casseroles, Katherine placed her fork to the side and hissed at Slade, "Would you please quit staring at me!"

There was more mischief in Slade's dark eyes than Jeb's had ever held. That was disconcerting in itself. Slade was rarely anything but somber. His response to her demand was even more disconcerting. "All I'm doing is imagining what I'm going to do to you when we get back up to our room."

Katherine blushed furiously; then she turned her full attention to her meal.

Slade chuckled wickedly. "Good. I want you to hurry up and get finished. I can't wait much longer."

Somehow Katherine found her appetite was not as great as it had been just a little while earlier. Slade had turned her thoughts from food quite effectively.

When he had her alone in their room he began to unbutton the back of her gown. Katherine sighed and leaned against him, wondering once again what it might have been like for them if there had never been a Maggie or a Wolf Killer in their lives.

Reaching around her, Slade eased the bodice of her gown to her waist, then cupped her breasts through the thin material of her camisole. She arched into his hands, feeling his breath grow more ragged against her temple. His thumbs rubbed lightly against her nipples, and the burning warmth started low in her belly.

She turned to face him, and he lifted his hands to her jaw, cradling her face while he kissed her. Her mouth seemed to open to his tongue of its own accord, while the warmth within her turned into a blaze.

Dimly, she knew when Slade eased her gown from her hips. With equal skill he removed her undergarments; and then pressed his palm between her thighs. Craving his touch, Katherine parted her legs. But that was not enough.

Slade chuckled as she writhed against him; then he lifted her and carried her to the bed. She watched him with heavy-lidded eyes as he stripped, and the look nearly drove him insane. She was like no woman he'd ever known, and he never seemed to get enough of her.

He moved into her open arms and open legs, groaning as his flesh slid into her. Their lovemaking was wild and rough and good as it had been for a week. Each time Slade tried to make love to her tenderly, she would nip and bite and drag her nails across his back until he was out of control.

Slade knew she was hurting deep inside, and he knew that when they made love the pain was assuaged, if only for a while. And he wanted to ease her pain more than he'd ever wanted anything in his life.

When they both lay spent and gasping Slade recalled the look in her eyes that morning when she had said, "It's time for me to go home."

He'd been expecting it now that Jeb was out of danger, but expecting it hadn't made it any easier to face. He had wanted to say something, anything, that would change the fact of their parting. But he was afraid. There was always the chance that Jeb was right—that he would be wrong for Katherine, that he couldn't settle down. He couldn't forget the fact that for over ten years he had hunted a man with single-minded purpose. Vengeance had been the driving force in his life. He wasn't sure, now, what would replace it. He wasn't sure if anything could. And he couldn't bear to destroy Katherine's life by taking a chance and making a mistake. As it was, it would be hard enough for her to rebuild from the past. She didn't need him to make it any worse.

Slade pulled her tighter against him. "Everything's ready for us to leave in the morning."

The breath caught in Katherine's throat, and for a moment she forgot the need to breathe. The agony was too great. Then she drew a deep breath and nodded slowly.

Neither of them slept much that night.

Somewhat to her surprise, Katherine discovered it was quite difficult to say good-bye to Jeb. "Take care of yourself." She heard a bit of poignant regret in her words that she couldn't help. He was a link with Slade. One more broken link. "I'll miss you, Jeb."

"Oh, I imagine I'll be around now and again." He'd already started thinking of her as Slade's woman. He expected to see as much of her as he did of Slade.

Katherine smiled sadly, knowing what he thought, but knowing the truth was something different.

Slade's parting with Jeb was in character. "Get your ass out of bed. I'll be seeing you again in a few days."

Jeb grinned. Now that he was feeling better it was getting to be damned pleasant in bed. At least at times.

The barest hint of dawn was breaking when Katherine followed Slade out of Austin. They turned southwest, toward New Braunfels.

For Katherine it was a bittersweet journey. She was going home, and she was no longer sure what home meant to her. Or even where it was. Wolf Killer was dead. The day would come when the world of the Comanche would be no more. Shea had only her. Katherine tried to think rationally, tried to plan a future for Shea and herself, but all thoughts led to the painful realization that Slade would not be a part of that future. And each time her mind shied from that knowledge.

The only time she found any peace was when Slade thrust his hard body into hers and she could forget everything except what he did to her, how he made her feel. But it was a precarious peace and did not last through the morning that followed each night.

Nor did Slade find any peace. He made love to her with the aching certainty that in a day or two he would lose her forever. Nor did he sleep much. He didn't want to waste what precious moments he had left to hold her in his arms. He held her and watched her sleep and fought the urge to howl his pain to the world.

Deliberately, Slade traveled slowly, and Katherine knew that he did. And she knew why.

Late on the third day after they had left Austin, they reached the edge of the Bellamy property. Katherine stopped her mare and looked at Slade. "I'm home," she said simply. Something inside her knew it would be easier for her if they parted here, away from the eyes of others. "I'll go alone now."

"Is that what you want?" Slade asked roughly. He wanted her to say no—and didn't know what he would do if she did.

"It's best." Katherine was afraid to say more. The agony was too great, the tears too close.

Slade looked at her, drinking in every feature, every nuance, from the straight, wheat-colored hair to the silvery eyes that watched him now with sorrow in their gray depths. "Take care," he said hoarsely.

Katherine nodded, then clucked to Sadie, glad the mare knew the way home from here. Katherine could not have guided her for the tears in her eyes.

Slade watched her ride away, his throat burning. But he did not call her back.

Katherine had not yet reached the house when she saw the buckboard coming toward her. She glanced back, but Slade was no longer there. Realization pierced her heart. It was done. Holding Sadie in check, she waited.

Yates drew even with her and halted the team. Katherine wondered where he was going so late in the day while she endured his stare and waited for him to speak. There was condemnation in his eyes. For the first time, she felt self-conscious in his presence.

Ben thought of all her aunt had been through worrying about her, wondering if she would come back with that murdering Comanche buck to take the little girl away. His eyes missed nothing, softening a little as he perceived her weariness. "You coming home?"

She stared at him for a long minute, then lifted her shoulders. "I don't know, but I've come for my daughter." Despite the softening of his gaze, she sensed the challenge.

He took his gaze from her and stared across the land that lay waiting for the spring. "Been gone a few months. Things change."

Katherine felt threatened. "No one can change the fact that Shea is my daughter."

"No. Can't change that hair of yours either— or the color of your skin." He rubbed his jaw. "Your aunt's married now. Mr. Shanley. He's a good man. Thinks a lot of that little girl of yours."

"I understand, Ben." And she did. This wasn't going to be easy, whatever she decided to do.

Ben flicked his reins at the team, and Katherine turned Sadie toward the house, wondering what awaited her there. The sun blazed orange in the west, the sky glowing with blended evening colors, some harsh, some as soft as a child's kiss. Katherine's longing for Shea intensified.

In spite of everything a feeling of home welcomed her as she approached. The interior of the barn held a well-remembered scent of dust and hay. She wondered if Sadie would feel stifled by the barn after her long weeks of freedom on the trail. Katherine wondered the same about herself. Would she feel stifled by life in New Braunfels?

Katherine grained Sadie lightly and placed a pail of water in the stall. Slapping the mare's hip lovingly, she straightened her shoulders.

At the house, her hand automatically reached for the door. She stopped, slowly lifted her closed hand, and knocked. She had told Slade she was home, and the place welcomed her, but she felt like a stranger standing there.

Ford opened the door. His eyes lit up at the sight of her. "Kate. My God, Kate!"

Katherine's eyes widened as Elizabeth came to stand beside him, an apron covering her gown neatly. But she had no more time for thought as Ford wrapped her in a fierce embrace. Her arms closed about him as fiercely, and tears once more burned in her eyes. It seemed years instead of months that she had been so filled with fear for Ford's safety that she had followed a stranger, leaving her life behind her, just to find him.

When he finally released her Katherine caught her breath and tried to look beyond him. "Where's Shea?"

Ford frowned slightly. "Well . . ." He glanced at Elizabeth. "Well, she's not here exactly."

"Where is she?" The words exploded from Katherine's mouth. "Where's my baby."

"Easy, sis. She's fine. She's with Aunt Dee."

"But where is Aunt Dee?" Katherine was exhausted and bewildered, and she wanted her daughter.

"She and Doyle are back at his farm. She's real happy, Kate."

Elizabeth pulled Ford away from the door. "Bring her in, Ford. She's worn out, can't you tell?"

Ford's happy smile faded to quick concern. Elizabeth was right; Katherine did not look well. He hesitated, looking at his sister. "You're alone?"

Slowly, Katherine nodded. She knew he was asking if Shea's father was waiting somewhere for her to return with Shea. But she wasn't ready, yet, to speak of Wolf Killer.

Within moments, Ford had Katherine seated at the table in the room Katherine had always thought of as Aunt Dee's kitchen, while Elizabeth made a pot of tea and cut thick slices of bread and cheese.

Katherine wanted to tell them she didn't want anything except to see her daughter, but she felt so incredibly tired. Ford took the chair across from her. His look of concern was blended with a look of pride. "I reckon you've guessed that Elizabeth and I are married now."

Katherine smiled at the pretty, dark-haired girl who was watching her so anxiously. "Yes, since I know Aunt Dee would never let you live here in sin. And I'm glad for you."

"We wish you could have been here, but I wasn't sure . . ." His voice trailed away, and he colored slightly.

"I know." Katherine's voice was gentle. "You weren't sure if I would be coming home."

"I'm glad you have."

Elizabeth placed a cup of tea in front of her. "And I'm just as glad. I've missed you as much as Ford has." It was true. Katherine had been her best friend years before Ford had taken that place.

Seeing Katherine's hesitation, Ford frowned. "You are home, aren't you, Kate?"

346

Katherine sighed, knowing she had to warn them. "I'm not sure I'll stay. I doubt if anything has changed for me or Shea." She didn't miss the fact that Ford and Elizabeth exchanged looks, but neither of them said anything at her words. A tingle of alarm touched her clear to the soul. "I want to see her, Ford."

He placed his hand over hers on the table. "You will, Katie. I'll take you first thing in the morning, but you're exhausted right now."

She couldn't argue with that. The events of the past weeks were catching up to her with a vengeance. She could scarcely keep her head upright. But there was something she had to know. Looking Ford straight in the eye, she asked him, "Am I going to have to fight for my daughter, Ford?"

Ford's heart went out to her. He could see what the past few months had cost her by the lines of strain around her mouth and the dark circles under her eyes. "No, Kate. Shea is your child. You won't have to fight for her."

Katherine nodded wearily. "Then I'll sleep now." She smiled at Elizabeth as she got to her feet. "I'm so glad you're here. You're good for Ford." She shot her brother a hard look. "Maybe he'll stay home where he belongs now."

Ford had the grace to blush. He'd cost his aunt many a sleepless nights. But he'd cost Katherine a great deal more than that.

"I think he will. And we're so glad *you're*

347

home," Elizabeth said softly, wanting Katherine never to doubt her welcome here and wondering what had happened to the fierce Katherine who had left New Braunfels in the fall.

Alone in the room that had always been hers, Katherine discovered that, even as tired as she undoubtedly was, she could not sleep. She opened a chest and withdrew a small framed picture of her parents. It was an inexpertly done daguerreotype that evoked no sadness in Katherine. The man and woman posed so stiffly in no way resembled the warm and laughing parents she called effortlessly to mind through memories.

The picture was nestled in a stack of Shea's baby clothes, light, lacy garments that brought tears to Katherine's eyes. She had done so much for love of Shea, but she had failed in what Shea had needed most from her. Katherine had yet to give her a secure future in which she would be loved and welcomed by more than her family.

When Katherine finally slept she dreamed of Slade, and cried in her sleep.

True to his word, Ford rode with Katherine to Doyle's farm early the next morning. Along the way, Katherine told him of the deaths of Rusk and of Wolf Killer.

"I'm sorry, Katherine. I'm sorry you've been

through so much. Aunt Dee and I have worried about you." He sensed there was far more that she hadn't told him. And probably never would.

She sighed. "I hurt Aunt Dee when I left, Ford. She might not have forgiven me yet."

"There's nothing for her to forgive," he said evenly. "You'll see, Kate. Nothing will matter between the two of you but that you are near her again."

"It will matter if I can't stay, Ford. I'll hurt her all over again, and I don't want to do that."

Ford didn't have an answer, because he knew she was right. He didn't want her to leave, didn't want to witness his aunt's agony over losing her beloved Katherine once more and, along with her, the little girl she had come to think of as her own daughter.

Doyle Shanley's farmstead was on the far side of New Braunfels, and Katherine rode deliberately through town. Some of those she had called friends years ago greeted her with only a hint of reserve; some met her eyes without speaking. A few, a very few, looked intentionally away. Katherine schooled herself not to be bitter, but she noted the angry set to Ford's mouth.

"What did you expect?" she asked.

"They'll forget in time, Katherine."

But she could tell he didn't really believe that. "How much time? How much time will it take, Ford, for them to forget that I spread my legs for a Comanche buck?" She spoke with deliberate crudeness, determined to make him understand that she knew what these people were thinking when they looked at her.

"But you didn't." A wealth of frustration was in his voice.

"They can never know that," she reminded him. "They'll always have to believe that—for Shea's sake."

"Then you need to believe something for Shea's sake," Ford said raggedly. "These people have come to accept her."

Katherine shook her head. She had seen their disdain.

"It's true. I know you're thinking about taking Shea and moving away, but we're all the family you and that little girl have. Doyle and Aunt Dee are all the family she's had for months. They love her, and Doyle has made damned sure that if anyone in New Braunfels has a problem with Shea's Comanche blood, they'd damned well better keep it to themselves."

"What are you saying, Ford?" Katherine demanded. "That I should give my baby up? Was that what you and Elizabeth were looking so funny about?"

It was, but it didn't sound right when Katherine said it. Ford fixed his eyes on the road ahead. "I'm not asking you to give her up. I'm just asking you not to take her away. For Aunt Dee's sake. For Shea's sake."

They rode in silence for some minutes; then

Ford tried again. "Do you remember what I told you when you found me with the Comanche?"

"I remember," Katherine said quietly. She recalled every hurtful thing. "You think I am responsible for how these people feel about me, and about Shea."

"Only partly. They've opened their hearts to Shea, Kate. Give them a chance before you uproot her."

Katherine didn't know how to answer him, so she said nothing. She wasn't sure she was capable of making any more choices about anything. Not just yet.

Dee's new home was a neat square sitting firmly at the base of a sloping hill. Her wash was on the line at the side of the house. It was spotless and neatly arranged, as was everything to which Dee set her hand. Curtains hung at every window. The barnyard appeared well tended.

Ford hung back as Katherine knocked. Dee opened the door, then gasped with joy to see her beloved Kate's face, sunburned and wind chapped and so very welcome. Their embrace spanned the chasm of their separation. Dee stepped back to study her niece, her eyes seeing the wounds that Katherine still carried with her.

"Ah, Kate," she said, stepping back from the door. "Come in, sweetheart. And you, Ford. How's my Elizabeth?"

Katherine followed her aunt into the house,

glancing about while Ford answered Dee's inquiry concerning his bride. The house was well built and lovingly tended by Dee, but it was far smaller than the one in which she had reared her sister's children.

Katherine turned to face her aunt. "Where's Shea?" She tried to keep the fear from her voice, but she could not disguise the hunger.

"Asleep—again. Doyle chased a fox from the hens this morning long before dawn. The shots woke Shea, and she was too bright-eyed to sleep again until just a little while ago. She dozed off playing on the floor with the pots." Dee's words slowed. "Shall I wake her?"

Katherine heard trepidation in her aunt's voice, saw it in her eyes. Dee had clearly lived in dread of the day Katherine would come for Shea. "No. Of course not, but I'd like to slip in and see her."

"I'll take you."

Ford remained behind while Katherine followed her aunt down a narrow hall to a small bedroom. Dee left her at the closed door, but Katherine suspected her aunt fought an urge to follow her in, to be sure Katherine did not leave with the child while she was not looking.

Katherine entered the room and closed the door quietly. Shea was sprawled across the bed. Her dark hair was slightly damp, for the room was warm. Katherine was surprised that the ache she held inside did not ease at the first sight of her daughter. Perhaps she had missed her too much for too long for the effects to vanish in an instant.

Gently, Katherine parted white dimity curtains, allowing weak winter sunlight to fall on the sleeping child. Shea stirred, and in spite of her intention not to wake the child, Katherine spoke her name.

Fussing sleepily, Shea rolled onto her belly, her knees drawn up beneath her.

Unable to restrain herself any longer, Katherine picked her up. Shea's eyes opened and focused on Katherine. Unexpectedly, she arched backward, away from Katherine.

There was fear in her face. "Mama!"

"It is Mama, love." Katherine tried to reassure her.

"Mama!" The word was louder, more frantic. "Mama!"

Dully, Katherine realized that it was not to Katherine that Shea was calling. The door opened, and she turned to stare accusingly at her aunt.

"You taught her to call you 'Mama'!"

"No, Katherine. It came to her naturally after a while. A bairn needs her mother."

"I am her mother!" In anguish, she yielded to Shea's struggles and watched as the little girl ran to her great-aunt. Her steps were no longer the uncertain ones Katherine remembered. She felt the loss of her daughter's sweet infancy.

Dee stooped to lift the sobbing child, then looked at Katherine. "You were not here," she reminded quietly as she straightened and left the room.

Katherine sank to the bed, stricken and, finally, defeated. She had lost everything: her hope of a life with Wolf Killer; Slade; now Shea. Sobs rose up in her throat, but she swallowed them, fighting the pain, not wanting those who waited beyond the door to hear and come to her. She had to deal with this loss alone. Their love could not ease the hurt.

Katherine had no idea how much time passed before she left that room, dry-eyed and resolved, if not at peace. Dee and Ford waited for her in the kitchen, and Doyle waited with them. Katherine's gaze went to him first, for Shea was nestled against his chest. Her gaze lifted to his pale, tense face. He was afraid. She looked at her aunt and saw terror in Dee's dark eyes too.

"I'm not going to take her from you." Her voice sounded raw, even to her own ears.

Doyle said nothing, unable to believe, to even comprehend.

Dee fought sudden hope. "Katie?"

Slowly, Katherine unfastened the thin gold chain from her neck. The tiny cross Dee had given her so many months ago sparkled in the sunlight streaming through the windowpane. Dee's words, never forgotten, echoed in the room. *Shea is your daughter, but I will not give her up to anyone who cannot show me this.* Dee would never have to give her up now.

Katherine reached out, handing the chain and cross to her aunt. "Shea deserves you and Doyle. She needs a family. I can't give her that." Tears clogged her throat, and she looked at Ford. "Take me home, Ford. Please."

Katherine walked from the room and did not look back.

Chapter Twenty-seven

Slade returned to Austin only to find that Jeb had left his sick bed, intending to return to Fort Lancaster. Boredom had prompted his decision, or so the note said. Looking into the lovesick gaze of the girl who handed him the note, Slade had the feeling Jeb had been escaping, pure and simple.

"Damn fool," he swore under his breath.

The girl touched his sleeve tentatively. "Do you think he'll ever come back through here?" Her pretty blue eyes sparkled with tears.

Slade shook his head and answered gently, "Maybe in a year or two. Maybe never. He's an unpredictable cuss and not worth your tears." At the moment, Slade could cheerfully have strangled that "unpredictable cuss." This wasn't the first broken heart Jeb had left behind him, and Slade doubted seriously that it would be the last.

He didn't waste any time in Austin. There was nothing to keep him, except memories of Katherine that were far better forgotten. With every mile he traveled, he found that more difficult to do. She haunted every moment, with her soft gray eyes that had seen too much and lips that trembled as she waited for his kiss. She was too vulnerable to the blows life had dealt her, and he was too vulnerable to thoughts of her.

He rode into Fort Lancaster a few days later and went straight to see Captain Harding.

Harding greeted him gladly. He always had need of Slade one way or another. "Drink?" he offered, lifting a bottle of his best brandy.

"You know Rusk is dead?" Slade watched as gratification lit the other man's austere features.

Harding nodded. "I've seen Welles's report, but there were no details. What happened?"

"He forced Katherine Bellamy to leave Camp Colorado with him. I took exception to that and followed."

Harding slowly sank to a chair, motioning Slade to do the same. There was something in Slade's eyes that he didn't like, something to do with the Bellamy girl. "Did he hurt her?"

"No."

Harding sighed. He knew Slade fairly well. Whatever was there would remain Slade's secret. "The girl was lucky you were with her when Rusk got his hands on her."

"Lucky? I doubt if he would have touched her if it weren't for me."

The captain did not miss Slade's self-recrimination. "Rusk thought she meant something to you?" The outlaw wasn't the only one to think that.

Slade nodded. "That's my guess."

"And you killed Wolf Killer, as well."

"Actually, Jeb fired the shot."

Harding waved a hand in dismissal. Wolf Killer was dead; that was the important thing. "What now?"

Harding had worried for days after Slade left Fort Lancaster with the girl. Worried that Slade wouldn't be back. Welles had seemed to be of the same belief, and no one knew Slade better than Jeb Welles. Harding had been damned relieved to see Slade walk into his office, but the doubts were back. Slade didn't have the look of a man glad to be where he was.

Slade didn't answer, so Harding repeated, "What are you going to do now?"

"Nothing," Slade said slowly. "Anything. I'm ready for my next assignment."

Harding smiled broadly. "Well, I need someone to head north for a while. The army has requested a backup of Rangers on the Oregon Trail. Seems some immigrants have decided to settle there, to the displeasure of the Kotsoteka Comanche. This is going to be uncomfortable."

Slade smiled back cynically. *Uncomfortable* was Harding's euphemism for damned dangerous. As he rose to leave, a poster lying on Harding's desk caught his eye, and he paused to pick it up. Bold letters advertised for a lawman willing to provide protection to the citizens of a small town in the New Mexico Territory. Ignoring Harding's brow, lifted in query at his actions, Slade folded it and tucked it in his shirt pocket.

He knew the captain's eyes were on his back as he strolled out the door.

Hours later, Slade sat alone in the quarters always kept ready for him. Propped against the wall, feet stretched out on the bed before him, he watched the sunlight slide slowly across the room as day faded. He sat and tried not to think. And when he could not keep from thinking, he tried to accept.

Just before dark, Jeb, still covered with the dust of the trail, burst into the room with a jug of whiskey. "Damn, man, took you long enough to get back." He stopped short at the raw look of pain in Slade's eyes. "Shit."

Slade gave him a twisted grin. "Yeah. Shit."

"Well, reckon you need this." Jeb lifted the bottle, ignoring the fact that he was still on duty.

"Reckon I do."

Half a bottle later, Jeb commiserated, "I tried to warn her away from you."

"Warn her?" Slade knew he wasn't drunk yet, but he wanted to be. He took another long drink. "Warn her about what?"

"That you'd expect something from her. That you'd expect more than she had to give."

Slade started to deny Jeb's words, then shrugged. What the hell difference did it make? "It's done," he said flatly. "Over."

Jeb looked at him. "It ain't over for you." Any other man wouldn't have dared, but Jeb knew all of Slade's past, all of his demons. As Slade knew Jeb's. "If you feel like that, what'd you let her get away for?"

Slade glared back in outrage. "You're the son of a bitch that told me it'd be a mistake!"

"Well," said Jeb reasonably, "what the hell do I know?"

"Damn well nothing!"

"I'll admit I've never understood women," Jeb said, "but I sure as hell like 'em." He watched Slade's morose expression for a moment. "Look, Slade, if she's what you want, just go back after her."

"No."

"Then I will," Jeb said reasonably.

"I'll kill you, you son of a bitch!"

Jeb peered at him. "Not for me, you ass. For you."

Slade was sober when he reported to Harding's office the next morning, but he looked and felt like hell. He didn't feel much better when he walked out carrying his orders.

Jeb waited for him on the parade ground. "Where you headed?"

"North. The Kotsoteka Comanche are raising hell with the immigrants. I reckon the army likes the way I speak Comanche. Anyway, Harding thinks I can help 'ease some of the tension' along the Oregon Trail." Slade wasn't particularly happy with the assignment. He didn't care if he never saw another Comanche.

Jeb had a pretty good hunch how he was feeling and clapped him on the shoulder in commiseration. "I'll see you when you get back."

"Good," Slade returned cryptically as he mounted the buckskin the private led up to him. "You'll like New Mexico."

Perplexed, Jeb pushed his hat back on his head and watched Slade ride away.

Chapter Twenty-eight

Warm April air touched Katherine's cheek with a soft caress. She lifted her face to the late afternoon sun, breathing in the fragrances of spring. Light, sweet meadow flowers mingled with the spice of pine needles. High above her, a wild goose called, and she opened her eyes to watch his solitary flight.

The span of his wings looked poignantly alone against the wide blue of an empty sky. A piercing feeling, part bittersweet memory, part stark loneliness, caused Katherine to wrap her arms about herself and turn away. She really should be returning to the house anyway. Elizabeth fretted when she left for long walks by herself. No matter how often she tried to tell Elizabeth to simply enjoy some time alone with Ford, her brother's wife fussed. Unlike Katherine, Elizabeth did not enjoy being alone.

Ford met her halfway along the path to the house. Seeing past the ready smile she gave him, he knew Elizabeth was right in her worries. Katherine, beneath her smiles and laughter and conversation, remained unhappy. He fell into step beside her and reached for her hand.

Ford's hand, large and callused, reminded Katherine of Slade. Everything reminded Katherine of Slade. She sighed.

Ford squeezed her fingers lightly. "Things are going to get better, sis."

"I've been home five, almost six months," she said quietly. "Nothing's changed."

No argument of Ford's could stand the test of truth. Nothing *had* changed. "Shea's happy," he said, knowing Katherine thought the little girl's happiness worth every sacrifice.

"She was happy before I came home," Katherine reminded him.

"What you did was very unselfish." Ford knew it had been the hardest thing his sister had ever done—and that it had made her unbearably sad.

Katherine stopped and turned to face him, still clasping his hand tightly. "I gave Shea what every little girl deserves: a mother and a father and a secure home where she's loved more than anything." That was all Katherine had ever wanted to give her. "Aunt Dee and

Doyle love her as much as I do. They can give her what I'll never be able to."

"I know what it cost you," Ford said roughly. They all knew. "Damn it, Kate," the words burst from him in frustration, "I want you to be happy."

"I'm not unhappy, Ford."

But that was a lie, and they both knew it. Her eyes told the truth.

"You're planning to leave, aren't you?" He'd fought the truth for days. He didn't want to lose Katherine. If the thought of leaving wasn't already there, he didn't want to put it in her head. But Elizabeth said Katherine was too restless, too unhappy to stay, and several days ago Katherine had insisted on signing a paper relinquishing her half of the farm to Ford and Elizabeth.

"Leaving has crossed my mind, Ford," she admitted. "I love you and Elizabeth, and you've been good to me, but there's really nothing to keep me in New Braunfels."

"But this is home. And we're your family. Me and Elizabeth and Doyle and Aunt Dee. And Shea." Shea, who now thought of Katherine as her Aunt Kate.

"It doesn't *feel* like home. Not anymore. Not for a long time." Katherine dropped his hand and touched her palm to his jaw. "I've got to find a life for myself. I've got to find a place where I'll belong, where no one will look at me and label me as Wolf Killer's white squaw. You

365

know I've tried here, Ford," she said quietly. "Folks don't mean to be cruel, but they're never going to let me forget, not entirely."

"I'm sorry. Damn, Katherine, I'm sorry." Ford felt so helpless. The family had banded around Katherine, and Doyle had worked his magic on folks. Katherine was never ostracized, but Ford knew she was right. New Braunfels would not forget. And this time, it was no fault of Katherine's. She had tried. Perhaps if she was to marry, have a husband and children of her own . . . but Katherine showed no interest in any man. And she had intimidated the few who had dared to come calling.

"Starting over isn't a scary thought for me, Ford." Katherine wanted so much to reassure him. "It's kind of exciting."

"But where will you go?"

"West, I think. There's free land to be had. I've got that money you insisted on giving me for this place, and Aunt Dee came up with some outrageous lie about an inheritance so she and Doyle could give me some money. . . ."

"You've talked with Aunt Dee about this already?" Ford sounded hurt.

Katherine smiled. "She guessed before you did, that's all."

"Even with money, you can't work a place by yourself," Ford protested.

That takes a man. The unspoken words hung in the air, but Katherine stiffened her shoulders against them. "I can hire out whatever I need done, same as any man would do when he's trying to get a place started. I'm not helpless, Ford, and you and Aunt Dee can't protect me forever. But I can understand you wanting to," she added softly.

Ford thought of the way she had ridden out after Slade to find him, to "protect" him, and he smiled wryly. Yeah, she understood that. He thought of all the arguments he could put forth about what she planned, but he knew it would be a waste of time. Katherine had her mind made up. Again.

"When are you planning to leave?"

Katherine smiled in relief. She had hated the thought of having to fight Ford over this. "As soon as you and I figure out the best place. There's all kinds of possibilities." She'd been poring over government land advertisements in secret for weeks.

Before Ford could answer, Elizabeth called to them from the porch. Ford glanced toward the house and groaned. "Elizabeth's going to have my hide for agreeing to this."

Laughing at his dismay, Katherine caught his hand in hers once more and started walking toward the house. She felt lighter of heart than she had in months. Starting over. Yes, she could do that.

Two days after her conversation with Ford, Katherine sat in Dee's kitchen, playing with Shea. Though it still hurt to ride away from each visit and leave her, the pain was no longer biting. Katherine knew her decision was best for Shea. One day the little girl would have to know the truth about her father, but Katherine trusted Aunt Dee to know when that was. For now, Shea was the only child and beloved daughter of Dee and Doyle Shanley. And Katherine was her "Aunt Kate."

Right or wrong, Katherine knew she would never reveal that Shea was not her daughter. It would serve no purpose save to cheat Shea of the one security she had now. Jeane Pearson, her brother, and their parents were dead. Any relatives who remained could never be the family that Dee and Doyle would be. Katherine could not take the chance that any would try.

Dee sat across the table from her niece. Her heart was heavy at the thought of losing Katherine so completely to another place, but it also sang with relief that she would never have to lose Shea. "Are you and Ford still arguing?"

"Of course," Katherine retorted. "He wants me to move back east." She made a face and quoted her brother, "Where there are civilized people."

"That's not so bad an idea, Kate."

"But that's not what I want, Aunt Dee. I want excitement, a challenge. Can you see me settling in a town where all the women have afternoon teas and Sunday socials?"

"Well, and what's wrong with that?" Dee questioned indignantly. As a matter of fact, she had attended a few teas in New Braunfels lately. She and the daughter, whom no one dared snub now. No one wanted to risk Doyle Shanley's wrath. And, truth be told, Dee suspected Shea had charmed a few unsuspecting hearts. Where Doyle's threats would have found no purchase, Shea's sunny smile had.

"Nothing's *wrong* with it, Aunt Dee. It's just not what I want."

"Do you know what you want?" Dee asked quietly.

Katherine nodded slowly. She wanted to forget Slade. She wanted not to long for Shea when the evening shadows slid across the farmlands. She wanted not to hurt. But all she said was, "I want to make a new life for myself. One that's so busy and so full that I fall asleep on my way to bed."

"Are you running away, Kate?"

A shaft of pain went through Katherine at the words, and Slade's voice echoed within her. *Are you running back to the Comanche—or away from the whites?* "Maybe I am running from the past," Katherine acknowledged, "but not from myself. Not this time."

A little while later, she kissed Shea good-bye and hugged her aunt. "It'll be dark soon. I'd better leave or Ford will ride after me. Tell Doyle I said hello."

"I'll tell him." Dee smiled. Her fears that she would be caught between her husband and her

niece in a battle for Shea had never material-
ized—thanks to Katherine's loving wisdom.

She watched Katherine ride away and
hoped somewhere, someway Katherine could
be happy again.

Katherine had the same hopes.

Elizabeth faced the stranger and wished desperately that Ford was around. Or Katherine.
Katherine was afraid of no one and nothing.
And this stranger frightened Elizabeth, though
she could not have said why. All he'd done was
knock at the open door and wait, hat in hand,
for her to answer his knock.

Studying him, Elizabeth decided perhaps her
fear was because she had never seen a man
with such a hard look to his face. "Yes? May I
help you?" she inquired with as much firmness
to her voice as she could manage.

Slade turned the hat in his hand almost nervously, studying the dark-haired girl. He hadn't
seen her the one time he'd been here before.
Ford's wife, maybe? He acknowledged her pret-
tiness, but he hungered for Katherine's strong
beauty. He hungered for Katherine, period.

The girl was still staring at him wide-eyed,
waiting for his response. Slade realized she was
afraid of him. Her fear made her cheeks paler
than fresh cream.

He cleared his throat. "I'm looking for
Katherine Bellamy."

Elizabeth's heart thudded. This man could

not mean any good for their Katherine. He was too rough, too hard. "She's not here." Elizabeth forced herself not to look away from his steady regard.

At her words, Slade's heart dropped to his feet. "Does she still live here?" A dozen possibilities crowded his mind. Had she moved away with the baby? Had she married? What would he do if he couldn't find her now that he had finally accepted that he couldn't live without her?

"Why do you ask?" Elizabeth wasn't going to place Katherine in danger, even if she risked herself to protect her friend. Katherine had suffered far too much already. She prayed Katherine wouldn't ride up before this man was gone from here. "What do you want with Katherine?"

Eyes narrowed, Slade stared at her for a long moment. Ford's wife—if that's who she was—wasn't going to tell him anything. "Tell Katherine I'll wait just north of here. Until daylight."

"Wait for what?" Elizabeth asked sharply. This man confused as much as frightened her.

"Just tell her." Slade turned to go, wondering what he would do if Katherine never showed.

Ford had not yet returned from the fields when Katherine arrived home. Spring planting consumed every daylight hour for him and Doyle and Yates. The three of them had decided to work both farms together, dividing their time equally between the two places.

Elizabeth met her on the porch, and Katherine felt a tingle of alarm at her expression. Elizabeth rarely frowned, but she was frowning now. "Is something wrong?"

"I don't know," Elizabeth said slowly. "Someone was here asking for you. A man."

"Did he say what he wanted?" Katherine asked, fighting the insidious hope that threatened to destroy her hard-won peace.

Elizabeth looked at her strangely. "You."

Katherine's heart began to pound. "Did he give his name?"

Elizabeth shook her head. She didn't like Katherine's expression. She didn't like any of this, and she wished Ford was home.

"Describe him for me, please, Elizabeth." Katherine's voice was filled with a hopeful urgency that would not be quieted.

"Katherine, you're flushed," Elizabeth scolded. "What's going on?"

"Please, Elizabeth!"

"Very well, but I couldn't see much of him beneath that beard. He had on leather leggings, a wool shirt, and he carried a very wicked-looking rifle."

Katherine closed her eyes against the sudden fear that swept through her. What if it was only Jeb? "His eyes?" she asked softly.

"Brown. And," Elizabeth added, "very hard-looking."

"Slade." His name was a whisper on her lips. Elizabeth looked at her in dismay.

"What else did he say?"

Elizabeth hesitated. What should she do?

"Elizabeth, please," Katherine pleaded, certain there was more.

"He said . . . he said he'd wait for you just north of the farm." Elizabeth's fears were realized as Katherine whirled away from her. "Katherine, wait!"

But Katherine was already running back down the porch steps.

"Katherine, stop! Where are you going?"

For one brief moment, Katherine paused in her flight. "I'm going home, Elizabeth." And she knew it was the truth. Wherever Slade was would be home for her. "Tell Ford . . . just tell him I love him, and I'll be happy."

"I'll tell him," Elizabeth whispered, but she knew Katherine couldn't hear her. She had already disappeared into the barn.

Elizabeth was still watching a few moments later when Katherine rode Sadie out of the barn and disappeared into the dark.

Chapter Twenty-nine

Slade watched the flickering flames of his campfire and listened to the night birds calling to one another. They were peaceful sounds, but lonely. He thought of every reason why he shouldn't be where he was. The same reasons he'd told himself over and over not to come. But here he was.

Stacked up against his need for Katherine, the reasons just weren't good enough. It didn't matter that he didn't know what kind of job, what kind of life waited for him in New Mexico. It didn't matter that he wasn't sure he knew anything about living the kind of life a wife deserved. A wife and child, he reminded himself. It didn't matter that they were both misfits. If he could talk Katherine into leaving with him, he would.

Whatever mistakes they made in the future, they could make together. The only thing he wasn't sure of now was how he would survive if he couldn't talk Katherine into going with him. Of if he *would* survive that.

Harding had told him he was a fool for thinking he could settle in one place. Jeb had grinned, wished Slade luck, and said he'd be along when his current enlistment was up.

Slade thought of the way the woman, Ford's wife, had reacted to him. Maybe that's how any decent woman would act, or maybe it was because of Katherine that she acted that way. Maybe Katherine had harsh memories of him. Maybe she had said harsh things.

Slade had turned everything over in his mind a hundred times. He'd made love to Katherine, and he'd left her. So what if she hadn't asked him to stay? Neither had he asked her to go— or said that he'd be back. Maybe she hated him now.

Nearby, the buckskin lifted his head, and Slade froze, listening and waiting. The buckskin blew softly, then dropped his head.

Slade's heart started pounding as he forced his shoulders to relax against the tree behind him. Someone waited in the darkness beyond the circle of light from his campfire. Katherine waited.

"Come ahead," he called without waiting for her to call to him.

Katherine nudged Sadie forward, suddenly

terribly afraid. Her feelings were too strong, too much out of control. If he had not come for her, if he rode away from her once more, she did not think she could bear it.

Slade was on his feet by the time she reached him. She slid from Sadie's back and stood looking at him. He had a lean and hungry look that reached clear to his soul. She could see it even through the beard that hid his expression and the night that hid his eyes.

Tears filled Katherine's eyes, but she could not take a single step toward him. There were ghosts between them. Maggie's ghost, and Wolf Killer's.

Then Slade lifted his arms to her, and the ghosts faded. Katherine stepped into his embrace. The sweetness of his hard arms enclosing her was almost more than she could bear. Her own arms encircled him, her palms pressing into his back, pressing him closer and harder against her.

She lifted her face and felt his lips close on hers. Slade's kiss was hard and almost bruising—his way of branding her, of claiming her.

Katherine Fierce Tongue was no more. Katherine Bellamy had been born again. The past faded into memory, and her future belonged to Slade.

TIMESWEPT ROMANCE

TIME OF THE ROSE
By Bonita Clifton

When the silver-haired cowboy brings Madison Calloway to his run-down ranch, she thinks for sure he is senile. Certain he'll bring harm to himself, Madison follows the man into a thunderstorm and back to the wild days of his youth in the Old West.

The dread of all his enemies and the desire of all the ladies, Colton Chase does not stand a chance against the spunky beauty who has tracked him through time. And after one passion-drenched night, Colt is ready to surrender his heart to the most tempting spitfire anywhere in time.

_51922-4 $4.99 US/$5.99 CAN

A FUTURISTIC ROMANCE

AWAKENINGS
By Saranne Dawson

Fearless and bold, Justan rules his domain with an iron hand, but nothing short of the Dammai's magic will bring his warring people peace. He claims he needs Rozlynd—a bewitching beauty and the last of the Dammai—for her sorcery alone, yet inside him stirs an unexpected yearning to savor the temptress's charms, to sample her sweet innocence. And as her silken spell ensnares him, Justan battles to vanquish a power whose like he has never encountered—the power of Rozlynd's love.

_51921-6 $4.99 US/$5.99 CAN

HISTORICAL ROMANCE
HUNTERS OF THE ICE AGE: YESTERDAY'S DAWN
By Theresa Scott

Named for the massive beast sacred to his people, Mamut has proven his strength and courage time and again. But when it comes to subduing one helpless captive female, he finds himself at a distinct disadvantage. Never has he realized the power of beguiling brown eyes, soft curves and berry-red lips to weaken a man's resolve. He has claimed he will make the stolen woman his slave, but he soon learns he will never enjoy her alluring body unless he can first win her elusive heart.

_51920-8 $4.99 US/$5.99 CAN

A CONTEMPORARY ROMANCE
HIGH VOLTAGE
By Lori Copeland

Laurel Henderson hadn't expected the burden of inheriting her father's farm to fall squarely on her shoulders. And if Sheriff Clay Kerwin can't catch the culprits who are sabotaging her best efforts, her hopes of selling it are dim. Struggling with this new responsibility, Laurel has no time to pursue anything, especially not love. The best she can hope for is an affair with no strings attached. And the virile law officer is the perfect man for the job—until Laurel's scheme backfires. Blind to Clay's feelings and her own, she never dreams their amorous arrangement will lead to the passion she wants to last for a lifetime.

_51923-2 $4.99 US/$5.99 CAN

LOVE SPELL
ATTN: Order Department
Dorchester Publishing Co., Inc.
276 5th Avenue, New York, NY 10001

Please add $1.50 for shipping and handling for the first book and $.35 for each book thereafter. PA., N.Y.S. and N.Y.C. residents, please add appropriate sales tax. No cash, stamps, or C.O.D.s. All orders shipped within 6 weeks via postal service book rate. Canadian orders require $2.00 extra postage and must be paid in U.S. dollars through a U.S. banking facility.

Name _____

Address _____

City _____ State _____ Zip _____

I have enclosed $_____ in payment for the checked book(s).
Payment <u>must</u> accompany all orders.☐ Please send a free catalog.

FROM LOVE SPELL
FUTURISTIC ROMANCE
NO OTHER LOVE
Flora Speer
Bestselling Author of *A Time To Love Again*

Only Herne sees the woman. To the other explorers of the ruined city she remains unseen, unknown. But after an illicit joining she is gone, and Herne finds he cannot forget his beautiful seductress, or ignore her uncanny resemblance to another member of the exploration party. Determined to unravel the puzzle, Herne begins a seduction of his own—one that will unleash a whirlwind of danger and desire.

_51916-X $4.99 US/$5.99 CAN

TIMESWEPT ROMANCE
LOVE'S TIMELESS DANCE
Vivian Knight-Jenkins

Although the pressure from her company's upcoming show is driving Leeanne Sullivan crazy, she refuses to believe she can be dancing in her studio one minute—and with a seventeenth-century Highlander the next. A liberated woman like Leeanne will have no problem teaching virile Iain MacBride a new step or two, and soon she'll have him begging for lessons in love.

_51917-8 $4.99 US/$5.99 CAN

LOVE SPELL
ATTN: Order Department
Dorchester Publishing Company, Inc.
276 5th Avenue, New York, NY 10001

Please add $1.50 for shipping and handling for the first book and $.35 for each book thereafter. PA., N.Y.S. and N.Y.C. residents, please add appropriate sales tax. No cash, stamps, or C.O.D.s. All orders shipped within 6 weeks via postal service book rate. Canadian orders require $2.00 extra postage and must be paid in U.S. dollars through a U.S. banking facility.

Name_____
Address_____
City _____ State_____ Zip_____
I have enclosed $_____in payment for the checked book(s).
Payment **must** accompany all orders.☐ Please send a free catalog.

FROM LOVE SPELL

HISTORICAL ROMANCE

THE PASSIONATE REBEL
Helene Lehr

A beautiful American patriot, Gillian Winthrop is horrified to learn that her grandmother means her to wed a traitor to the American Revolution. Her body yearns for Philip Meredith's masterful touch, but she is determined not to give her hand—or any other part of herself—to the handsome Tory, until he convinces her that he too is a passionate rebel.

_51918-6 $4.99 US/$5.99 CAN

CONTEMPORARY ROMANCE

THE TAWNY GOLD MAN
Amii Lorin

Bestselling Author Of More Than 5 Million Books In Print!

Long ago, in a moment of wild, rioting ecstasy, Jud Cammeron vowed to love her always. Now, as Anne Moore looks at her stepbrother, she sees a total stranger, a man who plans to take control of his father's estate and everyone on it. Anne knows things are different—she is a grown woman with a fiance—but something tells her she still belongs to the tawny gold man.

_51919-4 $4.99 US/$5.99 CAN

AN HISTORICAL ROMANCE
GILDED SPLENDOR
By Elizabeth Parker

Bound for the London stage, sheltered Amanda Prescott has no idea that fate has already cast her first role as a rakehell's true love. But while visiting Patrick Winter's country estate, she succumbs to the dashing peer's burning desire. Amid the glittering milieu of wealth and glamour, Amanda and Patrick banish forever their harsh past and make all their fantasies a passionate reality.

__51914-3 $4.99 US/$5.99 CAN

A CONTEMPORARY ROMANCE
MADE FOR EACH OTHER/RAVISHED
By Parris Afton Bonds
Bestselling Author of *The Captive*

In *Made for Each Other,* reporter Julie Dever thinks she knows everything about Senator Nicholas Raffer—until he rescues her from a car wreck and shares with her a passion she never dared hope for. And in *Ravished,* a Mexican vacation changes nurse Nelli Walzchak's life when she is kidnapped by a handsome stranger who needs more than her professional help.

__51915-1 $4.99 US/$5.99 CAN

LEISURE BOOKS
ATTN: Order Department
276 5th Avenue, New York, NY 10001

Please add $1.50 for shipping and handling for the first book and $.35 for each book thereafter. PA., N.Y.S. and N.Y.C. residents, please add appropriate sales tax. No cash, stamps, or C.O.D.s. All orders shipped within 6 weeks via postal service book rate. Canadian orders require $2.00 extra postage and must be paid in U.S. dollars through a U.S. banking facility.

Name _____

Address _____

City _____ State _____ Zip _____

I have enclosed $_____in payment for the checked book(s).
Payment <u>must</u> accompany all orders.☐ Please send a free catalog.